The Hook

The Hook

James Pack

VaudVil

Tucson

All rights reserved. Printed in the United States of America by VaudVil. An imprint of Pack Enterprises LLC, Tucson, Arizona.

Cover photo by George Desipris from Pexels.

ISBN 979-8-9859342-2-9 (hardback)
ISBN 979-8-9859342-3-6 (ebook)
ISBN 979-8-9859342-4-3 (paperback)

Other Titles by James Pack

The Morbid Museum (Short Stories)
Corbin's Catacombs (Poetry)
Black Chaos (Poetry)

Part One
Crescent

*"Each that we lose takes a part of us; A crescent
still abides, Which like the moon, some turbid night,
Is summoned by the tides."* — Emily Dickinson

One
October 28, 1976

John and Martha Abbott were driving to Hallowell, Maine early Friday morning down Outlet Road. They did so each week and it was the only activity they did together.

"We don't need to give out any damn candy." John said.

"The grandchildren love getting sweets when they come over so we're getting sweets at the store." Martha said.

"Then they'll tell their friends like they did last year. And like last year, they'll come overlooking for candy. When we don't give them any, they'll cover our house and yard in toilet paper and eggs. I spent two days cleaning that mess. No candy!"

"They'll do it anyway if we don't have any candy. But if we get enough candy for everyone, we won't have a problem."

"If I point my shotgun at them, we won't have a problem."

"Johnathan Abbott! You will not do any such thing. If I see you point that thing at any children, you'll be sleeping in that old barn for a month."

"I won't load it. I'll scare them away, that's all."

"Oh, buy some extra candy, you cranky old man."

"I'm not cranky, I'm cautious. All these kids listening to loud music, worshipping Satan, having orgies in meadows…"

"Johnathan!"

"Well they do! They're heathens!"

"Is that a car parked up ahead?"

"One of the doors are open. They might be having car trouble."

"Oh, pull over and see if they need help. You're handy with engines."

"Alright."

"Is someone laying by the trees? Are those bullfrogs?"

"I've never seen so many. You wait here."

"Be careful! You're not a young man anymore."

"I never would have noticed if you hadn't said something. Thank you."

John walked around the car. A back-seat door hung open and the headlights were on.

"Has it been here all morning?"

He walked toward the tree line where the bullfrogs gathered. He moved many of them with his feet to avoid stepping on them and clear a path to walk. Martha took a step from the pickup.

"What is it, John?"

"Stay there! Bullfrogs can be ornery!"

John stopped. His mouth hung open. He took two steps backwards before running back to the truck hopping over frogs.

"John, what's wrong? You're scaring me. You've gone pale. What did you see?"

"I gotta call the Sheriff. I can tell him about it or I can tell you, but not both. I don't have it in me to say it twice."

"Say what twice? What did you see?"

John drove fast before Martha could see anything.

"They're dead, Martha. Will Evans youngest boy and his wife. I forget their names."

"The young couple who had a baby on the way. What about the baby?"

"I gotta call the Sheriff."

"John? John! What happened to the baby?"

"They're dead, Martha."

"John. Don't drive so fast. It's dangerous."

"I gotta call the Sheriff."

John drove in silence to the closest pay phone. Martha watched him.

"Wait here."

"John. John!?"

He fidgeted in his pocket for change, dropping several coins. He paused a moment then ignored the lost change and ran to the phone.

"Kennebec County Sheriff. Davis."

"I need to speak with Sheriff Bazinet, it's an emergency."

"He's not in the office. I can transfer you to Deputy Wells. Or you can hang up and dial 911 for emergency services."

"Deputy Wells please."

Martha watched John from the car as he continued fidgeting and looking restless.

"This is Wells."

"Deputy. This is John Abbott. I'm at a payphone off Outlet Road. Something awful has happened. I can't even describe it. At first, I thought someone abandoned the car or some kids were messing around, but, well, they're dead. They're both dead."

"Alright Mister Abbott. Slow down. Start at the beginning and tell me what happened."

"My wife and I were driving into town, and we saw a car on the side of the road. A Ford Granada, a couple years old. One of the doors was open. I went to look. No one was there, but the headlights were still on. I looked around and saw them by the trees. They had bullfrogs all around them. I've never seen so many bullfrogs, Deputy. But they were lying there. I know them. It's Will Evans youngest boy and his wife. She was pregnant, but something… You have to see it. You have to send someone now. I mean right now."

"Okay. Okay. I'll get some deputies together and I'll look at it myself."

"And you'll tell the Sheriff."

"I'll report to him about it myself."

"Thank you. Thank you. Uh, what should I do? Should I wait."

"Stop by the Sheriff's office later today if you can and give a formal statement. For now, try to relax. We'll take care of the situation.

"Okay. Later today. Okay. Should I go now?"

"Whenever you feel comfortable. Deputy Davis will be at the front desk all day."

"Okay. Thank you."

John hung up the receiver and said thank you under his breath. His hand shook as he walked back to Martha.

"We're going to the Sheriff's Office. No candy today."

"Do we need to go see the Sheriff or are you avoiding the store?"

"I have to give a statement, Martha. We'll go to the store after. I still need shave cream."

The constant movement of the steering wheel in the '51 Chevy helped calm John's nerves. Martha didn't notice his hands shaking.

"Can I sit with you when you give them your statement?"

"That might help."

***

Deputy Jedediah Wells was the second deputy to arrive. He immediately requested more deputies and officers from Hallowell and Augusta Police. In his report, he detailed taping off the scene, but chose not to describe the scene in detail.

"Dispatch, this is Wells. I need every available unit out on Outlet Road."

"Wells, this is dispatch. Sending boys your way."

"You better get some local police too. We'll need help to search the woods. Get someone from MCU."

"Roger. We'll keep you posted."

"Thanks, Pam."

Deputy Wells stepped out of his patrol car to examine the scene again.

"You think it was an animal attack?" The other deputy said.

"Animals don't usually pull people from their cars. You can see nail scratches in the back seat." Deputy Wells said.

"Oh, shit."

"And why would an animal tear open one person only to break the neck of the other?"

"It doesn't make sense."

"Don't let anyone near the bodies. Only the Medical

Examiner and detectives from Major Crimes. No one should see this. And Jerry, if any reporters come sniffing, keep them away and tell them there was an accident on the highway."

"Yes, sir."

"Run the police tape around the car and tie it off on the trees. Go a couple feet into the wood line. Everything happened right there by the road. After that, we'll sit tight until other deputies get here."

Detective Russel Vaughan arrived a short time later followed by a couple deputies. He was a detective for the Sherriff's Major Crimes Unit. He often worked with the Hallowell and Augusta Police Departments. Everyone recognized him. No one stopped Detective Vaughan from passing the police tape. He provided a more detailed and graphic description of the murder scene.

"A 1972 Ford Granada sits on the side of the road. The rear passenger side door is open. Scratch marks on the back seat indicating someone pulled a victim from the car. One of the rear tires is flat. A tire iron lays behind the vehicle near the trunk. Nothing else in or around the vehicle appears out of place.

"Question – Did the killer take advantage of the blowout or cause the blowout?

"Two bodies lay at the tree line. The male has a broken neck, probable cause of death. The Medical Examiner will verify. The body does not appear to have any lacerations. There's no skin or fabric under the fingernails. Nothing to suggest he struggled with the killer.

"Question – Was he killed behind the car then dragged to the tree line?

"There are marks in the ground from where someone dragged the female from the car. There are no marks on the ground near the male's body. The female has blood and entrails pulled from her stomach. Small pieces of bone lay within the blood. The bone bits look chewed. The first deputy on the scene stated there were many bullfrogs around the bodies.

"Question – Did the killer feed any animals?

"Question – Why was the male's body ignored?

"Question – Was the female carrying a child?

"Question – If the female was pregnant, why was the child pulled out?

"The only marks on the ground are from dragging the body and from the bullfrogs."

***

My name is Samantha Belcher, and I am a reporter for the Kennebec Journal in Kennebec County, Maine. I arrived at the scene after all the deputies and officers. My office kept a radio set on police frequencies to get leads on stories. The local police always recognized me and rarely let me pass. Most of them felt women didn't belong at a crime scene.

"Hold it, Belcher. This ain't one you want to see."

"Jerry, I don't have time for your shit. Let me pass." I said.

"This ain't like anything else we've had. It's bad. It's real bad."

"Go get Wells. I'll wait here."

"He ain't gonna let you pass neither."

"Either. Go get him."

"Okay, but I warned you."

I saw him mouth the words 'I tried to tell her' to Deputy Wells. Wells sighed then put his hand up, nodding his head. He rubbed part of his nose by the corners of his eyes before walking over.

"Sam." Wells said.

"Deputy Wells." I said.

"Why don't you call me Jed? We've known each other since grade school."

"Wells sounds better. It rolls off the tongue easier."

"Fine. I'm not letting you see this crime scene."

"You afraid I can't handle it or afraid I'll manage better than all your boys?"

"I'm not even letting most of them see it. It's that bad."

"How much do you want?"

"I'm not letting you pass the tape."

"I've got 53 bucks."

"Keep it. You can't bribe me on this one."

"Then give me a statement. Something I can use."

"Why do you keep acting like some big city reporter? People don't want to know about all this awful stuff."

"But they have a right to know. You can't stop the freedom of the press. You can't stop the spirit of journalism."

"You sound like a damn salesman. Can't you ever talk to me like a friend?"

"We haven't been friends for years, and you know damn well why."

"You can't guilt trip me into letting you pass. It's gruesome."

"Some people like gruesome."

"One Augusta officer puked."

"Sounds like a rookie. I've seen a body before. I can handle a bad smell and a little blood."

"Deputy Stevens."

"Yes, Sir."

"No civilians cross the tape, especially this one."

"You're a piece of work, Wells."

"You too, Sam. I have work to do."

"Dammit Wells. May I please have a statement for my article?"

"The official statement is there was an accident on Outlet Road involving a male and a female. We will not disclose their identities until we've spoken with the families."

"You have a lot of officers and deputies out here for one accident."

"It's unusual and requires more pairs of eyes to ensure we don't overlook or miss anything."

"You are so full of shit."

"That's the official statement."

"Anything else?"

"That's all. I need to supervise. Call me later."

"He's still an asshole. What do you think, Jerry?"

"That's Deputy Stevens, Ma'am."

"Well, Deputy, I got 53 bucks. What do you say?"

"Ma'am, are you attempting to bribe a state official?"

"Relax Barney Fife. Mind if I ask the other officers some questions?"

"Well, I mean, as long as you stay behind the tape."

"You got it Barney."

"My name is Jerry! I mean Deputy Stevens!"

"It sure is."

In hindsight, I should have heeded the warning. I've never been one for doing as I'm told. Well behaved women never make history. But when I can't guilt trip Wells, I know it's serious. They had a special van on site for the people who take photos and samples at crime scenes. I threw on one of the crew's jackets and hats and walked under the police tape. Hot cop Jerry Stevens never noticed.

I saw the car first. It looked fine and I wondered if the engine stalled. I considered carbon monoxide, but why did they need so many officers? They put one of the bodies into an ambulance. The other was still on the ground. The female. I knew her. Sarah Evans. She was pregnant. I froze. Someone stepped away bringing the whole body into view. I would have screamed if I hadn't been gagging and crying.

"Who the Hell is throwing a fit? Dammit Sam!" Deputy Wells said.

"Sarah! It's Sarah! Her baby. The baby!" I said.

"I know, Sam. I know. That's why I didn't want you to see it."

"Why didn't you stop me!? Why didn't Jerry stop me!? Jerry you bastard!"

"Stop yelling at Jerry."

"Well it's his fault! He didn't do a good job of watching me! Why didn't you tell me it was Sarah!"

"Then you would have demanded to cross the tape."

"You're damn right, Wells!"

"Please don't print anything until I talk to her family."

"I would never do that to her. Oh God! I need a drink."

"It's nine in the morning!"

"That never stopped me before!"

I don't know if I felt upset about losing a friend or because of the terrible way they died; her and the baby. Or it was a little of both. The rest of the story, the real story, isn't my own. The real story is about a man, a stranger to Hallowell, a stranger to Maine. A veteran coming back from deployment looking for his wife and daughter. When I asked permission to print these events, he asked me not to use his name. This story is not my own, but I'm the only one who can tell it.

Two
October 29, 1976

Ernest Kemp arrived the day after the bodies were found. This is his story. He was an outsider to Kennebec County. Residents accused him multiple times for the murders. Even the ones that happened before he came to Maine.

I'm sharing his story with his permission. Many events I did not witness. Some of them are too outrageous to believe but this is the way Ernest tells the story. People will sometimes embellish stories to captivate their listeners, but I have no reason to doubt Ernest's claims. Even the fantastic ones.

Ernest always started his story with his taxi ride into Hallowell.

***

'If You Leave Me Now' by Chicago played on the radio. The cab driver looked at Ernest through the rearview mirror.

"You military?" The driver said.

"Yeah. Navy." Ernest said.

"You from around here?"

"No. First time in Maine."

"What brings you here?"

"I'm looking for someone."

"You Military Police or something?"

"What? No. I'm trying to find my wife and daughter."

"They move here while you were over there? In Vietnam?"

"Something like that."

"What'd you do over there?"

"I was a Navy Hospital Corpsman. A medic."

"You saved anybody's life?"

"Some. Not all."

"I'm glad somebody was tryin' to do somethin' good over there."

"You from around here?"

"Ayuh. Lived here all my life."

"I might be here awhile. Where's the best place to stay?"

"Most stuff is downtown. Hallowell ain't a big place, but she's been around a long time."

"Most places on the East Coast are pretty old."

"Well, we got old Hallowell verified as a historic landmark a few years back. It used to be the only good things this town had were antique shops. We're getting a little better each year."

"Why'd you stay if it wasn't that great?"

"Didn't want to go anywhere else."

"There's no place like home."

"Ayuh. There's a lot a history here. Hallowell, I think, used to include Manchester, Augusta, and Chelsea, but I don't remember. This part of Hallowell back then was called 'The Hook' or 'Hallowell Hook.'"

"Why's that?"

"Most people think it's somethin' to do with the river downtown, but I don't know. I'll stop jabberin' all this nonsense. How long were you in the service?"

"Twelve years. Most of that I was stuck on a boat or submarine. Felt like I was in a sardine can."

"I don't think I could handle that, close quarters n' all. You on leave or somethin' like that?"

"No. I served. I'm done. I want to build a life with my family."

"Good luck with that. I'm divorced so I hope you have better luck than I did."

"Thank you and I'm sorry to hear that."

"I ain't sorry. Best thing I ever did for myself. Anyway, this here's a good spot to stay. I hear the owners are nice, but I've never met 'em."

"I appreciate it. Here you go. Keep the change.

"Hey thanks! Welcome to The Hook."

"Thanks. Take care."

Ernest saw a 'Rooms for Rent' sign in the window of an antique shop. He hoped the rooms would have antique furniture.

"The cab driver said this is the best place to stay." Ernest said.

"That it is young man. How long you plan on staying?" The shop owner said.

"A couple weeks. I'm looking for someone, but I don't know how long that'll take."

"Who you looking for? Maybe I can help."

"My wife and daughter. Linda and Amy Kemp."

"The names don't ring a bell. The rooms are $56 a week over the shop here. You can come and go as you please through the back stairs."

Ernest surveyed his room. It had the basic needs, a bed, nightstand, dresser, a rotary phone, a radio, a lamp, a small refrigerator, a coffee pot, a gas space heater, and a bathroom. He was disappointed with the room's modern furnishings. He unpacked his military duffle bag. He sat on the bed and dialed zero on the phone.

"Operator?" Ernest said.

"How may I direct your call?"

"I'd like to make a long-distance call to TUrner 3-4001."

"Stay on the line while I connect you."

The phone rang three times.

"Kemp Residence." A woman said.

"Hello Mom."

"Oh Ernie! It's so good to hear from you. Have you found Linda and Amy?"

"Not yet. I just got into my room and called you first thing."

"Where are you?"

"I'm in Maine. A small town called Hallowell. An old friend of Linda's said she was coming here."

"Was that friend in Ohio? You said Linda had family there."

"Yes. She visited and went to Maine, they said."

"Well, I hope you find her soon and come back home."

"I'll make sure to call when I do. How's dad?"

"He's like always. Still refuses to retire and won't stop working."

"I figured. Send everyone my love. I was calling to let you know where I was."

"Thank you, sweetie. Take care of yourself. I love you."

"I love you too, Mom. Bye."

"Bye, sweetie."

Ernest remembered passing a general store in the taxi. He locked his room and walked down the street. The store buzzed with chatter as he entered.

"I don't care. I still think Reagan is a better choice." An older man said.

"It don't matter now cause Ford beat him in the primaries." Another man said.

"I guess it doesn't matter as long as Carter doesn't win. I don't even like peanuts. I like almonds."

Two girls were looking through a small rack of shirts.

"This one looks neat." The first girl said.

"It's okay. We should go to the city. They have better clothes there."

The store clerk noticed Ernest as he looked around the store.

"Can I help ya?" The clerk said.

"A pack of unfiltered Luckies please." Ernest said.

"That's a half dollar."

"Thank you. Most of the people in town shop here?"

"Just about everyone."

"You know a woman named Linda with a baby girl?"

"Name don't sound familiar. There's a lot a women with baby girls though. Why do ya ask?"

"My wife brought my daughter out here while I was on my last tour. Just trying to find them."

"Where you in Nam?"

"Cambodia actually. And I'm happy to never go back."

"Never heard of it."

"It's a country next to Vietnam."

"What'd ya do over there?"

"I was a Corpsman in the Navy. I helped the doctors take care of people and saved a few Marines in combat. Lost a few too."

"I'm sorry son. I served back in '42. I'll ask around. Maybe someone knows your wife. She might be in Augusta. It's just a few minutes North."

"Thank you."

Ernest checked his pockets for matches and looked around the store.

"I shit you not. A full-grown black bear was in our kitchen." A man said.

"What'd ya do?" A woman said.

"I got my shotgun, but the bear had already walked outside. It was like it didn't care about us." The man said.

Ernest walked outside with a cigarette and matches in hand overhearing other conversations.

"Just tell me you got some leads." A woman said.

"I'm not on duty. And I can't discuss details of an ongoing investigation." A man said.

They both stopped talking when Ernest passed.

***

That was me talkings with Deputy Wells. That was the first time I saw Ernest but didn't know who he was. I had no idea how involved he would become in the investigation.

***

Ernest smoked his cigarette and walked along the street. He looked at everyone he passed. He felt someone was watching him. Across the street, he saw three women looking at him, a blonde, a brunette, and a redhead. The brunette woman in the middle turned and walked away. The other two followed. He wondered if they knew Linda. He considered following them but thought it was just small-town people noticing someone new. He put out his cigarette and returned to his room.

Three
October 30, 1976

The next day, Ernest went to the Hallowell Police Station.

"Help you?" The officer said.

"Yes, sir. I'm looking for my wife." Ernest said.

"How long has she been missing?"

"She's not missing. A friend in Ohio said she moved up here."

"Are you separated?"

"No, sir. I just got out of the Navy. I'm trying to find her and my daughter."

"She didn't tell you she was moving?"

"We're from California. She wrote a letter about visiting family in Ohio. She was gone by the time I got there."

"She in some kind of trouble?"

"None I'm aware of. Her letter was vague."

"Do you know when she came up here?"

"Maybe a couple weeks ago."

"I'll see if we got files on her. What's the name?"

"Linda Kemp. Maiden name is Rosemont."

The officer returned several minutes later.

"Sorry pal. We don't have anything on her."

"Do you have any suggestions where I can look or who I can ask? No one I've met so far knows her by name."

"She might be using a different name. You got a photo?"

"Nothing recent."

"Not much can be done short of asking everyone in town.

She might be in Augusta. Try the librarian first."

"Why the librarian?"

"She's the nosey type. Likes to gossip. She hears everybody's business and tells everyone else."

"Any other places?"

"The local bar. Bartenders talk to a lot of people and hear lots of stories."

"Okay. Well thanks for your help."

"Have a nice day, sir."

Ernest had never known Linda to be a drinker. She always called it poison for the body. He hoped the librarian would be more helpful than the police. The librarian sat at her desk near the front door of the library.

"Excuse me. I was told you could help me find someone." Ernest said.

"There's a phone book out with the payphone." The librarian said.

"She isn't in the phone book. She only got into town a couple weeks ago.

"The library isn't a dating service."

"I'm aware of that. I'm looking for my wife. A friend of hers said she moved up here. Linda Kemp. Do you know her?"

"I don't. And if I did, I wouldn't tell you. I support any woman trying to get away from her husband."

"She's not trying to get away from me. I just got out of the Navy."

"Maybe she didn't want to be around a baby killer."

"I never killed anyone. I was a medic. I saved lives!"

"Shhh! Keep your voice down. This is a library."

"Can you offer any help or not?"

"Try Augusta. But if she doesn't want you knowing where she is, you should leave well enough alone."

"What's it like being an angry old crone?"

"Well I never…"

"I bet you haven't."

"Get out of my library!"

"Shhh! Keep your voice down."

Ernest left fast while the librarian gasped with her hand on her neck. He smoked his last two cigarettes and went back to the general store.

"Hiya." The store clerk said.

"Unfiltered Luckies please. Keep the change." Ernest said.

"Thank ya!"

Two kids in Halloween costumes ran into the store excited and giggling.

"Don't be runnin' in my store now."

"Sorry, sir."

"Can I help ya with anythin' else?" The store clerk said.

"I think I need to find some work around here. Know any hospitals or doctors that need people?" Ernest said.

"I don't of any here in town. You might try Augusta."

"Everyone keeps saying that."

"Any luck findin' the misses?"

"None yet. That's why I'm looking for work. I might be here a while."

"I could use some help around the store."

"You'd hire me?"

"Ayuh. Ya look like ya can lift heavy stuff and yer military, so I trust ya."

"I appreciate it. When do you want me to start?"

"Tomorra' or Monday is okay with me."

"Okay. I'll start tomorrow."

"Okay. Three dollars an hour alright?"

"Sounds great. I'm Ernest by the way."

"Call me Joe. Nice ta meet ya."

The two children in costumes sped past Ernest on his way out bumping into him.

"Sorry, mister."

"I told ya kids no runnin'!" Joe said.

Ernest returned to his room after finishing another two cigarettes. He grabbed the phone, put his left index finger on zero and turned the dial to the left. He watched it spin back in place.

"Operator?" Ernest said.

"How may I direct your call?"

"CRest 2-4178 please. Long distance."

"Stay on the line while I connect you."

The phone rang five times.

"Rosemont Residence."

"Hello Beatrice. It's Ernest."

"Hello Ernie. Have you found our Linda?"

"Not yet. A friend of hers said she came to Maine. That's where I am now."

"Well, if anyone can find my baby girl it's her husband. Honestly, I don't know why she left. And you're sure she didn't say anything to you in her letters? Have you gotten any other letters? She really has no right to run off like that with your child. It's just shameful. Oh, and you're such a dear for not being angry with her. I don't know how you do it." Beatrice said.

"Well, I don't know why she left so I'm holding any judgement until I speak to her. Right now, I just want to see her and Amy. She's barely a year old and we've never met. I just want to meet her." Ernest said.

"Of course. I can't imagine what you're going through. That must be hard."

"I'm doing okay. Well, I don't want to keep you too long. The long-distance rates are ridiculous."

"Never mind that. We can afford it. Just don't call us every day. Tell me how you are. What's Maine like? I've never been so I'm very curious. What's the weather like up there?"

"It's a lot colder here than San Bernardino. People talk a little funny, but that's no big deal. There's a lot of old buildings. Some have probably been around for 200 years."

"That sounds interesting. We have a few churches that old out here, but I've seen them all. I'll have to talk Herbert into traveling out there. You know, he's never interested in going anywhere. Sometimes he can be a real bore. A couple years ago we were on vacation…"

Ernest held the phone away from his ear. Beatrice's voice echoed through the room. He sat down rubbing his face.

"…and all Herbie wanted to do was sleep in the hotel room or sleep on the beach. He never wants to go anywhere with me.

Sometimes I don't think he's attracted to me anymore. Oh, listen to me. You don't want to hear about your in-laws' marital issues. But take my advice. When you find Linda, make sure you take her places, or she'll think you're a bore like her father. I don't want that for you two. You're so good together. And Amy is just the sweetest little baby. You should be proud. Oh, I'm so sorry. You just said you haven't met her yet."

"That's okay Beatrice. I need to go. I have some errands to run."

"I've just been babbling on. You go ahead and take care of things. And you call me first thing when you find Linda and tell me she's alright."

"Okay, I'll do that."

"And you take care of yourself Ernest. This is all hard to go through on your own. If you need anything, you let us know."

"I survived the war. I think I can handle Maine."

"Of course. You're a strong man, but even strong men need help sometimes. You just take care of yourself, okay?"

"Okay, I will."

"Okay, hun. We'll talk to you later."

"Okay bye."

"Bye Bye Ernie. It was good to hear from you."

"You too."

"Okay Bye now."

"Bye."

There was a brief silence before Beatrice hung up.

"Why is she so exhausting to talk to?"

Four
November 1, 1976 - Letter from Ernest

Dear Linda,

It's been almost a week since I left Ohio. All you told anyone was you were going to a small town in Maine called Hallowell. Was that a lie? Did you go somewhere else? Somewhere no one will find you. I hope that's not the case. But I do wish you had left an address or phone number. Did you know where you were going in town? Or did you figure that out when you got here?

I still don't know why you left. Your last letter was vague. You told me more in that letter than you told anyone else. That's why I'm not angry you left without saying much. What are you running from? You said you needed to get away from your family but didn't say why. I didn't tell your family what you said. I told everyone you didn't say why you left.

How's Amy? I can't wait to meet her. How big is she now? Has she started crawling or walking? Has she said her first word? I'm so nervous about being a father. To be honest, I'm scared. What if she doesn't like me? What if she cries when I hold her? What if I spoil her too much? I don't even want to think about when she starts asking those difficult, awkward questions. What if she's like your mother and never stops talking?

I spoke to your mother the other day on the phone. She chewed my ear off without caring about the long-distance charges. Is she one of those people who's always on the phone? I can't imagine what it'd be like living your whole life around your phone. I'd rather talk to someone in person. Lately, I haven't wanted to talk to anyone. Most conversations I have or overhear are so irritating. I can't stand the sound of anyone talking.

Everyone in Maine talks funny. You've noticed, I'm sure, the way everyone says yes or yeah. It's hard to describe. I want to ask why they say it like that, but I'm afraid that would be rude. It feels like most people don't like me. I don't know if it's because I was in the war or because I'm new in town. Some people are nice, but it feels like everyone else is judging me. Do they look at everyone like that?

A few days ago, these three women were glaring at me. I thought they might know you and recognized me. But that doesn't explain their hateful looks. Have you seen them around? They look a little younger than us. A blonde, brunette, and a redhead. The brunette was followed by the other two like she's their commanding officer or something. It was creepy. I swear they were staring into my soul. It's difficult to explain the feeling I had. Almost like ice rolling down my spine. I'm not sure I want to see them again.

Something weird happened yesterday too. I suspect it was a Halloween prank. I walked down to the general store and there had to have been six or eight bullfrogs on the sidewalk. They either didn't notice or care about the people walking around. Women were screeching. Little kids wanted to play with them. One older woman tried to move them off with her broom. The bullfrogs paid no mind to her shouting "Shoo." It was strange but funny.

I don't know how long it will be before we find each other. That's why I started working at the general store. Joe, the owner, mostly has me moving boxes and stocking shelves. He gives me a discount on everything in the store too. That makes it easy to get groceries. I'm so used to MRE's, the simplest meals taste like gourmet cooking. The room I'm renting doesn't have a kitchen. It has a small fridge and a coffee pot, but the owners let me use their kitchen anytime I want. I'm trying not to take advantage.

I think people don't like newcomers around here. Every time I ask someone a question, whether it's about you or something else, they all tell me to try Augusta. It feels like everyone wants me to leave. I had an argument with the librarian. A police officer said she was a gossip. I'm sure she's told everyone about our exchange. I got angrier than I should have. She called me a baby killer. I never killed anyone, but it still hurt. None of these people understand what the war was like.

That's not true. Joe was in World War II. I think that's why he's so nice to me. Most people ignore me. Every now and then I get some dirty looks from other people. I hope I don't have to stay here long. I'm home sick. I didn't have much time at home before I left for Ohio to find you. Why didn't you stay there longer? Were you afraid your family would come for you? They said you left without a word. Why'd you tell your friends in Ohio you were coming to Maine? And why'd you choose Hallowell? Do you know someone here? Have you been here before? I thought you grew up in Ohio. You said you'd only been to Ohio, California, and everywhere in between.

This whole situation is frustrating. I have plenty of money saved up, but that won't last forever. I plan to use it to buy us a house, a new car, everything we need. None of that matters until I find you. This is more stressful than all the search and rescue missions in Cambodia. It's all the unknowns. All our missions, we had intel on where someone was held. We had a plan to get them out. I don't have a plan. That's why this is difficult for me. Where are you, Linda?

Love always,
Ernie

Five
November 2, 1976

"Ha! See that? Ford's in the lead. He's gonna' continue what Nixon started." The first man said.

"I want Ford to win as much as you but Nixon's a crook. Watergate is the biggest shame our country has had." The second man said.

"He resigned. That was the descent thing to do. And Ford kept up the good work."

"Why you guys arguing over a guy who can barely stand up better than a toddler?" The third man said.

"Don't make fun of Ford for fallin' a couple times. I've fallen plenty." The first man said.

"That's cause your old ass needs a walker."

Several people laughed while watching the election coverage in the general store.

***

Most people didn't have a television. They preferred the radio, but they enjoyed a sense of community at the store. Big events always had large groups huddled around the small television. I would often attend in the hopes of overhearing something for a story. I could always find someone willing to share. That's the day I first met Ernest. He tells the story with more glamor.

***

Ernest was behind the counter. He organized the shelves. Making sure everything faced forward and pulled to the front. The mundane work was a nice break from military life. He tried to ignore the chatter from everyone watching the election.

"Excuse me."

Ernest turned to see a brunette in a business suit.

"Where's Joe?" She said.

"He went to the bank for change. Can I help you?" Ernest said.

"That depends. Have you heard anything about what happened on Outlet Road?

"I don't know where that is. I'm not from around here."

"Are you that Army guy who pissed off Nancy?"

"Navy actually. And who's Nancy?"

"The librarian."

"Oh! Yeah, we had a disagreement. I guess news around here spreads fast."

"Don't worry. Most people don't put much stock in what she says."

"But some do?"

"Not many."

"You know a lot of people in town?"

"I meet a lot of people in my line of work."

"What work is that?"

"I'm Samantha Belcher. Reporter for the Kennebec Journal. That's why I want to see Joe. Find out if he's overheard anyone talking about things they shouldn't talk about."

"Ernest Kemp. Nice to meet you."

"Likewise. So, you haven't heard anything? How long you been working here?"

"A couple days. I've only been in town a couple more than that."

"What brought you here?

"I'm looking for my wife, Linda. She came up here just before I came home. Didn't leave a forwarding address."

"She just up and left without a word?"

"She left me a letter saying she was visiting family in Ohio. She had a friend tell me she was coming here. She didn't want her family coming for her. Her letter was vague. I don't know why she left.”

"That is strange. I can ask around if you want.”

"I'd appreciate the help. She has our baby girl with her. I haven't met her yet. She's barely a year old.”

"I'm sorry. I'll definitely help. Why haven't you seen your daughter?”

"Two-year tour in Cambodia. I just got back.”

"Wow. That must have been hard. Not seeing your family.”

"Yeah. Then imagine getting home and finding out they left. I've been smoking a pack of cigarettes a day.”

"I hope you find them soon.”

"Thank you.”

"Stop botherin' my store hand, Samantha.” Joe said.

"I'll bother you now that you're here. Overheard anything about the accident on Outlet Road?” Samantha said.

"Only rumors.”

"Sometimes rumors can give me a lead.”

"Well I don't think werewolves killin' people is much of a lead.”

"Werewolves?” Ernest said.

"Kids makin' up stories.” Joe said.

"A couple people were killed. We've had it in the paper every day since it happened. Police are being extra quiet about the investigation. I think it's because they don't have anything.” Samantha said.

"What happened?” Ernest said.

"Thursday morning, two people were found on the side of the road. Their bodies mutilated. I saw it. That's an image I won't forget. Everyone talked about it all day. I'm surprised you didn't hear.”

"I got into town Friday afternoon. And most people don't say much to me. No one here likes outsiders, do they?”

"Murders got folks on edge.” Joe said.

The three women who stared at Ernest a couple days before entered the store. They walked with purpose. Their expressionless faces ignored everyone else. The chatter over the election stopped. They had the attention of the entire store.

"Ya don't see women like that every day." Joe said.

"You know them, Samantha?" Ernest said.

"I've never seen them before." Samantha said.

"I did a couple days ago. They were watching me for a moment. I get a weird vibe from those three."

"Nonsense, Ernie. Ya been around them oriental women too long. Beautiful women like that will make ya feel all kinds a things." Joe said.

"You okay, Joe?" Samantha said.

"Wazzat?"

"You're drooling."

"Oh, let a old man alone."

No one noticed the television announcing Jimmy Carter had taken the lead in Texas. The older men watched the three women. Ernest and Samantha watched them for different reasons.

"They look like they know exactly what they want." Ernest said.

"They're organized too. Did they plan out who was getting what beforehand?" Samantha said.

"You need a hand with anything Miss?" One man said.

"The blonde ignored him. She continued gathering items like she was the only one there. Defeated, the man returned to his seat by the television.

"I hate women like that. The pretty ones who think the world revolves around them." Samantha said.

"Most women I've met enjoy that, they like the attention. These women have no interest. They're something else. I can't explain it, but they make me uncomfortable." Ernest said.

"Most of the men here are uncomfortable."

"That's not what I meant. Something feels off about them. I don't trust them."

The blonde woman approached the counter with a few items.

"Do you have any hobblebush?" She said.

"What's that?" Ernest said.

"Ain't never heard of it." Joe said.

"I guess that's a no." The blonde said.

The redhead approached the counter.

"Do you have any buttonbush?" She said.

"Probably not. They don't have hobblebush." The blonde said.

"No buttonbush, but you can find 'em around town. My neighbor has 'em in her yard. She's the reason I heard of 'em." Joe said.

"Where does your neighbor live?" The redhead said.

"Uh…about four blocks South 'o here. Big yellow house. Ya ladies ever try gardenin'? I'm sure you could grow all tha stuff ya need." Joe said.

"We don't have that much time." The blonde said.

The redhead elbowed her in the side.

"What was that for?" The blonde said.

Her whispers were still loud enough for everyone to hear.

"We'll talk later." The redhead said.

The brunette approached the counter with several bags of candy. She looked at the items on the counter.

"We're missing a few things." She said.

"They don't have everything we need." The redhead said.

"Ya might try Augusta. The stores there are bigger 'n this one." Joe said.

"That won't be necessary. We'll take these items." The brunette said.

Joe tallied up all the items. Among the candy were several herbs and spices.

"That'll be $12.75." Joe said.

The brunette dropped 20 dollars on the counter. Ernest bagged up the items while Joe counted the change.

"That's 13. 14. 15. And 20. Ya ladies have a nice day now." Joe said.

The three women left without a word, each with a paper bag. Chatter over the election resumed.

"Now Carter's in the lead? Damn you voters."

"That was rude." Samantha said.

"Ain't a friendly bunch, are they?" Joe said.

"They could have at least said thank you." Ernest said.

"They could have said anything." Samantha said.

"Who in the hell acts like that? Ya think they're hippies or somethin'?" Joe said.

"They didn't look like flower power kids. I'd know. I was one of them in college." Samantha said.

"Well that figures." Joe said.

"You protested the war?" Ernest said.

"I did. Not the people fighting the war. Too many men were sent over against their will. Were you drafted or did you volunteer?" Samantha said.

"Drafted. I served my time and I'm out now."

"Some weren't so lucky."

"Yeah. I know."

There was a brief silence.

"Ha! See that? Ford's back on top."

"You ever see those women before, Joe?" Ernest said.

"That's the first time I've seen them." Samantha said.

"I think I seen 'em somewhere in town a day or two ago." Joe said.

"I saw them a couple days ago, too." Ernest said.

"Maybe they got into town 'round the same time as you."

"You sure you don't have a crush?" Samantha said.

"I'm the only guy here that wasn't ogling them. All I know is I don't want to be alone with any of them. They make me uncomfortable." Ernest said.

"You said that. I'll admit they're weird. But I'll bet they're sweet girls if you get to know them." Samantha said.

"I don't have time to go meeting strange women. I need to find my wife."

"Ya got more stockin' to do, too." Joe said.

Ernest went to the back room. He carried a crate out to the middle of the store. He listened to Samantha probe Joe.

"You're sure you haven't heard anything? About the murders." She said.

"Girl I told ya I ain't heard nothin'." Joe said.

"Did Jed tell you to keep quiet?"

"If I knew somethin' I'd tell ya, okay?"

"Well thanks for nothing."

Samantha stopped on her way out. She turned and walked toward Ernest.

"Hey. I'll do what I can to help you find your wife." She said.

"Thank you. Is someone stopping you from getting your story?" Ernest said.

"What do you mean?"

"Who's Jed?"

"Oh! Sherriff's Deputy. We…have a history. Sometimes he helps me with a story. He's been trying extra hard to keep me out of this one. He says it's too dangerous for me. I told him losing my job would be dangerous."

"You'd really want to help me find my wife?"

"Of course."

"Then I'll help you with your story. I'm no reporter and most people don't talk to me. But I'll keep my ears open."

"I appreciate that. A favor for a favor. I'll see you around."

"Yeah. I'll be here."

Six
November 6, 1976

After having no luck for a week in Hallowell, Ernest went to Augusta. Everyone had suggested it. He assumed townsfolk wanted him to leave. It was Saturday night. There had been a lunar eclipse. The Augusta police weren't going to be much help until morning. He didn't expect to find her in one, but Ernest tried several local bars. That's where most people would be on a Saturday night.

"What'll it be!?" The bartender said.

"Jack and coke!" Ernest said.

"Buck 25!"

"Shit. Keep the change!"

The bartender gave a nod and punched in the money on his cash register.

"Hey! What's the best way to find someone in the city!?" Ernest said.

"Phonebook!" The bartender said.

"They've been in town a couple weeks! Not listed!"

"I don't know man! Ask around maybe!"

The music quieted. Drinkers were still shouting.

"Thanks." Ernest said.

Ernest found an empty corner table. He sat sipping his drink watching the crowd. He didn't want to keep shouting at people. A woman in a purple dress sauntered towards him. The dress stopped above the knee. Her blonde hair waved and curled like Farrah Fawectt.

"Hey handsome. You look lonely." She said.

"I'm not."

Ernest held up his left hand displaying his wedding ring.

"Where's your wife?"

"Waiting for me. I'm out exploring. New in town."

"Maybe I can show you around."

"Maybe another time."

"Yeah, whatever."

She walked to the bar and looked around. Her eyes met a guy at the other end of the bar. He walked over with a big, fake smile. She touched his arm. They fake smiled at each other. He ordered two drinks. Ernest finished his drink with one final gulp and left. He had enough of the mating rituals of people who didn't know what it was like to be in a fire fight. The loud music irritated him.

He tried other bars with the same result. Even filled with more alcohol, the civilians annoyed him. He failed three times to catch a cab. He walked back to Hallowell frustrated and drunk. He spent an hour imagining different scenarios in his mind. His thoughts ran rabid fire.

"What if she never came to Maine? I bet she stayed in Ohio. Or went somewhere else. Why would she lie to me? Why would she have someone tell me to come to Maine? I've been miserable since I got here. No one wants me here. My wife doesn't want me. My country hates me for protecting them. I never killed anyone, and they hate me for fighting in a war they know nothing about. They could at least ask me what it's like. None of these people understand. None of them care. I could die right here on the street, and no one would care. No one would miss me. My daughter will never know me. I'll never see her. What's the point?"

Ernest saw two people far off. They stood behind a car with the trunk open. It was dark and they were too far away. They carried something long and heavy into the woods off the side of the road. He stopped and waited for them to come back. Ten minutes passed.

They returned to their car. They put something in their trunk. One of them saw Ernest. They closed the trunk and sped off.

Ernest ran into the wood line. It was too dark to see. He assumed the worst.

"I guess I'm going to the police tonight. There has to be a payphone nearby."

Ernest continued walking home searching for a payphone. He found a gas station. He couldn't remember if he needed change to dial 911. He tried anyway. The phone rang and rang. Ernest grew impatient. He didn't have any dimes.

"911, what is your emergency?"

"Uh…well I'm not sure exactly. I saw some people take something long and heavy out of the trunk of their car and into the woods. It looked like a body wrapped in carpet." Ernest said.

"Stay on the line for the Sherriff's Department."

"Okay."

"Sherriff's Department. Wells."

"Uh…yeah. I saw some people take something long and heavy out of the trunk of their car and into the woods. It looked like a body wrapped in carpet."

"Where are you located, sir." Wells said.

"I'm on Whiter or Wither road. I'm not sure on the name. I'm not from around here. It's North of Hallowell. I'm coming back from Augusta.

"Do you mean Whitten Road?"

"That could be it. I don't know."

"You saw some people throwing out trash?"

"I'm not sure what it was. They were far off and it's dark."

"What kind of car did they have?"

"I don't know it was too far away."

"What color was it?"

"It was a darker color. Not black."

"Can you give me any details about the people you saw?"

"Nothing for certain."

"Have you been drinking tonight, sir?"

"I don't see how that's relevant."

"Please answer the question, sir."

"Yes. I had a couple drinks."

"Okay. I'm sure you saw something. But your mind is

probably playing tricks on you. I'll have someone drive out there and make sure everything's okay. The best thing for you to do now is go home and get some rest."

"But don't you want to know where I saw this?"

"We'll handle everything. We'll give the road a thorough search. You don't need to worry about anything."

"Why are you talking to me like I'm a damn child? You're not sending anyone out here, are you?"

"We'll have someone check it out. Just get yourself home now."

"Yeah, whatever. Someone could be dead, and you don't give a shit."

"It's a full moon and there was a lunar eclipse. We always get a lot of weird calls on nights like this. And they always turn out to be nothing. Unless there's something you haven't told me, we don't have much to go on. The best I can do is send someone out there. Please go home. If you remember something, call the Sheriff's Department on our non-emergency number. Ask for Deputy Jed Wells. Until then, get some rest. Okay?"

"Yeah. Okay. Deputy Jed Wells. Got it."

"Have a good night, sir."

"You too."

Ernest hung up the phone. He stood for a moment leaning against the wall.

"He thinks I'm some drunk crack pot making prank calls. Someone might be half-dead out there. The police don't care, and I can't find them. I'm useless. I can't save anyone's life anymore. I can't even find my wife."

Ernest started for home. His mind still racing. Reliving his failures. Trying not to think about the most recent memories. He focused on the people he saw. And their car. No definitive details surfaced.

"I guess the deputy was right. There's nothing to go on. Not enough intel. I'm still drunk. Maybe I'll remember more tomorrow. I need to focus on getting home. That's the primary mission right now. Everything else can wait."

He walked with more purpose. He cleared his mind. He

focused on his surroundings. He walked on part of the street to avoid getting too close to dark corners. He wanted to see someone if they tried a surprise attack.

He stopped and jerked his head towards a loud noise. A trash can had fallen over. It rolled to-and-fro with trash and a racoon tail sticking out of it. Ernest continued walking. His heart continued pounding for another ten minutes. He steadied his breathing. He needed to regain control of his body.

Ernest saw someone staggering down the street. The man's behavior suggested he was more drunk than Ernest. Ernest kept his guard up. He had seen people fake this act to get closer to their prey. He wouldn't go down easy. The man mumbled to himself shuffling towards Ernest.

"So, I says to the pickaninny that he was a stupid shit, and I don't like him. And he says he don't care what I like. And I threw a rock at him. Holy shit! Where you come from?"

He stared at Ernest with wide eyes. Ernest held the same expression.

"You with them, ain't ya? They been keeping an eye on me. It was a matter a time I suppose. I knew you devils would get me. You got a joint or maybe a cigarette?" The drunk said.

Ernest handed him a cigarette and got one for himself. He lit a match putting the flame on both cigarettes. They both stood a moment savoring the first drag. They didn't look at each other. The drunk broke the silence.

"I saw 'em once. The old hags. Back before the 95 was done. They said in 20 years they'd be young again. I said they was crazy. Ain't nobody gettin' younger. They gave me a little cackle. They said some funny words I don't remember. Then they said they cursed me. I said they was crazy again. They disappeared into the woods. Ain't seen 'em since."

The drunk took another long drag off the cigarette. He looked comforted by the habit. Ernest continued listening. He wasn't sure what any of it meant.

"My wife and kids left me. I lost me job. My dog died. All I had left was the bottle. Now I live in the cold. They cursed me all right. They cursed me good."

"I'm sorry." Ernest said.

"Oh, it weren't yer fault. I guess I deserve some of it. I deserve this too. Whatever 'tis you gonna do."

"I'm not doing anything and I don't know who you're talking about."

"Gonna wait and surprise me, is it? I don't expect that much kindness. Maybe that's the best way for both us. Easier on me if I don't see it comin'. How come they don't do it themselves?"

"I don't know." Ernest said.

"They curse you, too? This part of yer curse? You musta pissed 'em off real good. Them devils is somethin' else. You mind if I bum another smoke? Last request 'n all."

"Here's a couple."

"Yer a kind one, ain't ya? They don't make 'em like you no more. I shoulda' known my time was comin' with that eclipse. Don't know how but I felt it. Deep in my chest. Somethin' bad is comin'. I hope yer ready fer it. Them devils don't play nice. But you already knowed that, don't ya? They ain't never played nice."

The drunk lit another cigarette with the one he was finishing. He looked up to the dark sky. His eyes watered and he smiled.

"Well, I best be off now You'll find me again when my time comes. You watch yerself now. They may send someone after you like they did me. You look like you can give 'em a hell of fight though. Good luck to ya."

The drunk stumbled away mumbling a tune Ernest didn't recognize. He stood a moment finishing his cigarette.

"What the hell was that about? I've heard people talk nonsense before but that's a first. He must be delusional. Blaming all his problems on devils or hags or whatever. I've never seen anyone that far gone on alcohol." Ernest said.

He started home again. The chill in the air bit his face. The steam from his breath floated past his head as he moved through it.

"I guess the deputy was right about tonight being weird. I hope nothing else happens before I get home. If I see that drunk again, he might freak out and expect me to kill him. Or he might not recognize me and tell some other crazy story."

Ernest retuned home without another incident. He laid in bed reflecting on the night's events.

"That can't have been some random thing. Something has felt a little off since I got here but I thought it was because I'm an outsider. This town has a weird vibe. Why did you come here Linda? I'm still not sure you're even here. I better figure it out before something else weird happens."

Ernest approached the windows to close his curtains. He stood a moment peering outside. Down on the sidewalk, he saw a group of bullfrogs. Some were motionless. Some hopped a couple times then turned back to the rest of the group. He watched for a moment.

"Why are they out there? It has to be too cold for them."

All the bullfrogs hopped down the sidewalk a little way before turning into the grass. Their green bodies blended into the darkness.

Seven
November 7, 1976

Multiple reports went unnoticed because they called the sources unreliable. One of these reports came from a homeless man. Police labeled Stephen Currier a drunk and paid no attention to his statement. They had one of the newer officers file the report and put him in detox overnight. They released him the next morning. The rookie officer said he continued insisting the police search around the bend of the Kennebec River. His statement on the morning of November 7, 1976 read:

"I don't know what time it was. The town was quiet. Everyone was asleep. That's how come I heard it. The splashing. I had drunk a bottle of vodka and passed out behind one of the shops on Water Street. It was cold even with my blanket. I didn't notice at first anyone was there. I thought it was animals. I got up to find someplace warmer. That's when I saw them.

"Three women standing about waste deep in the water. It must have been freezing. They were saying something. I couldn't hear them. One of them was lowered back by the other two like she was getting baptized. She stayed under the water for a minute. She stood up slowly and wiped her face. Then one of the other women was lowered into the water. Then the third.

"They walked out of the water. I could see their breath and mine. I ran after them. I was gonna offer my blanket to keep them warm. When I got there, they was gone. I didn't hear a car. I didn't hear them go into one of the shops. They disappeared. I thought about looking in the water, but it was too cold. Something ain't right about all that. Something ain't right in this town."

The rookie officer recalled what Stephen Currier said about the appearance of the three women. He said one was blonde and they wore long black dresses. No other reports mentioned anyone in the river the night of the eclipse.

Eight
November 25, 1976

Ernest woke on Thanksgiving Day in the Hallowell police station. His only company were two men sleeping off too much alcohol. One of the officers hit the iron bars with his baton.

"Rise and shine, Cupcakes! Kemp! Detective wants a word." The officer said.

He led Ernest into a room with a long table, two chairs, and brutal fluorescent lighting. The officer left Ernest alone. There was a clock on the wall. He sat alone for 15 minutes. The detective walked in carrying a file and two cups of coffee. He set one down in front of Ernest.

"Good morning, Mister Kemp. This won't take long. Please sit down."

They both sat. The detective reviewed the file.

"When we spoke yesterday, you said on the night of the lunar eclipse you went to a few bars in Augusta. Some of the bartenders remembered you. We also verified your 911 call. I read the transcript. I need to fill some gaps to finalize my paperwork. What time did you leave for Augusta?"

"I left the general store a little after six. I changed in my apartment and called a taxi. It was maybe 6:30. It was a 15-minute drive. Maybe 20 minutes." Ernest said.

"Then you had dinner and made your rounds to all the bars."

"Yes."

The detective scribbled in the file then looked over

everything.

"Okay. That's all for now. Mister Kemp you are free to go. I may call you with some follow up questions."

"You never said why I was arrested."

"Officially you were never placed under arrest. We held you overnight while we verified your alibi. We found a child's body and got an anonymous tip that you were involved. The child died while you were still working. You're no longer a suspect."

"Why would anyone think it was me?"

"I suspect it was someone who thinks everyone in the war kills children. I wouldn't think too much about it. Good luck finding your wife."

Ernest sat a moment sipping his coffee. He couldn't make sense of the past 24 hours. He signed for his personal items. Everyone he passed walking home turned away. No one wanted to look at him. He passed the general store. It was closed for the holiday. He showered to wash off the holding cell smell. It reminded him of the drunks he spoke to the night before.

He walked over to the phone in his towel. It rang as his hand hovered over it.

"Hello?" He said.

"Happy Thanksgiving! I hope you're getting enough to eat."

"Hi Mom. Food isn't something on my mind at the moment."

"Oh. Is everything alright? You haven't found Linda, have you?"

"Not yet. And I spent the night in jail."

"What!? What happened? Did someone bail you out?"

"It was a 24 hour hold so they could check my alibi. Everything's fine. I wasn't arrested."

"Well, I'm glad to hear that, but what happened?"

"The last couple weeks have been uneventful. I worked and kept asking around about Linda and Amy. Yesterday the police picked me up at work. They said they had questions. They asked me about the night of the eclipse. I don't think you guys saw it out there. I told them my story and they held me there until they verified everything. I spent the night with a couple drunks.

"One of them slept the whole time. But he smelled awful. The other one gave me his whole life story. Bill was his name, and though not as bad as the sleeping drunk, Bill had a ripe odor about him."

"Well, those kinds of drinkers always do."

"Yeah. So, Bill told me about all his pets he's ever owned. I'd swear he kept talking after I rolled over to sleep. Anyway, this morning the detective told me everything I said checked out. Then they let me go. I just got out of the shower after getting home."

"I barely caught you at home."

"Yeah. I was about to pick up the phone to call when it rang. It made me jump a little."

"Well, why did they hold you? Did they ever say?"

"I guess a kid was killed. Someone said I did it, but I was working when it happened."

"How awful! The parents must be devastated."

"I suppose they are. I didn't ask for any more details. I don't know if it was a boy or a girl."

"That's all terrible. They must have something in the paper out there. A small town like that, I'm sure everyone knows about it by now."

"I got a lot of dirty looks this morning from the townsfolk. Most of them avoided me. I think I've got yesterday's paper somewhere. Yeah, there it is."

"What's it say?"

"Hold on. I'm looking."

Ernest searched the pages of the Kennebec Journal with the phone receiver wedged between his shoulder and ear.

"Here's something. Police have not identified the body of a young boy found early this morning in the Vaughn Brook River. A suspect was taken in for questioning, but no other details were released. The cause of death is still unknown. Police are treating this as a homicide investigation. Officers say they have no reason to believe this is related to the brutal murders last month."

"Is that it?" She said.

"Yeah. Maybe today's paper has more information. I'll

have to go out and get one. I have a friend who works for the paper, too. I can ask about it the next time I see her."

"Well, other than all that, how've you been?"

"I'm okay. I wish I could hold my baby girl. But otherwise, I'm getting by."

"I understand how you feel. Look, why don't you get some food. It's Thanksgiving after all. And I'm sure you're hungry after yesterday. And go get the paper. I want to know if the police are coming for my baby boy."

"Okay but I don't think they're worried about me anymore. I'll give you a call later tonight."

"Okay Ernie. Take care. And Happy Thanksgiving!"

"Happy Thanksgiving, Mom."

"Buh bye."

"Bye."

Ernest dressed and brushed his teeth. He didn't expect anyone to offer him a meal. He considered finding an open restaurant in Augusta. First, he wanted a newspaper. He was curious if his name was mentioned.

Most people were off visiting family, but a few still roamed the streets. Ernest found a newspaper dispenser. He inserted a nickel and a dime. He pulled the door down and removed one newspaper. The front page covered the Macy's Day Parade with an image of a Snoopy float from the year before. It listed the time and channel the parade would air.

He opened to the second and third page. In the bottom right corner of the third page read a small headline, "Body Found in River Still Not Identified." Ernest read the short article.

> *Police have not released the identity of the young boy found in the Vaughn Brook River early Wednesday morning. One suspect was taken into custody yesterday for questioning. Sources say this person has been cleared of all charges. Police are continuing to follow leads and are searching for a number of other suspects. When asked why the identity of the boy hadn't been released, Detective*

*Russel Vaughn of the Sheriff's Major Crimes Unit
had this to say.*

*'This is a difficult time for the family with the
holidays giving this a greater impact. The family
has asked us to withhold the boy's name until a
later time. We ask that the paper and the people of
Hallowell to respect the family's wishes.'*

*Detective Vaughn is hopeful the case will be
solved quickly. The Hallowell Police, Kennebec
County Sheriff, and Augusta Police are working
together on the case. As of today, officials do not
believe the murder is related to any other crimes. A
press conference is scheduled Tuesday morning to
discuss the details of the autopsy.*

*One local resident said they are pleased with
the quick action the authorities have taken with
this case. They said children should always take
priority.*

"Well, that didn't say much, did it. Mostly a repeat of
yesterday." Ernest said.

He reviewed the byline. The article was written by S.
Belcher. He wondered if she kept his name out as a courtesy or if
she was waiting to interview him. The only way to know was to
ask.

"I'll probably see her tomorrow. I'm sure she'll come by
the general store. Assuming Joe still wants me there. It doesn't
look good to have police take away one's employee during their
shift. I don't know if I can find more work if he lets me go."

Ernest carried the newspaper under his arm to free his
hands for a cigarette. He had three left.

"I think a walk to the gas station will do me some good.
I'll get some cigarettes. Maybe a sandwich. I'll go out to Augusta
a little later. I should go down to Portland sometime this weekend.
No one knows me down there. I'll get fewer stares. That'll be a
nice change of pace."

Ernest bought two packs of Lucky Strike cigarettes and a

ham and cheese sandwich.

"Is that today's paper?" The cashier said.

"Yeah, I'm done with it if you want it." Ernest said.

"Thanks. I only want the sports page. Everything else in the paper is bullshit."

"That's a fair assessment."

"Happy Thanksgiving to ya."

"You too. Thanks."

Ernest ate his sandwich walking back to his room. With only bread, meat, and cheese, it was a boring sandwich. MREs in the military had more flavor. He threw half of it away. He lit another cigarette in front of the trashcan. Something across the street caught his eye.

A dark green Buick. He walked past it to see the trunk. It resembled the car he saw the night someone buried something in the woods. It was dark that night. He never saw the car up close. Something inside him told him this was the car. He memorized the license plate.

"What was that deputy's name? Williams? No. Welsh? Dammit. Why didn't I write it down? The car might not be enough. This can't be the only Buick in town. I should wait and find out who owns it."

He leaned against a brick wall. He watched the car but looked around to look less suspicious. A few people walked past. None paid attention to Ernest. He was patient. He was focused. He was on mission. He occupied himself observing his cuticles. He bit a couple off. He always did this when his hands had nothing to do. He inhaled two cigarettes before anyone approached the car. A man approached the car.

Ernest's heart jumped. He held his breath, then sighed. The man passed the car without interest.

"Dammit. Relax. Someone's gonna notice. I'm just standing on a street having a smoke. That's all. Nothing to worry about. No one need pay any mind."

He lit a third cigarette. He walked at a slow pace to the end of the block furthest from the car. His chest started pounding.

"Nothing's happening. There's no one around. Why is this

happening? Why am I freaking out?"

He looked down the opposite street and saw the three women. The ones who made him feel uneasy.

"That's why my chest is pounding. What is it about them? I don't even know them. I feel this way around threats. People who might hurt me. What kind of threat are they?"

They all looked at Ernest, concern hovering on their faces. He felt their gaze pierce into his soul. They watched him until they passed him. He followed them with his eyes. They stopped at the dark green Buick. Ernest's heart raced. They got into the car and drove away.

He looked up and down the street after the car was out of sight. No one was around. No one saw them. He walked over where the car had been. He looked down the street.

"Where did they come from? What were they doing here? That has to be the car from the other night. There's no doubt. Those women are bad news. What the hell is that deputy's name?"

Nine
November 28, 1976 - Letter from Ernest

Dear Linda,

It's been six weeks since I got home from Cambodia. Six weeks and I've almost given up hope of finding you. The holidays are difficult when an entire town treats you like a pariah. It's hard to describe how alone I feel.

I miss you. I've missed you for the last two years. Every night all I wanted was to hold you in my arms. I miss the way you hugged me. The smell of your hair. Kissing you. I'm afraid I'll never have those things again. Will I ever see you again? Do you even want to see me? And what of Amy?

How was your Thanksgiving? I didn't do much. Woke up in jail. Someone accused me of a crime. I was innocent so they let me go. No harm. No foul. The rest of the day was uneventful for the most part. I talked to mom on the phone. I told her what happened with the police. Later in the afternoon, I found a restaurant that was open and had a nice warm meal. One of the best I've had in a long time. I called it an early night and slept like the dead.

The next day, Joe, my boss, asked me what happened with the police. I told him everything. He said he wasn't worried. He knew I'd come out on top. I was just happy to still have my job. I think he gave me extra work to do because of it though. The store gets extra merchandise for the holidays anyway. I guess it all worked out.

I haven't heard from my friend who works at the newspaper. I think she put some effort into keeping my name out of the paper with this whole police thing. I thought she would have tried to talk to me by now. Maybe work has her doing all kinds of stuff.

I'm running out of ideas on where to look for you. I feel like I've asked everyone in this town. Most of them won't talk to me after the police thing. They've told people I'm no longer suspected of any crimes and still people think I'm guilty. I went to Portland, Maine yesterday. No one knows me there. It was a nice break. No one avoided me. No one gave me dirty looks. No luck finding you either. There are some nice little shops though. Maybe we can visit Portland together sometime. We'll roam all the shops together. You, me, and Amy.

Maine is beautiful in the fall. Most of the leaves are gone now. But for a while there were lots of yellows, oranges, and reds. I guess you've seen it too. I like to smoke outside. I like the cool air on my throat. I watch the wind blow all the leaves around and feel the chill on my face. It's a nice change from the humidity in Cambodia. And I'm not carrying 50 pounds of gear. I had to change my socks three times every day. We were always moving. I couldn't sleep most nights because I felt anxious. No one could predict when we might run into the enemy. Even on calm days when nothing happened, everyone was on edge waiting for the other shoe to drop.

I thought about you and wrote you letters every day. I hope you got them all. Sometimes thinking of you was the only thing that would calm me down enough to finally sleep. That was the only thing that kept me going. I think it's the only thing that keeps me going now. Writing these letters. I guess I need someone to talk to and that's what these letters do for me. It's an outlet. A way to keep from bottling things up.

The truth is I'm scared I'll never see you again. Maybe you don't want to see me. I hope that's not the case. You've been a part of my life for so long. I don't know how to go on without you. Maybe that's the point of all this. It's a test. A test that will help me overcome whatever I need to overcome. I think I live in my head too much. I've spent so much time thinking about you. Imagining being with you and doing things we haven't done yet. I'm afraid

I don't know you like I thought I did. I think I know you well but maybe I'm wrong. Maybe I don't know the real you because I ignored the parts I didn't like. I'm certain I love you. I have no illusions about that. Everything else is just noise. Sometimes too much of that noise is overwhelming.

I don't like being in crowds anymore. I'm not sure anyone likes it, but it's been difficult lately. I get annoyed or irritated. I can't stand hearing other people talk. It's all bullshit. There's no meaning behind any of it. It's just more noise. I like things to be quiet. Something about living through a fire fight makes you want everything to slow down and be quiet.

It's like the old men who spend all day in the general store. They bicker and complain about anything and everything, but they never shut up and do anything. I think they like to hear themselves talk. Maybe they're hoping someone will listen. Nobody wants to hear about it but sometimes I wish I could tell someone about the war. Sometimes I just want to be heard. Do you exist if no one hears you? I guess my point is I don't want to listen to them, and they don't want to listen to me. Some days I take extra smoke breaks to avoid the noise.

Maybe I'm overthinking everything. Maybe I listen more than I should to things I don't like. I don't feel like I'm adjusting to civilian life well. I still roll my clothes. I'm still up at four in the morning. I still put hospital corners when I make my bed. I haven't used any of the skills I learned since I came back. It's like I have to learn how to live again. It's like everything is starting over. I hate it. I hate change.

Do you remember when we first met? I had some leave after my first year in the Navy. There was a carnival. I think it was to raise money for a school or something. You were selling cotton candy. I hate cotton candy but I bought six different things so I could keep seeing you. You thought I was drunk. I told you I was stone sober. You ignored me for a while. Maybe you weren't interested. Then an older gentleman passed out from the heat. You saw me take care of him.

I never told you what that man said to me. He thanked me for being kind. He said the world needed more kind people. I told him not to thank me. It was my training. I knew how to help. He asked if I was going to Vietnam. I nodded. His eyes started to water. He said, "I hope you make it home, son."

I went over to get more cotton candy. You asked if I was sure I wanted another. I said I didn't want another, and I only wanted to see you again. You rolled your eyes and said, "Oh!" But I saw you smile too. You know, I've never had that much luck trying to ask a girl out. It was meant to be, I think. Good things don't last forever, do they? Is our good thing over? Is that why you left? Is there someone else? Another man? Is that why you don't want your family to know?

After all this time, I never thought it might be another man. I've thought all kinds of things. But never that before. I guess you got tired of waiting for me. I got a Dear John letter when I was in basic training. It had only been four weeks after I left. All I'm saying is, I understand if you found someone while I was gone. I hope that's not why you've run off. I hope we can still be a family. I want to meet and get to know our daughter. I hope you'll give me that much."

Love Always,
Ernie

Ten
December 4, 1976

After the boy's body was found, everyone called the police and the paper with wild theories. Each one more insane than the last. One person said it was the government. Another person said aliens. Someone else claimed both government and aliens. People claimed to have information about the murders in October. Ernest became an outlet for the town's anger. Everyone wanted someone to blame. Someone to punish.

"Hey Samantha! Why don't you ask him why he did it? Why'd he kill those people?" One man said.

"I've never killed anyone!" Ernest said.

"He wasn't even in town when the first murders happened." Samantha said.

"Is that what he told ya?"

"Well, where were you that night?" Samantha said.

"Don't try to turn this on me. I ain't the one on trial."

"No one's on trial! You're making blind accusations. You got any evidence?" Samantha said.

"Well…he killed people in the war! He's a murderer."

"I never killed anyone! I was a medic! I administered first aid on the battlefield! I saved lives!" Ernest said.

The store fell quiet. People were thinking of responses.

"I couldn't save everyone. I regret that."

The silence grew awkward. Some men sat down losing interest.

"If it wasn't him, who did it?"

"Finally, someone is asking the right question." Samantha said.

"You don't gotta be sassy 'bout it." Joe said.

"Shut up Joe." Samantha said.

"It could be someone from Bangor. I hear they got a crazy house up there. One of 'em coulda escaped and come down here to kill folks. It could happen."

"Anyone have any ideas they didn't make up out of thin air?" Samantha said.

"What about those three odd women?" Ernest said.

"What women?"

"The blonde, brunette, and redhead. They came in about a month ago. Everyone stared at them." Ernest said.

"I never saw any three women like that."

"You asked them if they needed help. You were drooling all over them." Samantha said.

"Hogwash!"

"You remember them, don't you Joe? They bought a bunch of candy and herbs." Ernest said.

"Ayuh. I remember. They asked some odd questions too. Why you bringin' them up?" Joe said.

"What if they killed that boy? Or the couple from before?" Ernest said.

"For what?" Samantha said.

"I don't know. But they give off a weird vibe. And I think I saw them dumping something in the woods a few weeks ago. Dammit! I keep forgetting to call that deputy. What was his name? Welsh or something."

"You mean Wells? Jed Wells?" Samantha said.

"That's him." Ernest said.

"Now who's pullin' stuff outta' thin air?" The man said.

"What?" Ernest said.

"You're making stuff up. Quit lyin' and confess!"

Ernest froze. Those words brought back a memory. One Ernest didn't know he had.

***

"You lyin' to me? You know I hate that. You might be my

53

son, but I'll whip you into next week if you lie to me."

"It's the truth daddy! Honest. I didn't…"

"Well who did boy!? Things don't just up and break. How'd it break?"

"I don't know."

"You better come up with an answer quick. Do I need to get my belt?"

"No, sir."

"Tell me what happened."

"I don't…"

"And don't say you don't know. That's no answer. What happened?"

The boy stood still with tears rolling down his cheek.

"You better answer me."

The boy remained silent.

"So, that's how it's gonna be? You think you can end the conversation when you want? Gail? Gail! Bring my belt. The boy doesn't wanna' confess to what he did wrong."

"I didn't do nothing!"

"Quit lyin' to me!"

***

Ernest blinked and shook his head.

"You okay? You went blank for a second." Samantha said.

"Sorry. Yeah, just remembering something. It's not important."

"See that? He got stuck tryin' to think up a new story. You're full a' bologna!"

"Maybe those women did do it. Maybe they didn't. It can't hurt to talk to them." Ernest said.

"How you gonna find a bunch of imaginary women?"

The small crowd in the general store roared with laughter.

"I don't know but I'll find them." Ernest said.

The men doubled over with laughter. Some gasped for air. Others coughed from the strain on their throat.

"Don't listen to those jackasses. When the real killer is found, they'll say they knew it wasn't you the whole time. They're so full of it." Samantha said.

"I'm tired of everyone in this town treating me like a bag of shit." Ernest said.

"I know. But things will get better."

"It doesn't feel like it."

"Sometimes it doesn't but things still get better. Trust me."

"Tall order. I don't trust anyone. Especially them."

"You shouldn't trust them. But me? I kept your name out of the paper. Doesn't that count for something?"

"I guess. Don't you just want my story for yourself?"

"Only if you want to tell me your story."

"I don't know what I want anymore."

"I know the feeling. So, what are you gonna do?"

"I haven't decided. I guess all I want is to see my wife and daughter."

"I meant what are you gonna do about finding those women?"

"Oh! I don't know. I see them at random. I saw their car once."

"You get the license plate?"

"Yeah."

"When you're done here, we'll pay a visit to a friend of mine with the Sheriff's Department. I think you talked to him already."

"You mean Wells? What was his first name?"

"Jed."

"Yeah. That's the deputy I talked to on the phone. Let's go see him."

"He's not working today, but he can help us out. He owes me."

They drove to Jed's house. He rinsed his car with a water hose. He looked confused as Samantha's car stopped in front on the street. He turned the water off as Samantha left her car.

"No. No! You don't come to my house to get your story." Jed said.

"That's not why I'm here. A friend of mine needs your help." Samantha said.

"What kind of help?"

Ernest stepped out of the car.

"Deputy Jed Wells? You spoke to me on the phone the night of the eclipse." Ernest said.

"Look, I'm not on duty. Can this wait 'til tomorrow?"

"We think it has to do with the boy that was found." Samantha said.

"Shit. Alright. I'll put on some coffee."

"You're an angel." Samantha said.

"I'm a pushover is what I am."

Jed's kitchen was an ugly yellow with flowers on the wallpaper. He lit the fire and put a percolator on the stove.

"Okay. What's the story?" Jed said.

"You told me to contact you if I remembered anything about what I saw that night. I think I found the car. I saw it in town on Thanksgiving."

"Okay. What's that got to do with the kid?"

"I think they're the ones who did it. The people I saw."

"You think they killed the kid?"

"Yes."

"You saw them in the car?"

"Yes. All three of them."

"Three?"

"I only saw two of them that night but they're always together."

"Who?"

"The three strange women in town. The blonde, brunette, and redhead."

"I don't know who or what you're talkin' about. I found out what you saw that night. Some folks that live just outside town we're drinkin' and huntin'. One of them got hit with some buckshot. They took him home to clean him up, but it was bad. They took him to the hospital. What you saw was them throwing out the bloody throw rug. We had them dig it up and charged them a fine. It was down the street from where you called that night. There weren't any bodies."

"What kind of car do they have?" Ernest said.

"A brown Buick. So, who do you think killed that kid?

What three women?"

"You haven't seen them around? Most of the guys in town drool all over when they walk by." Samantha said.

"That sounds like somethin' I'd remember. What about 'em?"

"They're really odd." Samantha said.

"They make me uncomfortable." Ernest said.

"That's not enough to accuse someone of murder." Jed said.

"It made more sense when I thought they hid a body."

"You can still look up their license plate, right?" Samantha said.

"I need a reason. Something better than they make someone uncomfortable."

"You got a call about reckless driving. You'll pay them a visit and tell them to be careful." Samantha said.

"I won't visit anyone. But I can check if the driver has a record. If they have a record, I can bring 'em in. That's no guarantee. I need evidence to charge someone with murder."

"Get us a name. We can do the rest."

"Okay. But we never had this conversation."

"Everyone knows we talk. They'll figure out how I got the information."

"Then don't admit to it. It's called confidential informant for a reason."

"I don't need you to explain how this works. This isn't my first rodeo."

"Then put on your big girl pants and take this seriously."

"What the hell is that supposed to mean?"

"It means if there's a killer out there, I don't want you pissing him off."

"How do you know it's not a woman?"

"Eh…we don't know anything. I only want you to be careful."

"I can handle myself."

"So can I, and my family still tells me to be careful because they care about me."

"Jed, you old softy. If I didn't know better, I'd say you were flirting with me."

"Dammit Samantha. Please take this seriously."

"I am taking it seriously."

"Then act like it!"

Silence grew in the kitchen with the tension. The only noise came from the percolator. Ernest broke the silence.

"Is the coffee ready?"

"Ayuh." Jed said.

"Can you help us with the plate number?" Ernest said.

"Ayuh. What's the number?"

"I wrote it down."

Ernest pulled paper from his pocket and handed it to Jed.

"Green Buick?" Jed said.

"Yeah. You've seen it?" Ernest said.

"No. But I might know who owns it. I'll let you know what I find out."

"Can you find out tomorrow?" Samantha said.

"I'll try. I might not get a chance until the next day. I'll call you when I have something."

"I know you can't give details, but do they have other suspects?" Ernest said.

"You mean besides you. I don't know. Detective Vaughn heads the investigation. I'm not involved."

"Isn't he on the Outlet Road case?" Samantha said.

"Ayuh. As far as I know he's investigating both. The guy's a work horse. Some of the other officers joke that he never sleeps. He's always cheerful. I don't know how he does it."

"I hope he can handle it." Ernest said.

"He's the best we got. I think he's giving the kid's case priority, but he still has leads on the other one."

"He doesn't come across as a detective." Samantha said.

"What do you mean?" Ernest said.

"He's charming and personable. He doesn't have that gaze like most cops. Where it looks like they don't believe anything you say."

"Most people lie to the police. That's why we have that look." Jed said.

"Be he doesn't?" Ernest said.

"No. It's like he's trying to listen instead of reading you. You know?" Samantha said.

"So, what do we do now?"

"You two can do what you want but somewhere else. I'm enjoying the rest of my night off." Jed said.

Eleven
December 11, 1976

"A little higher now. A bit more. Hold that. That looks good. Tie it off." Joe said.

"Isn't this sign a bit much?" Ernest said.

Ernest stood on a latter in front of the general store. A large sign reading 'Merry Christmas' stretched across the building.

"We hang it every year. It's tradition. Some folks say it don't feel like Christmas until they see the sign." Joe said.

"It's kind of big and bulky."

"Ayuh, but we can't afford to get another made. Now bring that ladder inside we got more stuff to hang."

"You mean I have more stuff to hang."

"That's why I'm payin' ya. Unless you wanna stand outside draggin' folks in to buy everythin'."

"Definitely not."

"Then quit your gripin'. The tree will go in that corner over yonder. The small wreaths and snowflakes hang over all the shelves. Christmas lights in the windows, the door, and around the freezers. Have fun." Joe said.

Ernest spent the whole afternoon decorating. He enjoyed this. Few people talked to him and he stayed busy. He hadn't heard from Jed or Samantha in a few days. The three women hadn't been around either. He fought with a cluster of Christmas lights.

"This thing is pissing me off. I must be stupid if I can't untangle this rat's nest. I can't find those women. I can't find my wife and daughter. I'm not good for anything except grunt labor.

Everyone in this town hates me. Half of them hate me for being an outsider. The other half think I'm a murderer. I don't want to be here anymore. I haven't gained anything from this place except more pain and frustration."

He shook the lights with vigor. Only a couple feet came lose. He dropped them to the floor. He rubbed his face and sighed.

"Hey Joe. I'm gonna grab a coffee and have a smoke. These lights are pissing me off."

"Alrighty. I don't need you shoutin' in front a customers."

"I've never done that."

"And you won't if you calm down. Don't take too long. I want those lights up before we close."

"It'll get done. If I can handle getting shot at, I can handle some tangled Christmas lights."

"That's the right attitude. You're doin' a great job with that decoratin'. No need to get flustered."

"Thanks Joe. I'll be right back."

"I'll give them lights a talkin' to while yer out."

Ernest chuckled out the door lighting a cigarette. His thoughts continued running back and forth.

"I hate Christmas. I hate that everyone else loves Christmas. I only have bad memories from this time of year. It's not the greatest thing ever. No one decorates for an entire month for any other holiday. It's all bullshit. I wish I could go somewhere they don't celebrate all this shit. Everyone's smiling and snuggling each other. They must be faking. No one's that happy."

He got a coffee at the restaurant down the street from the general store. The first sip burned his tongue. The steam felt good on his face. The paper cup warmed his hands. He held the coffee to his face without drinking. He savored the aroma.

"All coffee is better than military coffee."

He walked back towards the store. The brisk air pierced his throat. The coffee was still too hot but warmed his throat. The steam from his breath mixed with the steam form his coffee. Something caught his eye.

He watched a blonde walk down the street. She was alone. She didn't look like one of the three. His heart raced.

"What's wrong with me? Am I going crazy? I never used to act this way. Not even in Cambodia. I don't remember my chest pounding so much. Am I out of shape? It's been a while since I've gone running or done any exercise. That must be it. I should see a doctor to be sure. What if I've developed some medical condition? Older men have heart problems and still live normal lives. I guess it could be stress. Everything has me worried these days. I haven't taken any time off. I've been looking for Linda. I haven't enjoyed anything. I should see a doctor anyway. Maybe it's nothing."

Ernest took his time with a cigarette. It took a lot of effort not to suck it down. He wasn't eager to return to work or the tangle of lights. He watched everyone up and down the street. It was a busy day in Hallowell. Christmas shopping got done. Deliveries were made. Kids lingered in different places talking.

"Hey! We should go see that new movie 'Rocky' at the cineplex." The first kid said.

"What's that?" The other said.

"It's a show about a boxer."

"Oh! My pop read a review in the paper. He wants to see it."

Ernest hadn't heard of the movie but was interested in boxing. The last film he saw was 'Blazing Saddles' with Linda. That was the last night they were together before he shipped out. He was to report for duty on the U.S.S. Oriskany. And aircraft carrier nicknamed the Mighty-O. He was to return in six months, like always. Then the boat sank and a platoon of Marines lost their corpsman. He was reassigned.

"I could have got out then. Left the military and could have seen when my baby girl was born. Why did I go with the Marines?"

He stared off at nothing specific. Someone walked into him. He got shaken back to the present.

"Sa…sorry." A man said.

The man stumbled away. He tried not to walk into everything on the sidewalk. He stopped a moment and leaned on a wall. Ernest watched the man. Not thinking. Observing.

"Why do I keep meeting all the drunks in town?"

The man attempted to walk again and fell back against the wall in panic. Three bullfrogs hopped past him on the sidewalk. The man looked terrified and confused.

"Hey! Hey! What the hell are you doin'? You know where yer s'posed to be. Now go on!" The man said.

Ernest remembered his first night in Cambodia. His first firefight.

***

A man shouts at Ernest over rifles and explosions.

"Hey! Hey!"

The man claps his hands in Ernest's face.

"What the hell are you doin'!? You know where you're supposed to be! Now go on!" The man says.

"But I haven't had SARC training, Gunnery Sergeant!" Ernest says.

"Well, you're in the shit now so you better figure it the fuck out! My Marines need medical attention! Move your ass! If they die, I'll kill you myself!"

"Yes, Gunnery Sergeant!" Ernest says.

Ernest starts running. He dives to the ground after a grenade blows a few feet from him. He looks up and sees the injured Marines. He crawls to them to avoid rounds flying overhead. One Marine holds his left arm.

"Fuck, it burns!" The Marine says.

"Hold on! I'm gonna wrap a tourniquet on your arm to stop the bleeding!" Ernest says.

"Take the bullet out!"

"That can wait 'til no one's shooting at us!

Ernest tightens a strap around the Marine's arm. He puts some of the blood on his finger and writes 'T 1324' on the Marine's forehead.

"It still burns!"

"Here!"

Ernest pulls out a small needle and stabs it into the Marine's arm.

"What the fuck is that!?"

"Morphine! You'll feel better! You! Stay with him! When

the morphine kicks in he's gonna get stupid! Don't let him shoot his foot off!" Ernest said.

"Where you goin'!?"

"To see if anyone else got shot!"

Ernest squats and duck walks to a Marine on the ground. Another Marine shouts at the one on the ground.

"Get up Jones! Keep shooting!"

"He's dead Marine!" Ernest says.

"What!? Bullshit!"

"He got a bullet to the face! He's gone!"

"Motherfuckers!"

The Marine screams firing blindly in three different directions. Ernest doesn't know where the enemy is and doesn't want to know. He passes more Marines.

"Whoo! This is where we separate the men from the boys! Let's get these sum'bitches!" Another Marine says.

"Fuck! My rifle jammed again!"

"That's why you gotta clean that shit every day!"

"I do clean it every day shitbag!"

The sound of rapid gunfire forces everyone's heads down. The vegetation around them is mutilated. A tree branch creaks as it falls behind them.

"You don't see that every day!"

***

"You don't see that every day." Joe said.

"Huh. What?"

Ernest jerked back to reality. Joe stood next to him. They both watched the drunk shout at the bullfrogs.

"Go on! Git! Get outta here!"

"Why's he screaming?" Ernest said.

"He's drunk. And bullfrogs hibernate in the Winter. I ain't never seen 'em this late in the year. They gonna' freeze tonight if they don't find a warm place to sleep." Joe said.

"The longer you stay in a place, the more weird shit you see."

"What's that?"

"Nothing Joe."

"Oh. Well, them lights are waitin' for ya."

Ernest sucked one more drag off his cigarette. His hand shook as it rose to his mouth. He ignored it and flicked away the cigarette. His body felt heavier. He moved slower. His head hurt. He didn't remember it hurting before. He glared at the pile of Christmas lights. He hated them. He wanted to throw them in the trash. He thought of stomping out all the little bulbs.

"Joe, you got any Tylenol in the back?" Ernest said.

"We out of it on the shelves?"

"No. I want some. I got a headache."

"Oh. Take a bottle off the shelf. You can pay me later."

"Thanks."

He walked to the shelf taking his time. Anything to avoid the tangled mess of lights was helpful. He found a bottle. He struggled and strained himself to get it open. He removed the cotton ball and swallowed two pills dry. He put the bottle and the cotton ball in his pocket. He returned to the lights. His chest pounded.

"These lights don't want to cooperate. It's like they're laughing at me. Like they tangled themselves on purpose. Why would anyone wad all this shit together anyway? Do they forget this happens every year? Or do they not care as long as they don't have to deal with it? This is all bullshit. Civilians are inconsiderate savages. I don't know how Joe is so friendly with everyone. Maybe he's been here long enough to get to know everyone. I bet if people knew me, they wouldn't stare so much or give me dirty looks. But I don't want to talk to any of them. I don't need to get to know them. I don't plan to be here long. But I can't do anything right. I've been here six weeks and can't find my wife and daughter. What's the point?"

Ernest fought with the mess of lights for half an hour. He made progress. Despite overcoming the obstacle, he grew more frustrated. He began hanging the lights in the windows. People watched outside. Some people watched inside.

"They're gonna stare at me all day and not offer any help. What the hell is so exciting about this?"

A woman and her son stood near Ernest watching.

"Look Billy. Christmas lights. Isn't that fun?"

The boy looked disinterested.

"Can I help you with something, ma'am?" Ernest said.

"No, thank you."

She stared as Ernest worked with a giant grin on her face. Her son fidgeted.

"Excuse me. I need to move the ladder over here."

"Oh. I'm so sorry. We're in your way. Come on Billy. Let's get out of the man's way so he can finish hanging the pretty Christmas lights. I just love Christmas. All the decorations and the presents and the snow. Isn't it just wonderful?

"Uh-huh." Ernest said.

The woman continued telling Ernest why she loved Christmas. He had no interest. He wanted to finish working and go home. Her son Billy had about as much interest in Christmas as Ernest.

"Maryann, I pay him to work not to socialize. Let the man alone or he'll never get them lights hung." Joe said.

"Oh, hi Joe. I was showing Billy the lights. Say hi Billy."

The boy waved while hiding behind his mother.

"That woman is too bubbly for me. I should thank Joe after she leaves." Ernest said.

Joe walked around with Maryann while Ernest finished hanging lights. She finally left as the store was closing. Ernest tested all the lights.

"Looks like they're all working." Ernest said.

"Boy that woman's a chatterbox. Wow! It looks good in here. Ya did a hell of a job. Ya should be proud."

"Thanks Joe. I'm ready for a nap."

"A nap sounds real nice. Okay, I'll lock up. See ya tomorrow."

"Goodnight Joe."

Twelve
December 25, 1976

Ernest sat in his room in darkness. Without lights, his room was darker than outside. A small orange glow from the tip of his cigarette was the only light source. He sipped the last of a drink. Ice clattered around the glass. He stared out the window.

Earlier that day he spoke to his mother. The usual holiday discussions. He told her he still hadn't found Linda and Amy. He lied and said he was doing fine. He lied and said he had dinner plans that evening. Later he spoke to his mother-in-law. She did most of the speaking. Ernest listened without interest. The highlights of his day ended.

He got more ice from a small bucket. He poured another glass of Jameson Irish Whiskey. He sat down sipping his drink. Starting the second glass made his face feel numb. He didn't want to feel anymore. He sucked his cigarette in his right hand. The whiskey glass rested in his left.

"I hate this holiday. They say spread good cheer and call this the season of giving. If I was dying on the street, they'd all walk past me. They're all hypocrites."

Ernest sipped his whiskey. He listened to the ice clink on the glass. He sucked his cigarette. He listened to the burning as he inhaled. It was too dark to see any smoke. The only other sound was a ticking clock. He focused on the noise.

Tick. Tick. Tick.

The consistent rhythm was soothing. Ernest opened a window to release the uncomfortable warmth in the room. He savored the cool air on his face. He heard voices from the street.

"What is that thing?" A woman said.

"It's the new Polaroid SX-70 camera." A man said.

"Is that one of those instant cameras?"

"Ayuh. I got it for Christmas. You take the picture. Pull out the photo. Then wait a few minutes. You watch it develop."

"Far out!"

He heard a thump outside his room. He opened the door to investigate. Christmas music played down the hall. A man and a woman stumbled away from Ernest. They giggled. The man noticed Ernest.

"Hey man. You like to party?"

The man touched his nose. Ernest stepped back into his room. He shut and locked the door after hearing the woman say, "Guess not." Their muffled laughter irritated Ernest. He finished his whiskey in one gulp.

He heard more laughter outside his window. People attempting to sing '12 Days of Christmas.' They were too drunk to succeed. Ernest poured another glass of whiskey. He lit another cigarette. The noises outside and outside his room stopped.

"Thank God."

His room echoed the sound of the clock.

Tick. Tick. Tick.

The clank of ice on glass. The burning of tobacco. These peaceful noises were short lived. Laughter erupted down the hall from his room. Someone had arrived to the party. The door down the hall closed. The music and laughter left as fast as they came.

"I'm gonna' have to deal with that all night. All I want for Christmas is some peace and quiet."

"Hey!"

Someone was yelling outside. Ernest went to the window. They weren't looking at him. He shut the window. He surveyed his room in the darkness. He had no decorations. No tree. No presents. He always thought those things were for the benefit of children.

Without much to do, he laid on his bed. He had books to read but nothing interested him. He considered joining the party down the hall. He didn't feel much like socializing. He sat up and rubbed his face. He sipped more whiskey and sucked his cigarette. He paced back and forth several times around the room. His thoughts started moving as fast as his body.

"This is ridiculous. I'm too wired to sleep. I don't want to go out or be around people. None of them want me around anyway. All the restaurants are closed. If I had a car, I'd go for a drive and listen to the radio. I could write another letter to Linda, but what's the point? I've nowhere to send it. Goddammit! Why didn't she say where she was going? She doesn't want me to know. She doesn't want me around. No one wants me around. When I got home, no one cared that I was leaving again. Hell, they encouraged it. They liked not having me around. Everyone in this town hates me too. They all want me to leave. Everyone's happier when I'm gone. Maybe the world is better off without me."

He stopped moving. He inhaled the last of his cigarette; his hand shaking. He went to the bathroom and splashed water on his face. He stared a moment at his reflection; his furrowed brow, the beard he had grown in the last few weeks, his brown eyes., and the dark circles under them. A water droplet fell from his chin. He dried his face with a towel and took a breath. He pushed his chin sideways cracking his neck.

He stared at his dresser. He sipped his whiskey and looked at the dresser again. He wasn't sure how long he stared. He opened the top drawer. His socks and underwear, rolled to the size of a fist, each looked up at him. He moved some to the side to reveal a revolver.

Ernest held a Colt Python. It glinted light from outside on its bright nickel finish. It had a four-inch barrel. He held the wood finished grip and opened the cylinder. It wasn't loaded. He looked at the box of .357 magnum rounds. He closed the double-action revolver returning it to the drawer. He stared. He hesitated then shut the dresser drawer.

He sipped more whiskey and lit another cigarette. He sat in the dark silence. He glanced at the dresser and continued sipping his whiskey. He finished the pack of cigarettes and the bottle of whiskey before sleeping.

Thirteen
December 31, 1976

An uneventful week passed. Ernest worked then went home to his room every day. He wanted to avoid the cold. He wanted to avoid people. Another year was coming.

"1977. Another year without my wife and daughter. Another year stuck in some shithole all alone. At least no one's shooting at me. Not yet anyway. If someone else dies, the town might try to hang me in the street."

The clock read a quarter to ten when Ernest laid down for the night. The bed was warm and comfortable. He dozed off fast.

He was startled awake by loud noises outside. They sounded like gunfire. In a disoriented panic, Ernest stumbled to the dresser. He grabbed the revolver. His attempt to open the box of rounds knocked them all over. With two rounds in his hand, he stopped. He heard laughter. There were a few more cracking pops. Someone lit fireworks outside. The clock read five after midnight. He dropped the rounds in the dresser drawer. He sat on the bed. His breaths were quick and heavy. His chest pounded and vibrated his whole body. He had forgotten the revolver was still in his shaking hand. He closed the cylinder and dropped it on the bed. He rubbed his face and took several deep breaths. He heard more laughter and party favors down the hall from his room. He poured himself a glass of whiskey. He took several deep breaths and clenched his shaking fist.

"I hate the holidays."

He sipped more whiskey trying to calm down. He opened

and closed his fist multiple times. He picked up the revolver. He held it a moment. He remembered how he felt on Christmas. He still felt that way.

"I fuck up everything. I'd probably fuck this up too. There'd at least be one poor bastard's life my death would fuck up. The guy who'd have to clean up my mess. I wouldn't wish that on my worst enemy."

He opened the cylinder making sure it wasn't loaded. He returned it to the dresser drawer. The noise of fireworks subsided. Ernest remembered a Marine who died in a hospital bed. This was before he was transferred to a Marine unit.

***

"Things are looking good. Your wounds are healing well. And you'll get to go home once the doctors release you." Ernest says.

"What if I don't wanna go home?" The Marine says.

"You'd rather go back to the jungle? Back to the fight? What if you get killed or…?"

"Yeah, so what? What if that's what I deserve? After what I did, I should get put down."

"What'd you do?"

The Marine is silent. He looks away fighting back tears.

"Corporal Lewis. Talk to me. What happened to you?"

"A couple weeks ago, my unit marched through some small village. The locals were families. No one had guns or anything. They said the Viet Cong were around. So, we held up there waiting for some action. We waited a while. Then some Vietnamese kid started walkin' into the village. None of the locals knew him. He was small too. Like he only just learned to walk. He had a vest or somethin' on. We had heard of kids with bombs killing US Troops. Our Captain gave the order to stop the kid before he got to the village. Everyone hesitated. No one wanted to kill a kid. The Captain shouted. Put the kid out of his misery he said. I took the shot. He fell backwards. Everybody was quiet for a while. Then the bomb the kid was wearin' went off. There was nothin' left of the kid."

"You think you don't deserve to go home because you

killed a kid? The kid had a bomb. You saved your unit and that village.”

"Was it worth killin’ some kid? He was barely a toddler.”

“You were following orders.”

“That don’t make it right!”

“Okay. I’m gonna find you someone who can help you with this. Someone you can talk to.”

“I don’t wanna talk anymore.”

“I’ll have the doctor check on you. I’ll be right back.”

“Whatever man.”

Ernest leaves the ward and finds a nurse.

“Excuse me. Can we get a shrink or Chaplain or something? There’s a guy who isn’t coping. He doesn’t want to go home. I think he…”

A gunshot fills the ward. Ernest and the nurse run towards the sound. Corporal Lewis lays motionless. A pistol in his right hand. Blood and brain matter are splattered on the wall behind him. People are screaming. Orderlies enter then stop. Ernest stares at the scene. One hand covers his mouth.

“I tried to help him. I did. I wasn’t much help. I was trying to find a doctor. I tried. I tried.” Ernest says.

The nurse rubs his shoulder.

“It’s not your fault.” She says.

“There must have been something else I could have done.”

“You did everything you could. We can’t save everyone.”

***

In his room, Ernest stared at the revolver.

“We can’t save everyone. I learned that the hard way. Sometimes we can’t even save ourselves.”

He closed the drawer. He swallowed the rest of his whiskey and poured another. He lit a cigarette.

“Happy New Year. I guess I should think of a New Year’s Resolution. Finding my wife and daughter is a pretty good one. Maybe finding out why those women are so weird. Getting out of Maine sounds like a great plan, too. My patience for the dirty looks and “Ayuhs” is wearing thin. Am I ever going home?”

Ernest stood in the dark. The festivities had quieted. The

champagne and alcohol had finally put people to sleep. He finished his cigarette. Then he finished his whiskey. He laid in bed. Eyes open staring at the ceiling.

"I can't end up like Corporal Lewis. I don't know what to do anymore. But I'm not giving up. I won't quit. I'm done when the mission is done."

Fourteen
January 1, 1977 - Letter from Ernest

Dear Linda,

Happy New Year! I hope we find each other soon. I want to spend as much time with you as possible. That's my resolution. That's all I want. To see you and Amy. The holidays are difficult without you. Being in a strange town with no family or friends would give anyone a hard time.

Being around other people has been hard. I can't stand most of them. Most of them don't talk to me but I overhear their conversations Some people out there are dumb.

The other day, this guy said we left Vietnam because Nixon resigned. I told him the US left about a year before Nixon resigned. He didn't believe me. He said my facts were wrong. I said I was there. I remember when we left. He ignored me and walked away. These people have no idea what they're talking about. And you can't correct them. They assume you're personally attacking them.

I try to avoid most conversations. Especially during the holidays. Everyone wants to talk about being cheerful and loving the holidays. They call it a beautiful, magical, happy time. I don't have much to be cheerful about. Maybe I feel that way because I didn't sleep much last night.

People set off firecrackers for New Year's at midnight. It woke me up. I thought someone was shooting at me. I almost loaded my revolver and fired out the window. People already hate me in this town. I'm sure that would set them off more. They'd probably tell me to leave town and never come back.

If I wasn't looking for you, I would have left by now. Some people still think I killed that kid. If the real killer is caught, I'm not sure if people will believe the police. They'll still say I killed him. Some people start hating something and they never quit. It's like they thrive on hate. Some people enjoy hating something. Some people want something, anything to hate. Maybe I do too. I hate a lot of things these days. I don't remember hating so much.

I had a nightmare a few nights ago. It startled me awake. I can't remember having a dream like that since I was a kid. Anyway, I'm running from something in my dream. I don't know what it was, but my adrenaline was pumping. I never see anything. Somehow, I know whatever I'm running from is bad and will hurt me. I kept running until I woke. I didn't feel afraid after waking. My chest pounded. My breaths were heavier than normal. I tossed and turned the rest of the night.

My mother used to say that dreams were the mind's way of filing events of the prior day to help you remember them. This nightmare had nothing to do with events of any day. I don't understand what it means. I guess it won't mean much unless I have the same dream again. Maybe there's no meaning. Maybe dreams have nothing to do with the events of your day.

I've been feeling down the past few weeks. Like I don't have a purpose anymore. I'm not sure what it means to do anything. I'm not interested in anything. I don't know what to do. Right now, the only thing I can think about is looking for you and Amy. That's all that keeps me going and every day I feel like I'm getting farther away from you. I'm out of ideas, out of places to look. I haven't bothered asking anyone in weeks. No one cares.

I haven't given up yet. Part of me feels like I'm close. Sometimes I get upset and think you're somewhere else. I think you lied to me. Deep down, I know you're here. I've been holding onto that more and more. Maybe years from now this will all be trivial. The only thing that matters is finding you. Everything will be fine once I find you. Everything.

Love Always,
Ernie

Fifteen
January 1, 1977

Ernest stopped writing when the phone rang. He sighed before picking up.

"Hello." He said.

"Ernie! Happy New Year!"

"Owe! Mom, why are you screaming? It's five in the morning."

"Oh. I'm sorry sweetie. Happy New Year."

"You don't need to whisper either, mom."

"Will you make up your mind, young man?"

"Are you drunk? What time is it there?"

"I don't know. Your father and I just got home. We went to this really fancy lounge place. You gotta go there when you get home. They make really good drinks there. I was flirting with the bartender all night, so I think he made them extra strong."

"Mom, I don't want to hear about that."

"Well fine mister grumpy pants. How were your holidays?"

"The holidays were fine. Everything is fine."

"They don't sound fine. Oh, sweetie I forgot. It must be hard without Linda. I shouldn't have called."

"It's okay mom. It's nice to hear from you."

"Well thank you but I should go to bed. I drank too much…"

"How about I call you later today after you get some sleep?"

"That sounds nice. Are you sure you're okay? You know

you can talk to me about anything."

"Yeah mom. I know."

"Okay. We'll talk later. Happy New Year sweetie."

"Happy New Year Mom. Goodnight."

"Goodnight."

Ernest's eyes were dry and heavy. He swallowed the remainder of the whiskey and laid down. He felt comfortable. He felt relaxed enough to sleep.

He slept through the whole day and forgot his mother called. He forgot to call her. He spent the rest of the day in pajamas. He wouldn't leave until the next day for work.

Sixteen
January 2, 1977

Ernest went to work lethargic and unmotivated. He didn't look forward to speaking with anyone.

"Mornin' Ernie. I haven't seen ya since last year." Joe said.

"Morning. You're proud of that joke."

"I been sayin' it to ev'rybody. They all laugh. They're just being polite. Sometimes the bad jokes cheer folks up better 'n the good ones."

"I'll take your word for it."

"You do that and get them milk crates stocked. Lots a folks do grocery shoppin' after New Year's. Don't ask why. Damned if I know. But that's what they do."

"You got it Joe."

The day dragged. People came in for groceries, but business was slow. Kids came in asking for sodas and candy.

"Ernie, can ya get more sodas from the back?" Joe said.

"Which ones?"

"All of 'em."

"Mister Evans. My pop says you were in the great war. Is that true?" A boy said.

"That's right. And Ernie there was in Vietnam."

"Wow."

"Why do you ask, son?"

"I was thinkin' about the service. My pop said I should talk to someone who served."

"Who's yer pop?"

"Uh, Bill Abbot, sir."

"Ah, you're Bill's boy. What's yer name?"

"Henry, sir."

"Okay Henry. What ya wanna know?"

"I guess first I wanna know how the draft works."

Ernest placed a crate of unopened soda bottles on the counter.

"The draft ended almost four years ago. You don't have to worry about being drafted." Ernest said.

"Oh. But I can still join if I want to, right?" Henry said.

"Sure. And as long as the Russkies don't start nothin', your mom and pop don't gotta worry 'bout ya." Joe said.

"Which branch were you in?"

"I was Army. 101st Airborne. Ernie there is just out the Navy."

"Which is better?"

"We got pride in who we served with. I'll tell ya Army's best. He'll say Navy's best."

"No, I won't." Ernest said.

"Ya gotta pick 'em yerself son. Choose what's best for what ya wanna do."

"Thanks mister Randall."

"How old are ya?"

"I turn 17 next month, sir."

"Then ya got plenty of time to get yer wits about ya. It's a big decision. Don't make it too quick."

"Yes, sir. Um, can I ask another question?"

"Ask as much as you like."

"Do you know anything about women?"

"Oh, I can tell ya a lot about women but none of it makes any damn sense to me. Ya should be thinkin' 'bout girls yer own age." Joe said.

"It's not like that sir. I thought some women were actin' strange is all. I'd ask my momma, but I saw them out in the woods where me and my friends was settin' off M-80s. My momma would pitch a fit if she knew I was messin' with those things."

"Well, what d'ya see?"

"I don't know. There was three of 'em in a circle around a fire sayin' a bunch of weird stuff. I thought they were cookin' a rabbit, but it wasn't skinned or anythin'."

Ernest had stopped stocking and walked over to the boy. Henry looked uncomfortable with how close Ernest stood.

"What'd these women look like?" Ernest said.

"Uh…I don't know. Like, they were kinda far off in the trees." Henry said.

"Were they a blonde, brunette, and a redhead?"

"Ayuh. I think so. Why?"

"Where'd you see them?"

"I don't remember. But I think they live out there. Somewhere past the end of Central Street.

"Where is that?"

"It's past Hallowell town limits. Yer momma would be mad if she knew you was out there." Joe said.

"Please don't say nothin' to her."

"It's alright but you gotta' promise not to go out there again."

"I promise. Can…can I go now?"

"Run on home now." Joe said.

Ernest thought for a moment. Joe stared at him.

"Why'd you go and spook the poor kid?" Joe said.

"Those are the women I've been looking for."

"I thought you was lookin' fer yer wife."

"I am but those women too. Now I'm convinced they killed the kid they found in the river."

"Yer on that again. Dammit Ernie! Let it go. Find yer wife an' take her home. Don't get mixed up in that mess again."

"What if they are the killers and they kill again?"

"Let the police deal with it. We did our time. We served. We don't gotta do nothin' else."

They stared at each other in awkward silence. Samantha walked in on the tension.

"Woah. You boys okay?" She said.

"Ernie just don't know how to mind his own business."

Joe walked into the back room.

"What's that about?"

"I gotta lead on those three women. Joe says I should leave it alone." Ernest said.

"Well I hope it's a good lead because the car was a dead end."

"What do you mean? And I thought I would hear from you sooner. I left a message."

"I know. Jed took forever to get back to me. And then the holidays. Everything's been crazy."

"So, what happened with the car?"

"Jed knows the owner. He went and asked. The guy said he let three women borrow it."

"He just let them?"

"Didn't even ask for names. He handed them the keys without any questions. Jed asked why. The guy said he didn't know. They smiled at him and he gave them the keys. They took the car back the next day. He never saw them again."

"Weird. Some kid was just in here and said he saw them in the woods. At the end of Central street. Do you know it?"

"I think so. You just asked some kid if he saw them?"

"No. He asked us if we thought something was weird. They were standing around a fire and cutting into a rabbit, I guess."

"They were cooking rabbit. So what?"

"He said it wasn't skinned. And he said they were talking funny."

"That does sound a little weird. Should I get Jed to check it out?"

"We don't know if there's anything out there. But the kid thinks they live out there."

"What do you want to do?"

"I want to check it out myself. I can't really explain but I know when they're around. My chest starts pounding before I see them. It's like I can sense them." He said.

"You sayin' you got superpowers?" She said.

"No. I felt the same thing when I was getting shot at. I think they're dangerous."

"You work tomorrow?"

"Yeah. We get deliveries tomorrow."

"What about next week on Tuesday the 11th?"

"I can get the day off."

"Do it. We'll go find wherever they live. You think that kid can show us where he saw them?"

"He said he didn't remember exactly. What he saw must have freaked him out."

"Maybe we should meet in the morning, so we have plenty of daylight. Better pack a lunch too. Just in case."

"You've done this before?"

"Once or twice. Sometimes it takes a lot of work to get the story."

"Okay. When and where do we meet?"

"I'll pick you up here. Maybe eight? Eh, no, let's make it nine. Sound good?"

"I get up at six usually. That's if I sleep in."

"You're not in the Navy anymore. You can relax."

"It's gonna take a while to adjust."

"Anyway. I'll see you Tuesday at nine. Oh. Um. Well. It can wait. I'll see you Tuesday." Samantha said.

"See you later."

Joe returned from the back room.

"She given up on yer nonsense yet?" Joe said.

"You're the only one giving up on me."

"I just don't want to see ya killed for nothin'. Use yer head and don't get dead."

"That's a good motto. Mind if I use that?"

"Listen to it if nothin' else. But go ahead."

"Use your head and don't get dead. That's gotta ring to it." Ernest said.

Seventeen
January 11, 1977, 9:00 am

"Good morning, Mister Kemp." Samantha said.

"Morning."

"You're not a morning person are you."

"Not lately. How long is the drive?"

"About 30 or 40 minutes."

"I'll need coffee."

"I got a thermos in the car. Gonna' grab some snacks and water and be on our way."

Joe scowled at them as they made their purchases. He didn't say anything beyond good morning.

"Bye Joe." Samantha said.

"Meh." Joe said.

"What's his problem?"

"He thinks I'm gonna' get my self killed." Ernest said.

"Sounds like Jed. He's always telling me what I can and can't do."

"You two have history."

"Known each other since grade school. If I hadn't helped him with homework, he would have flunked eighth grade. We almost dated but it didn't work out."

"It sounds complicated."

"Not really. I wanted a career. He didn't understand that."

"Does he always tell you what to do?"

"Everyone does. I'm a woman so I'm obviously too emotional to make decisions. Everyone always knows what's best for you without knowing you. And if I tell them what's best for them, they tell me I can't possibly understand what they're going through."

"I've met some Marines like that."

"Right? You get it. The military always tells you what to do but you're not allowed to have an opinion. It's bullshit."

"Samantha?"

"What?"

"Can you start the car?"

"Oh! Sorry. I rant sometimes."

"Understandable."

"Will you get me some coffee from the thermos? There's a cup with a lid in the back seat."

"Sure. I'll have some too. How do you like it?"

"Black is fine."

"I like your style."

"Sometimes I add a little cream."

"I don't like your style anymore."

"Hey!"

"I'm teasing. But black coffee is the best."

"That's because you're a bitter old man."

"And I'm damn proud of that."

They drove through town for a few minutes in silence. Ernest focused on his coffee. He tried not to think about anything else. Samantha focused on driving. She'd wave to someone in a crosswalk now and then. Ernest listened to the turn signals and the gear shifter. He heard the heater blowing. The radio was off. An 8-track tape rested in the deck. He pulled it out. It read 'Elton John and Kiki Dee. Don't Go Breakin' My Heart.' He returned it to the deck.

"Not a fan?" She said.

"I've only heard it once on the radio." He said.

"Wanna hear it again?"

"I don't like 8-tracks. You have the record?"

"No. I got that for the car. I don't keep too many records. I never have time. I'm either not home or writing something."

"You live alone?"

"You gonna call me a whore if I say I do?"

"Whoa! Why would I say that?"

"Most men do. I'm in my 30s, never married, and I talk back. I'm obviously a whore with no morals."

"I didn't get married that long ago. It's not odd that you're not married yet."

"How old is your wife?"

"A couple years younger than me. She's probably the same age as you."

"That's unusual. Most men go for girls not women. Why her?"

"I've never met anyone I had more in common with. I guess it felt like destiny."

"That's sweet. I haven't met any sweet guys like that in this town. I'm good at finding jerks."

"Every guy is kind of a jerk."

"True. But I find the abusive ones too."

"Shit. I'm sorry."

"It's okay. It was ten years ago. And that son of a bitch died in a car accident a couple years ago. Everyone said he was a draft dodger anyway."

"Or he didn't pass the psych eval."

"I never thought about that. Anyway, most guys are awful and don't want me to have an opinion. I'm not the housewife type. Sorry if I'm ranting again."

"It's okay. I can relate. You're not supposed to think in the military. Just shut up and do what you're told."

"What was your rank?"

"It doesn't matter. There's always someone above you telling you you're wrong."

"Okay. You sound bitter."

"Yep." He said.

"You haven't started talkin' like a Mainer yet." She said.

"What?"

"You don't say Ayuh."

"I hate that."

"Why? That's how you talk like a Mainer."

"I don't wanna talk like a Mainer. I think it's annoying."

"That's because you didn't grow up here. I didn't stop until my second year of college."

"You pick it back up when you came back home?"

"A little. Most people don't notice one way or the other. They just talk without much thought."

"You could say that about anyone."

"Where'd you grow up?"

"California."

"Where in California?"

"San Bernardino."

Samantha waited for more. Ernest remained silent.

"What's it like there?" She said.

"Warmer." He said.

"You're just a fountain of information."

"What does that mean?"

"It's sarcasm. I'm saying you don't share much."

"I don't know you well enough to share the intimate details of my life."

"You're never gonna get to know me well enough if you don't share a little. It's a long drive. I'm not doing all the talking."

"Fine. What do you wanna know?"

"Where you grew up? Tell me about your childhood. What was little Ernie like?"

"Don't call me that."

"Okay. So, you're from San Bernardino, California."

"Yeah. My father runs a construction company. He's a prick. I have a sister I haven't talked to in a while. My mother is the only one I still speak to."

"Sorry if I brought up some bad memories."

"Don't worry about it. I'm more concerned about the present."

"Okay. What do you think we'll find out there?"

"I hope it's something useful. It feels like everything I do leads to a dead-end."

"I get a lot of leads for stories and most of them fall short. But I keep going. I always find the story. They're not always interesting enough for print. But I always find the story."

"I wish I had your optimism."

"You do. You just don't believe you do."

"What does that mean?"

"You were in the Navy. Did you give up when you hit a tough spot?"

"No. We kept going until the mission was complete."

"Exactly. Because you knew you could get it done. You don't have the same resources. It might take longer. But you'll get it done."

"Are you a motivational speaker?"

"No. But I'm getting this story with or without your help."

"Yes, ma'am."

They drove until the paved road became a dirt road. They parked and followed a trail into the woods. It led to a clearing filled with trash and used fireworks. There were several shattered bottles and busted tin cans.

"This must be where the kids were setting off M-80s." She said.

"There must be remnants of a fire somewhere. I'll check over here."

They split up checking the wood line. They walked towards each other. They met at the start of another trail. They followed it to another small clearing. A pile of charred wood sat in the center. Corpses of small animals in various stages of decomposition littered the area.

"Oh God! It smells like rotting paint." She said.

"Paint rots?"

"If it's milk based it does."

"The kid was telling the truth. And they weren't cooking the animals."

"I can see that. Can we get away from here?"

"Let's go this way." He said.

"What way?"

"There's another trail here. It's not as formed as the others."

"You sure you wanna go in there?"

"Would you rather hangout with the dead squirrels and

racoons?”

"Lead the way."

The vegetation was thick. The trail was new with snow patches and branches littering the way. It led to a small building. It's wood panels were old and dark. The forest had grown around the structure.

"This thing must be a couple hundred years old. I'm surprised it's still standing." Samantha said.

Ernest walked up the creaking steps. Each footfall made a different creaking sound. He pushed the front door open.

"Hello?" He said.

There was no answer.

"Shall we?"

"What the hell?" She said.

Dirt and leaves covered the floor. A rusty wood stove occupied a corner. There were three rooms beyond the main room. Two were empty except for dirt and leaves. The third room contained a single table covered in candles. All the candles were used, and the melted wax had connected them all to each other and to the table. The walls, floor, and ceiling were covered in markings carved into the wood.

"Cozy." He said.

"Speak for yourself. There's definitely something weird going on." She said.

"You think those women live here?"

"I don't think anyone's lived here for over a century."

"Maybe. But those candles aren't that old. Neither is that trail that led us here."

"I think Jed should look at this place."

"There's nothing here that will tell us anything about who uses this place."

"But someone owns this property. Maybe they know what's up with it. Or they let someone use it like the green Buick."

"What do you think these markings mean?"

"I've never seen them before. You?"

"Nope. I'm sure they mean something."

Outside carried the sound of crunching leaves. Tree

branches creaked.

"Did you hear that?" He said.

"I did."

They stood silent, waiting. The sounds stopped. They waited. Ernest mouthed the words 'wait here' and stepped with care towards the hall. He tip-toed to avoid creaking boards. He looked towards the front door. It sat open as they had left it. He motioned to Samantha to follow him. They moved slow towards the front door. Ernest held up his hand to stop. They listened. The wind blew outside. There were no other sounds. He twitched his fingers for Samantha to keep moving. He looked outside. No one was there. He looked at either side of the house. No one. He looked at Samantha and shrugged.

"Must have been an animal." He said.

"This place gives me the creeps. Let's go back to the car."

They followed the trail back to the clearing of dead animals, then back to the clearing of exploded fireworks. They returned to the dirt road. There were half a dozen bullfrogs resting in front of Samantha's car.

"What the hell?" She said.

"This town has a frog problem."

"It's too cold for them. They're usually hibernating."

"This town has a mutant frog problem."

"They're bullfrogs."

"Mutant bullfrogs."

"Just get them out of the way so we can leave."

Ernest tapped them with his foot one at a time to hop towards the tree line off the road. The other bullfrogs paid no attention to Ernest until he tapped them with his foot. They got in the car. Samantha made a U-turn and drove towards town.

Eighteen
January 11, 1977, 11:00 am

They drove a few minutes without speaking.

"So, what do you think?" Ernest said.

"About what?"

"That house."

"I don't know. You think someone is staying there? Is that who was walking around outside?"

"It was probably an animal. If someone's using that house, they're not living there."

"I can track down the property owner. Maybe they know something. Maybe they're the one using the house." Samantha said.

"How long to track them down?"

"The rest of the day to get a name and address. That's a guess. It could take a couple days. County Records isn't an easy place to navigate."

"I've never liked going through records. I had to keep track of the medical records for the doctors in the Navy. On the bright side, I knew where everything was."

"I don't think it's possible to know where anything is at the County Records."

They both went silent again. Ernest emptied the thermos of coffee.

"What's the next step? What do we do if that house is a dead end?" He said.

"We keep looking for new leads. But you saw the place.

There's no way that won't lead us somewhere. You have any other plans today?"

"Nope."

"You fancy a trip to the library?" She said.

"For what?"

"I wanna know what those symbols mean. I think I have seen some of them before, but I'm not sure. I have no idea what they could mean."

"I'm pretty sure the librarian still hates me."

"I'll talk to her so you can avoid her. As long as you're quiet in the library and reading, she won't bother you."

"How do you know she won't throw me out?"

"She believes reading makes everyone better. She respects books more than people. She refuses to disrupt what she calls the magical bond between book and reader."

"A librarian that's a book snob? I'm shocked."

"You'd do a lot better with people if you tried to relate to their interests."

"You're assuming I want to be better with people."

"Can you at least pretend you're not a cynical jerk?"

"No promises."

Samantha scoffed. Ernest smiled.

"But I will try." He said.

There was little traffic. They got to the library in good time.

"As soon as you walk in, turn left, and walk to the back of the main room. That's the history section. If we're lucky, she won't notice you." Samantha said.

Ernest did what she said. He heard her say good afternoon to the librarian and nothing else. He walked fast. He surveyed the subsections. There was World History, US History, Biographies, and Ancient History. Ernest skimmed titles in World History. Without knowing the origins of the symbols, he didn't expect to find anything. He wandered the maze of tall bookshelves. He took in the smell of old books.

"Every library smells the same."

His eye caught a book with something familiar printed on the spine. He squatted and removed the book. The title read 'Celtic and Scandinavian Symbols.'

"Hey." Samantha said.

"Hey. I think I found something. This symbol looks like one of them we saw at that house."

"This is the book I was coming to get."

"What?"

"Look. I wrote down the reference number from the card catalogue."

"That's weird."

"A lot of weird stuff is happening lately."

"I guess that means we should check it out. I don't have a library card."

"We can read it here." She said.

They sat at a long table. Ernest looked over Samantha's shoulder while she flipped through pages.

"Wait. Go back." He said.

"Where?"

"Right there. That's on the cover. Tri. Que. Tra. The Celtic Knot. What's that?"

"It says it's a symbol for eternal spiritual life. The knot is continuous. No beginning. No end." She said.

"This symbol was also in that room. How do you even say that?"

"It means 'Helm of Awe.' A symbol for protection and victory."

"Any of this make sense to you?"

"No."

"Why are there Celtic and Scandinavian symbols carved in the walls of an old building in New England?"

"You know as much as I do. I'll check out the book and take it home. Maybe there's something that will explain some things. I need to get back to the paper. I have other stories to work on. My boss would love an excuse to fire me. He's not big on female journalists."

"Why do you keep working there?"

"More women buy the paper now that a woman writes some stories. I feel good about that. And they won't fire me if they sell more papers. It could be a lot worse."

"Good luck at work. When do you plan to go by the County Records?"

"Later today. It'll be a good excuse to get away from my boss. He never complains when I say I'm looking up records."

"I can go through the book if you want. I have nothing else to do. I've probably asked everyone in town about my wife. No one will talk to me anymore."

"Oh. Um…look. I haven't confirmed this. It might be nothing. Someone told me they think they saw someone matching your wife's description. They were a little vague and I never followed up."

"That's okay. Where did they see this person? It'll give me something to do."

"Don't be upset if it's nothing."

"I'm sure I'll be fine."

"It was a trailer outside of town west of here. Off Shady Lane."

"Shady Lane?"

"It's a real road. I promise."

"If there's a small chance, I'll take it. You'll keep the book?"

"Yes. I'll let you know if I find something."

"You didn't say yes the Mainer way."

"I know. All that education forced it out of me. Talk to you later."

"Bye."

Nineteen
January 11, 1977, 2:00 pm

Ernest walked back to his room. He arrived as the phone rang.

"Hello?" He said.

"Ernie. I'm so glad I caught you."

"Hi mom."

"How are you? It must be so cold there. Are you keeping warm?"

"Yes ma'am."

"Oh, that's good. How are you sweetie? Any luck finding Linda and Amy?"

"Maybe. It could be nothing."

"Well what? What is it? Tell me."

"Someone saw a woman matching Linda's description outside of town. I was about to call someone to take me out there when you called."

"Well that sounds like a big deal. You've found them."

"I haven't found anything yet. It could be someone who looks like Linda. And no one mentioned seeing a child. I'll go find this woman and let you know if it's Linda or not."

"I'm sure it is."

"I don't want to get my hopes up and be disappointed."

"You need to be more positive, Ernie. I don't know how you can live with so much negativity."

"I'm not being negative. I'm being realistic. I'll call you tomorrow."

"Alright sweetie. Good luck."

"Thanks mom. Bye."

"Bye."

He dropped the receiver onto the base. It landed hard. The ringer vibrated and trailed off. His shoulders raised and lowered with a deep breath. He opened the desk drawer and removed a phone book. He thumbed to a spot in the book. He turned the page. He moved his finger down a list of numbers. The rhythm of the rotary phone filled the room as he dialed.

"Hello? Yes, I'd like to schedule a taxi pickup."

Ernest waited out by the street as the taxi pulled up.

"You call for a cab?" The driver said.

"Yeah." Ernest said.

"Where ya headed?"

"I don't know the address. It's a trailer in the woods off Shady Lane."

"I know Shady Lane. No sure 'bout trailers. You ain't from 'round here."

"What gave it away?"

"You don't talk like a Mainer. Why ya goin' to Shady Lane?"

"Someone I know might be out there. Or they just look like someone I know. I'm going to find out."

"It's quite a drive. It'll be expensive."

"That's not a problem."

"Okey. Let's see if yer friend is out there. You okay with country music?"

"I don't mind it. It's your radio. Play what you want."

"You an' me gonna' get along buddy."

The driver switched on the radio. 'Together Again' by Emmylou Harris played. There was no conversation for the rest of the ride. They turned down Shady Lane. The driver and Ernest checked each building they could see from the road.

"You said it was a trailer?" The driver said.

"That's what they told me. I don't know anything else." Ernest said.

They drove further North. The driver stopped at a turn to

their left.

"That's a trailer. Wanna check it out?" The driver said.

"You don't mind waiting?" Ernest said.

"Nah. I'll even turn the meter off until you get back in the car."

"I appreciate that. I'll let you know if it's the right place. Here. You can keep whatever's leftover."

"Twenty bucks!? Well, my shift just ended. I'll park here and read the paper. I'll take you home when you're ready."

"Okay. If it's not the place, you'll take me to the next one?"

"For twenty bucks you got me the rest of the night."

Ernest walked up the driveway. It made a loop in front of the trailer. A pickup truck rested in front. Inside the driveway loop sat a patch of snow. Three black birds pushed around a pinecone. One looked at Ernest and squawked. The bird's black eyes followed Ernest along the driveway. It squawked again followed by a series of croaking noises.

"I think that one's takin' to ya." A voice said.

Ernest turned from the bird to see an older man standing by the truck. He stood out from the white snow as much as the black birds.

"What are they? Crows?" Ernest said.

"Crows are smaller. Them are Ravens. They're smart little shits. That makes 'em more annoyin'. They come to pick through the garbage. I gotta put rocks on top of the trashcan so they can't open the lid."

"What do you mean it's taking to me?"

"Ravens will sometimes follow a person around for a few days. They'll follow folks to the store and the like. Don't be surprised if you see that one tomorrow. Don't be scared neither. They're harmless as long as you don't do 'em any wrong."

"Thanks for the advice."

"They don't like me much 'cause I shoo 'em away from the trash but they come back 'cause I don't hurt 'em. Is there somethin' I can help you with, son?"

"Someone told me there was a woman staying here. She has a baby girl. I think it's my wife and daughter. Is there someone else staying here?"

"Ayuh. What if she's not your wife?"

"Then I'll leave and apologize for bothering you."

"How'd you lose your wife?"

"She left while I was away in the Navy. She went to Ohio then came here. To Maine."

The man stared at Ernest for a moment. The trailer door swung open with a smack. A woman looking down at the steps stood in the door frame.

"Ed, I made some tea. Did you want any…"

She looked up. A mug fell and shattered at her feet.

"…milk." She said.

The three stood in silence.

"Linda." Ernest said.

"Er-Ernie."

From behind Ernest, the raven croaked like a frog.

Part Two
Gibbous

Twenty
January 11, 1977 - Samantha

I hoped I hadn't sent Ernest on a wild goose chase. My concerns for Ernest's adventure dissipated when I got back to work. My editor pounced on me as I passed his office.

"Belcher! Where's the child killer story?" He said.

"I'm following leads." I said.

"Follow them faster."

He followed me to my desk.

"What about the guy they arrested and let go? Did you interview him?"

"He didn't give me anything we can use. He's from out of town. He's here on personal business."

"What kind of business?"

"I'm not at liberty to say."

"Fine. You're covering the high school bake sale tomorrow."

"What? Can you give it to Molly? She loves that stuff."

"Molly has an assignment. Now you have yours. Get to work."

"I need to run to County Records."

"For what?"

"Following a lead."

"A lead on the murders?"

"Yes."

"Go. But I better see a story on my desk tomorrow morning."

He left. I wasn't sure if I'd have enough for a story by tomorrow. I drove to Augusta. I didn't have an address to look up a deed, but I knew George could help out.

"Hey Sam."

"Hey George." I said.

"What kinda' big story you got today?" George said.

"I don't know what it is yet. I need to find out who owns a property west of Hallowell. South of Granite Hill."

"Address or closest street?"

"Don't know an address. At the end of Central Street."

"Hmm. Most of that's county property. And there ain't much out there."

"There's an old shack out in the woods. I think some bad people are using it."

"Is that right? This about them kids that were killed?"

"Maybe."

"Let's see what we got."

George walked me back to the records room. Boxes upon boxes upon shelves towered between narrow paths. Everything was color coded by district, city, and town. Each box had its own number and date associated with it. It was impossible to find anything unless you knew the year, date, and document you needed. George opened a large book. It took both hands to open. The contents resembled a ledger.

"Thankfully, all property deeds are kept together. Red section. Boxes A1 through A7. Point out the place on the map and we'll get started." George said.

He pointed to a giant map of Kennebec County. It was broken into sections by zip code. I pointed on the line between 04347 and 04351. Hallowell and Manchester respectively.

"Hmm. We'll have to check both zips."

I followed George to the red section. He pulled a large box from the middle shelf resting at our waistlines. He waddled the box over to a table.

"Deeds are alphabetized by county. Then by town and city name. Then by zip code for each town. We'll start with Hallowell. If we're lucky, we won't have to look at Manchester." George said.

He thumbed through the many files. They made flap sounds as his fingers passed over them. He mumbled at each file.

"Here it is. 04347."

He opened the file and took the top half of documents. He handed the rest to me. I wasn't sure what to look for and read every document with care. Many were old. The handwriting was difficult to read.

"This will take all night." I said.

"Ayuh. The old deeds describe the property limits and don't give real addresses. Only the most recent deeds are in this box. The old ones are kept elsewhere." George said.

"Why are there still so many old deeds?"

"If the deed didn't come from a bank, or if it was a private owner who had no heir, the deed fell under the state and county. All the old ones are owned by the state."

I had never been so tired from doing so little. During my previous county records adventures, I was usually reading reports or eyewitness statements from a couple years past. Enough to keep my attention. This was so drool.

"We've been at this for thirty minutes. It feels like days." I said.

"Have patience. You'll find what you need." George said.

I skimmed a few more deeds trying to interpret the handwriting and make sense of the property's location. I found one that mentioned Central Street.

"This one says to the South ending on Central Street. And it extends to the North ending at the family pond. What's the family pond?" I said.

"I don't know of any ponds up there. But I think that's the deed ya want. It's an old one so that's state property. It's all forest. There could be lots of ponds out there."

"There's a small house on the property. An old one. Who built it and when?"

"Check the grantors on the deed. There weren't too many records back then, but the library has some old journals and newspapers. You'll have more luck there."

"Thanks for the help, George. The grantor on this deed is

a Daniel Vaughn. The grantees are Abella Skov, Carla Skov, and Malla Skov. Skov? That's an odd surname. And they never sold the property?"

"If it belongs to the state now, they probably died before selling. And no one made a claim for it."

"This keeps getting more interesting. Any death certificates this far back?"

"Nah. You might find their names in the Census. Most country folk died without anyone knowing."

"Thanks again. I guess I'm going back to the library."

"Happy to help."

I helped return the deeds to their box and gathered my notes. I don't always know where leads will take me. But I had a feeling this wasn't a dead end. There was no guarantee the library would have any answers.

"I'm back, Noreen. How far back do your newspaper archives go?"

"We have clippings from about the last hundred years or so." Noreen said.

"What about personal items like journals or diaries?" I said.

"I can't be sure how old many of them are. We do have a few items from the time Maine was still part of Massachusetts."

"Great! I'll search through old newspapers first. Would you be able to get me a list of titles of the journals and diaries?"

"Sure. Anyone in particular?"

"Does the name Skov sound familiar?"

"Surname Skov?"

"Yes."

"I'll see what I can find."

"You're a peach."

"Oh. Well. I know."

I prepared myself to sit for a long time. Scrolling through the microfilm of old newspapers is a tedious task. I've spent hours looking before and never found what I needed. I groaned when I saw the last person to look at the microfilm left it around 1923. I spent 20 minutes scrolling to get close to the end.

The oldest paper the library had was the Kennebec Journal

from March 1875. I started searching for Skov in Obituaries. I lost track of time. Noreen popped up behind me as I started January 1876.

"I have something. An incomplete diary. It belonged to a Malla Skov." She said.

"That's perfect. Why's it incomplete?" I said.

"Perhaps she passed before finishing. That's the only thing we have with that name. It was donated to the library by the Vaughn Family."

"Thank you, Noreen. Am I able to check this out?"

"It's part of our special collections. We don't normally check out those, but I'll make an exception for you."

"You're too good to me."

"Oh my. It's nothing. I enjoy helping others gain new knowledge."

She puttered away with a smug smile. I checked the diary for the last entry. I was more concerned with the date than what was written. July 12, 1877. I scrolled to the newspaper for that day. I had to stop and give my hand a break halfway through. No one named Skov in the obituary. I checked the next day. Nothing. I read some of the articles thinking maybe a death went unidentified. A headline caught my eye.

LOCAL SISTERS ACCUSED OF WITCHCRAFT

The headline had a sketch of the sisters beneath. I thought my eyes were playing tricks on me. The sketch labeled the sisters as Abella, Carla, and Malla Skov. The article stated they were suspected of witchcraft after several townsfolk fell ill and died. Authorities went to their home, but it was abandoned. But how could these three women in a sketch from 1877 look like the three women I saw in the general store a couple months ago? The three women Ernest believed were killing the children. I read part of the diary's last entry.

Carla held my things and was looking at this journal.

"I thought you got rid of this." She said.

"I never said I did."

"Your clumsiness proves that anyone can get their hands on this."

"I've told you none of our secrets are in there. It's mostly trivial things like what I did each day. It was something to talk to that wasn't one of you." I said.

"Is that how you feel about us? Get rid of it. We can't have anything linking us back to this town. Do you understand?"

"But why –"

"Malla, please! Listen to me this once."

We stared at each other for a moment. Bella looked prepared for an argument.

I gathered my notes and found Noreen.

"Has anyone read this diary?" I said.

"Not that I'm aware. It was said to have belonged to a friend of Elizabeth Vaughn from when she was a young woman. I never had interest in reading it myself."

"Thank you for all your help today. I think I have everything I need."

"Any time dear."

Nothing was making sense. I spent the rest of the day looking for any mention of the Skov sisters in the newspapers. There was nothing, except their home was taken over by the state. Their names never appeared again. As if they never existed.

I went home too tired to read through the diary. There was too much to think about. And not enough for a story. I had to get Jed to look at the house in the woods. If I could convince him, then I could write up something about police investigating an area in the woods pertaining to the murders. Without that, my editor wouldn't print anything I turned in.

Twenty-One
January 11, 1977, 3:00 pm

"I – I was afraid you wouldn't find me." Linda said.

"I was afraid I wouldn't either." Ernest said.

"I'm sorry I – I tried to wait. Wait for you. To come home. I couldn't. I had to leave."

"But why? Why the cryptic messages?"

"A lot has happened."

Muffled cries rose from the trailer.

"Is that Amy? Can I see her?"

"Of course. She's probably hungry. Um…"

Linda looked down at the shattered mug and hesitated.

"Don't worry about that. I'll clean it up." Ed said.

The raven croaked as Ernest stepped over the broken mug. The cries were loud inside the trailer. The furniture and walls were various shades of brown and red. He heard Linda in the back bedroom.

"Oh, look who's awake. Someone wants to meet you. This is your daddy, Ernest."

The baby cooed. Her cheeks were still wet from tears. She looked at Ernest with her big hazel eyes. She looked up at her mother then back to Ernest. A look of surprise and awe like she had never seen another person before. Ernest didn't move at first. Fear planted him to the floor. He forced himself to step forward. He held out his hand. The little girl grabbed his finger with her right hand. Gibberish flowed from her mouth like she was holding a conversation. She looked up at him and smiled. Ernest couldn't hide his tears anymore.

"Do you want to hold her?" Linda said.

Linda lifted the baby and she cried.

"I'm sorry. Amy, are you hungry?"

"No." Amy said.

"You want some milk?"

Amy nodded.

"Can you get the small cup by the sink? But only fill it halfway."

Linda handed Ernest the carton of milk.

"Can you say momma?"

"No."

Amy rubbed her eyes and moaned waiting for the drink. Ernest handed Amy the cup and she took it with both hands. She drank fast only stopping to gasp for air. Linda passed Amy to Ernest with no objections.

The rest of the world melted away. Ernest was holding his child. His baby girl. Seeing her for the first time. He kept crying feeling so many emotions. Relief. Fear. Happiness. Anxiety. Comfort. Sorrow.

"I'm sorry I wasn't there." He said.

"It's okay. You're here now. I've missed you." She said.

"I missed you too."

Linda kissed him. They both watched Amy with her milk. She was alert. Looking at everything.

"Did you come alone?" Linda said.

"No. I have a taxi waiting by the road."

"I meant my family. Did they come with you?"

"No. They're still in California. I talk to your mother on the phone sometimes."

"How are they?"

"Good. They're worried about you and Amy."

"What did they say when you got home?"

"No one knew why you left. They feared the worst."

"Is that what your family said too? Did they come with you?"

"They're in California too. Why did you leave?"

"Of course, they wouldn't tell you. I left to get away from your family. And mine. That's why I wrote a cryptic letter. I didn't want them to follow me."

"Then why'd you tell me you went to Ohio? They could have gone there and met your friends."

"I told my friends to only tell you I came to Maine. I showed them a picture so they wouldn't get fooled by someone pretending to be you."

"You went through a lot of trouble to get away from them."

"I did."

Amy burped.

"I think she's done." Ernest said.

He took the cup and gave it to Linda. She washed it right away.

"Oh, she's got some milk on her chin." Linda said.

Amy squirmed while Linda wiped her face with a paper towel.

"What really happened? Why'd you leave?" Ernest said.

"My belly was starting to show when we heard about your ship going down in the China Sea. The Captain who delivered the message said they were still searching for survivors, but things didn't look good. Everyone was upset. We all assumed you died. After a couple weeks, my mother told me to consider finding someone to help raise the baby. I was angry and stormed out. A few days later, your parents started telling everyone they would raise your child. Our families argued over who would get Amy when she was born.

"After six weeks thinking you were dead, they told us you were alive and on a special assignment. Everyone forgot about fighting over the baby except you dad. He was convinced everything was settled with you being alive. There weren't any problems until you wrote saying you were coming home in a few weeks. You dad started fighting for Amy again. I refused to give her up. I wanted a life with you and her. No one else. I went to my parents. They told me they never liked you and didn't want me around your family. I was so angry. I just left. I don't want Amy around our families."

"I'm not surprised about my dad, but your parents too. They never told me anything. They lied to my face."

"If they told you the truth, you would never tell them where I was when you found me."

"True."

"So... How did you get on a special assignment? What happened when your ship sank?"

"All Hell broke loose. I felt the whole ship shake from an explosion."

***

I got slammed into the wall. Alarms echoed through the corridors. Most of them filled with flashing red light. The ship had tilted. I had to support myself off the wall as I stumbled to the medical bay. Abandon ship cracked through radio speakers. I wasn't close enough to the medical bay to reach my usual life raft. I had to turn around and find the nearest one.

I made it to some stairs when the ship got hit a second time. I hit my head hard enough to pass out. I don't know how long I laid there. Less than a minute I'd guess. I stirred and someone lifted me up.

"On your feet Sailor. Keep moving."

The voice followed behind me. I saw others ahead of me. I followed to the life raft. My head had cleared when we reached the top deck. I was surrounded by Marines. I remembered we had picked them up a couple days before. They had suffered casualties and were waiting for more Marines. They never got those reinforcements.

By the time we arrived outside, the port side of the ship was hitting the water. Sailors were sliding off trying to open life rafts under water. I don't remember seeing any life rafts inflate. The Marines climbed up to the starboard side. Some dove into the water while others inflated life rafts.

"Hit the water Squid. We'll pick you up when we got a raft down there."

I jumped feet first into the ocean. I fell so long I didn't think I'd ever reach the water. It was cold. It surrounded me and slowed my momentum. I bobbed up and down looking every direction for the nearest raft.

"Over here Sailor."

I swam to the raft. Marines pulled me up.

"You with the Hospital Corps?" One of them said.

"Corpsman First Class Kemp. Anyone injured?" I said.

"Staff Sergeant Armey. We're all good. Our Corpsman's dead. We'll keep you around 'til we get a new one."

"That's better than drowning."

The Sun was setting. We spent the rest of our daylight looking for enemy ships and boats. We found a few survivors. Most of the crew died inside the ship. We spent about 14 or 15 hours in those rafts before we saw land. The ship sank in the South China Sea near South Vietnam. We had few supplies. The Marines knew of an Army Foreign Operating Base near the ocean. We walked for an hour. It was humid. The trees protected us from the Sun but not from the bugs. Sticky sweat ran down my body. I missed the ocean air.

We found the base. They fed us, gave us supplies, and let us shower and sleep. The next day we were told a platoon of Marines were nearby. They had also lost their Corpsman. I received orders to stay with their unit until their mission was complete. The mission took us to Cambodia. The war had officially ended for us in Vietnam. But the mission in Cambodia lasted almost two years.

***

"What happened in Cambodia?" Linda said.

"I'd rather not talk about it." Ernest said.

"Is it like classified stuff?"

"Something like that. So, why Maine?"

"Honestly, I picked a random place as far away from California as I could."

"Did something else happen? To make you leave?"

"No. I only wanted to get away from our families. That's the only reason I left."

"I understand why you're angry with your parents. But you should call them."

"I don't want to talk to them."

"I'm sure they were only concerned for you and Amy."

111

"I thought they would try to take her from me. I don't want to talk about this anymore."

"I'm sure they wouldn't…"

"Stop! Please. Let's talk about something else."

They stood in silence for a moment. Linda took Amy to lay her down. Ed walked in.

"Is that your cab out there?" Ed said.

"Yes, I forgot. I paid him extra to wait for me." Ernest said.

"Good idea. That raven is waitin' out there for ya, too."

"Thanks for the warning."

"So, where are you staying?" Linda said.

"A small, local place. Here's the number. I have to go. We have a lot to talk about, but let's not worry about that right now. We should plan some time to talk about everything. Our future. Do you like it here? In Maine?" Ernest said.

"It grows on you."

"My taxi is waiting. Give me a call. I work part-time at the general store. If I don't answer, I'm probably at work."

"Okay."

"Okay. Uh, it was nice meeting you. Ed, was it?"

"Yessir. Good to meet ya." Ed said.

Ernest walked out and the raven greeted him with a croak. He took deep breaths. He looked at his hand. He closed and opened his fist a couple times. He looked back once and saw Linda watching him in the window. The raven croaked again. The driver rolled down his window.

"Find what you were looking for?"

"Yeah."

He looked at the trailer again. The blanket of white snow covered everything. The black raven stared at Ernest. It tilted its head. It clicked its beak and flew off.

"Ravens creep me out." The driver said.

"Yeah."

"Where to now?"

"Back home. I gotta make a phone call."

"You got it. Name's Harold by the way."

"Ernest. Thanks for the ride."

"Anytime. Next time you need a ride, ask for me. I work most afternoons and evenings."

"I'll do that."

Twenty-Two
January 12, 1977

Ernest considered calling his mother when he returned to his room. It was early enough to call back home, but he had mixed emotions. Part of him didn't want to tell anyone. All he wanted was to find his wife and daughter. He'd done that. Nothing else mattered. No one else mattered.

***

He felt anxious after waking the next morning. He asked himself if he should call or not. He wanted his wife to call. He hoped she would call. He walked over to the phone then sat on the bed again. He tapped his heels. He bit at the cuticles on his fingers. He pulled a bit of skin too much drawing blood. He washed and dried his hands before getting a bandage. He looked at his fingers. Bits of skin were peeled back around all his fingernails.

"Have I always done this to my fingers?"

He looked at the phone. He took a breath and picked it up. He asked the operator to connect him to his mother in California.

"Ernie! You've never called so early before. Is everything okay?" She said.

"Yeah. I knew you were up. I need to ask you something."

"What is it dear? It sounds important."

"It is. Can you tell me again what happened before Linda left?"

"Well, I told you already, she left without a word."

"You didn't think she had a reason to leave?"

"Of course not. She disappeared out of the blue."

"So, you and dad weren't trying to take the baby from her when you thought I was dead?"

"Where – where is this coming from? I mean, where did you hear that? That's the most ridiculous thing I've ever heard. Have you talked to Linda?"

"She sent me another letter and told me you and dad fought with her parents over the baby. Everything calmed down when you heard I was alive. Then you started fighting over the baby again when you heard I was coming home."

"I see. Your father was concerned about Linda. He didn't think she was handling your death well. She was reserved and didn't talk much. She was always a little jumpy around us. Your father suggested taking care of the baby as a way to honor your memory. Linda's parents refused. They said it's her child, her body, her choice. Your father was furious."

"And what did Linda say?" Ernest said.

"You know, I don't remember her saying anything. The poor thing was still upset about your death. So, do you know where she is? How's the baby?"

"They're fine. I'll see them soon. What happened when you all heard I was coming home?"

"Well…uh…your… Your father thought that settled things and you, Linda, and the baby would stay with us. I told him you would probably want to find a place of your own. He said we'd talk about that when you got home. Linda refused to stay with us. Her parents said we'd never see the baby. A week later, she left. Her parents claim they don't know why. I don't trust them. That family is bad news. I'm convinced they want all the money you got saved up from your service."

"Well, you're right about one thing. Linda and I do want a place of our own to raise Amy. And it's not with you or her parents influence."

"Are you saying you're not coming home? Ernest? Ernest James! Answer me!"

"I'll call you when I have things figured out. Bye mom."

"Ern–"

He dropped the receiver on the base. He took a deep breath.

He rubbed the back of his neck. He stared at the phone with a blank expression.

"Let's find out the rest."

Ernest picked up the phone and had the operator connect him with his mother-in-law.

"Oh Ernie. I haven't heard from you in so long. I was getting worried. How are you? How's Maine? Are you still in Maine? Have you heard anything new about Linda and the baby?"

"Beatrice. Can you stop talking for a minute? I just spoke to my mother. She said you all were arguing over the baby before Linda left. I want to know what happened."

"Well…um…the thing is…it's not as simple as…Linda was going through a lot."

"I've never heard you struggle with saying anything."

"This – is a sensitive subject. It's complicated."

"Then simplify it for me."

Silence hung in the air for a moment. Ernest heard a deep breath in the receiver. He picked up the base of the phone and sat on his bed.

"Okay. I – I don't want to say anything bad about your father." Beatrice said.

"He's a dick. Say whatever you want."

"Okay. Well, when everyone thought you died, he started ranting about protecting his legacy. He wanted to raise the baby himself. Linda didn't say a word. She was grieving. I stepped in on her behalf. Your father said we had no right. I said he had no right. He grew angry screaming about legacies and carrying on the family name. Everything calmed down for a while, but we didn't talk to your parents after that. When we heard you were alive and coming home, your father told Linda you two would live with them. I told her to stay away from your family until you got home. Your father had made threats to take the baby. Linda became hysterical. I think it was postpartum. She accused me and Herb of taking the baby. I would never separate a mother from her child. I mean, could you imagine?"

"You keep saying the baby. Her name is Amy."

"Yes. Of course. Amy."

"What happened next?"

"Well, we confronted her. We told her she was hysterical, and we only wanted what was best for her and the bay…uh…Amy. For her and Amy. She calmed down. We all went to bed. She was gone by the morning."

"Why didn't you tell me any of this? Why keep it a secret?"

"Your mother and I talked, and we agreed we didn't want to worry you. It was bad enough your wife and child weren't here when you got home. That alone was upsetting."

"You should have told me."

"Would it have made a difference?"

"Yes! I've spent months trying to understand why she left. Now I know it's because both our families are insane."

"We were only trying to help her."

"Well, you failed! And you failed to help me!"

"Do you speak to your mother like that?"

"I'm pissed at her too so I probably will!"

"You will never find Linda if you keep yelling at people."

"I already found her and I'm not telling you where she is!"

"What? Well, how is she? Please Ernest."

"Goodbye Beatrice."

The ringer echoed when he slammed the receiver. He returned the phone to the table. He paced back and forth, from one end of his room to the other. He cracked his knuckles. He stretched his arms. He had to leave for work soon. His mind racing and angry. He lit a cigarette. He couldn't remember the last time he had one. He opened a window. The stuffy air in his room escaped. Cool fresh air seeped through. He inhaled the cigarette with the cool air. A snowplow rolled down the road. Piles and clumps of white powder collected on the sidewalk. He closed his eyes. He felt the cool air glide over his face.

Twenty-Three
February 1, 1977

Ernest stood at the register of the general store reading a newspaper. A case of beer appeared in front of him. Behind the case stood three boys who stood shorter than Ernest's chin.

"I'm not selling you beer." Ernest said.

"Joe sells it to us all the time." One boy said.

"I'm not Joe."

"Come on, man."

"No."

"Let's come back when Joe gets here. We'll get this cheese weasel fired."

"Yeah! You hear that cheese weasel?" The other boy said.

The boys laughed leaving the store. Ernest kept reading the paper and put the beer behind the counter.

"Okay. Thanks for coming in." He said.

The front door was propped open to let out the stuffy hot air in the store. One of the boys crept in. He hid behind each aisle checking if Ernest noticed him. He got to the back cooler. He grabbed a can and closed the door with care. He turned and Ernest stood behind him with the case of beer. The boy swallowed hard looking up at Ernest. He took the can from the boy.

"Beat it kid."

The boy ran outside. Ernest heard the other boys laughing hard. He returned the can and the case to the coolers then closed the front door with a jingle from the bell. He turned the page of the newspaper and continued reading. He enjoyed the first part of the day because not many people were in the store. Kids ditching school were a nuisance but nothing difficult. He had little interest in the newspaper, but it passed the time.

The door hit the small bell as someone pushed it open. Ernest used a box of matches to mark the last thing he read. He looked up to see Linda staring at him.

"Hey." She said.

"Uh, hey."

"You really do work here."

"It keeps me out of trouble. Do you need some things?"

"Oh no. I was running some errands. Ed has a package at the post office. And Amy needs new shoes. She keeps losing them. Well, she keeps losing the right shoe. I have a dozen left baby shoes."

"Where is Amy?"

"Ed's sister is looking after her while I'm running around. She's good with kids."

"Have dinner with me tonight."

"Oh, I don't know. That's short notice for a babysitter. Ed's sweet but he carries Amy with arms stretched out like she'll bite him. He's good with her. But he feels uncomfortable."

"Bring Amy. I want to see both of you."

"That's sweet but she's a handful right now. She gets fussy all the time. She always makes a mess. I dread taking her to a restaurant."

"You sound like you're trying to avoid me."

"No! Of course not. It's short notice. Maybe this weekend."

"What if I came to you at Ed's place?"

"No, I don't want to impose on him more than I already have."

"How do you know Ed?"

"My friend Evie who you met in Ohio, he's her grandfather. I thought she told you. Isn't that how you found us?"

"She never said. I've been here since October asking around. I got some help from the locals."

"I'm so sorry. I thought she told you. If Ed could afford long distance, I'd chew her out when I got back."

"That seems like important information to share. He wasn't upset about me stopping by unannounced was he?"

"No, he's happy you found us. He said he enjoyed having our company but won't miss Amy crying in the middle of the night."

"I have plenty of money saved up. We can get our own place. Right here in Hallowell if you want."

"You wanna stay here?"

"It's a nice place. The locals don't like strangers much but everywhere is like that."

"What about our families?"

"We can call them now and then. Write letters. As long as we're far away from them."

"They won't leave us alone. They'll demand we move back home."

"I never cared much for San Bernardino."

"Me either. But that's not enough for them. My parents think I can't take care of myself let alone a baby. Your parents, or at least your father, want to take Amy away from me. I don't want them involved in our lives. I'll do whatever it takes."

"I feel the same. That's why I suggested living here."

"I don't want them to know where we are."

"You want me to tell them I never found you? That I gave up and chose to stay in Maine. They'll never believe that."

"Then tell them you're still looking."

"That won't work. I didn't want to tell them I found you until I heard the truth. I told my mother I got another letter from you explaining everything and confronted her. She told me what happened. She didn't tell me before because she didn't want to worry me. Then I called your mother and told her what my mother said. She thinks you have postpartum."

Linda scoffed.

"My mother is a piece of work." She said.

"So is mine." Ernest said.

"I don't trust them. Not even my family."

"I won't let anyone take Amy. Why don't we look at some houses this weekend? We don't have to decide anything. It'll be fun looking at all the old houses."

"What about our families?"

"We can worry about that later. We've been apart for so long. We have to get reacquainted."

"Spending time together?"

"Like when we first met."

Linda smiled.

"Okay. I'd like that." She said.

Two women walked in the store. They saw Ernest and their bodies stiffened.

"Is Joe here?" One woman said.

"No ma'am. He'll be in tomorrow. Is there something I can help you with?" Ernest said.

"No. Thank you." She said.

She was curt. The two women browsed the soup aisle.

"What was that about?" Linda said.

"No one's liked me since I got here. Some people still aren't happy about the war."

"That's not a reason to be rude to you."

"That's not the only thing. Someone accused me of killing that kid a few months ago."

"What? What kid?"

"The one they found in the river. It was in all the papers."

"I don't read the paper. Unless it's the classifieds."

"Okay. Back in November they found a kid's body in the river. I think he was six or seven years old. He'd been murdered. Someone, I don't know who, told the police I did it."

"Were you arrested?"

"No, but they did question me. The locals tried to accuse me of another murder that happened before I came to town."

"Why would they do that?"

"The murders haven't been solved. People are scared. They want someone to blame."

"That's not an excuse to accuse random people."

"It makes sense in their minds because I was in the war, so they think I kill babies."

"What's that have to do with the war? You're not making

sense."

"I never saw this happen. The Viet Cong would send small children, one or two years old, barely able to walk, into villages with bombs. American troops noticed when this would happen and shoot the kid before they got to the village. A lot of guys had trouble dealing with killing a kid."

"Oh my God! That's awful."

Linda took Ernest's hand in hers and held it tight.

"I pissed off the librarian too. I'm sure that had a lot to do with everyone's opinion of me." Ernest said.

"Ed doesn't like her either. He says the only time she's pleasant is when she's reading."

"At least I'm not the only one who doesn't like her."

The two women approached the counter. They each had a bag of flour and two potatoes.

"Be careful young lady. He'll ask you about his wife if he hasn't already." One woman said.

"I am his wife." Linda said.

"Good heavens! You married this miscreant?"

"Yes. And we have a beautiful baby girl."

Linda removed a photo from her purse. The two women awed in unison.

"Isn't she precious?" The other woman said.

"Well, would you please ring us up for these items, sir?" The first woman said.

"Are you paying together or separate?" Ernest said.

"Separate of course."

She was curt and pursed her lips. Ernest punched the items into the register.

"That'll be fifty cents each." He said.

The first woman placed a fifty-cent piece on the counter. Ernest bagged the items while the second woman counted change. She handed Ernest one quarter, a dime, two nickels, and five pennies. The women took their bags and left without a word.

"That's what I've been dealing with for months." Ernest said.

"I didn't like her tone with you."

"I didn't like it either."

"Why don't you say something?"

"They'll hate me even more if I do."

"I'm sorry. If I hadn't come out here, you wouldn't be dealing with all this."

"You have nothing to apologize for. Once they catch who's killing these kids, everyone will leave me alone."

"I hope so. I think I'll run home to check on Amy."

"What about the post office?"

"Oh, I forgot. Okay, I'll call you later. We'll figure things out. Bye."

With the ring of the bell, she was gone before he could say anything.

"Bye. Maybe next time your husband can get a hug before you leave. Or a kiss. Any form of affection. I hope we can figure it all out." He said.

Ernest returned his focus to the newspaper. He finished reading unaware of how much time had passed. He was lost in thought when the bell on the door pulled his attention. The boys who tried to buy beer were outside.

"Hey there Ernie."

"Hiya Steve. More vodka?" Ernest said.

"Ayuh. Helps warm me bones at night." Stephen said.

"You can pay this time, right?"

"I'm offended by the accusation, young man."

"Answer the question, Steve."

"I got money ya damn G-man."

Stephen sauntered to the liquor aisle. He grabbed his usual bottle of cheap vodka. Then he got a case of beer from the cooler. He carried them at his natural slow pace to the counter.

"I've never seen you get beer before." Ernest said.

"Thought I'd expand my palate."

"Or did those boys give you money to buy beer for them? I'm not selling it to you."

"Ah Hell Ernie. Boys will be boys. Can I at least get the vodka?"

"How do I know you won't give it to them boys?"

"Don't be like that Ernie. You know I don't share my drinks with nobody."

"Get rid of them boys. Come back in an hour and I'll pay for your vodka."

"Ya mean it?"

"I mean it."

"You're a swell guy, Ernie. I'll see ya after a bit."

Stephen told the boys the bad news and returned their money. They all sulked off. As the door closed, Ernest saw a raven picking at some garbage on the sidewalk.

Twenty-Four
February 24, 1977 - Samantha

I spent all my free time at the library. I found little on the Skov Sisters beyond the journal. I hadn't read any of it. I had to move on to other stories for work. This limited my time at the library. No new information led to my editor ignoring me anytime I brought it up. He said it wasn't news anymore. I couldn't use it as an excuse to view records. I'd leave work for the library until it closed.

I tried my best to ignore everything when I got home. I didn't want to think about work. What little free time I had I used to decompress and escape. I'd watch television, make dinner, have a glass of wine. I'd wash dishes, take a shower, and go to bed. Every night. Even weekends. I worked every day. If I wasn't working on a story or at home, I was in the library. Sometimes for hours going through books and documents. All those hours led to nothing.

I found no mention of the Skov Sisters beyond the one article. For a century there was nothing about them or their family. Maybe the women I saw are their great grandchildren. I speculated the women changed their name and moved to another town. I had no leads. Nothing except the journal. I don't know why I hadn't read through it before searching newspapers. I felt uneasy looking at it. It was dark navy blue hardbound. It had little damage. The library took care of their books. Every time I held it, I felt nauseous. I didn't want to take it home.

I forced myself to reach deadlines early at work. This gave

me plenty of time for a couple days to spend reviewing the journal. I asked Noreen for the book, got out my legal pad and pen, and dove in. I don't know what I was expecting. Part of me thought all the answers would come to me. The journal read like any other from a young woman in the late 19th Century. The ordinariness of the text was underwhelming.

***

September 12, 1875

We went to the market today. We don't go to town often. We needed flour and chicken feed, but we made a day of it. I wanted to look at dresses. Carla said that was silly. She said we can make our own dresses. I told her I didn't want to buy any. I only wanted to look. She said no. I looked to Bella for support.

"We make dresses at home." Bella said.

I followed behind them. I didn't speak the rest of the day. They spent the afternoon walking around town gossiping. We never talk to anyone. We don't attend church or festivities. How do they know so much about everyone? Carla had always had this gift for looking at someone and knowing things about them. It's like she can see into their soul. Bella can sense what someone is feeling. She never knew why they feel something, but she can fell it too. Together, my older sisters can bring a grown man to tears without touching him. So, we avoid talking to anyone.

Because I stayed quiet, I heard what others say about us. They call us whores for never attending church. And for the way men look at us. Because we never married, they say we must commune with Satan and fornicate with animals. We've never harmed any of them and they say such awful things. Sometimes I think my sisters have no idea what is said about us. Other times I wonder if they enjoy making people afraid.

When we returned home, I went to my room to read. I heard my sisters speak about me.

"Honestly, she gets in such a mood when she doesn't get her way." Bella said.

"She's young. She doesn't know what her priorities are." Carla said.

Are all sisters this way? Am I acting like a child for being angry? I'd enjoy having a nice conversation with other people. People who don't scold me for having an opinion. I've lived to long not to be allowed a voice. Maybe that's why I'm writing this. To have a voice separate from my sisters.

***

This explained why there wasn't a lot of information about the sisters. They were outcasts. They didn't have much interest in being part of the community. I wondered if they were mentioned in other journals during that time. I asked Noreen to see everything they had.

"Every journal? That's a lot of reading." Noreen said.

"I want to find any other mention of the Skov Sisters." I said.

"What's so interesting about them?"

"They were accused of witchcraft then disappeared. I think they changed their names and moved to another town."

"Oh my! This is so exciting. I can help you look through some of these."

"You're a dream, Noreen."

There were several journals from men and women. None of them mentioned the Skov Sisters.

"Perhaps if we check older texts, we'll find mention of their family. Their parents or grandparents." Noreen said.

"How many texts do you have that are that old?" I said.

"Not many, but the oldest ones are from around the time of King Phillip's War. About 1670 or so."

"I guess since there's nothing left to check."

We read through a few journals from when Maine became

a state. Then a couple from the War of 1812 when Maine was part of Massachusetts. Then the Revolutionary War. Then the Colonial Wars.

"Most people didn't keep records back then unless they were wealthy. The family may have been poor." Noreen said.

"They appeared a hundred years ago and now three women who look like them appeared. None of this makes sense. That's why I need to find something. Anything." I said.

"Okay. Only a couple left. You read that one and I'll read this one."

She handed me a leather journal. The paper was rough on the edges. There were no lines. The handwriting was beautiful though difficult to read. The first page stated the diary belonged to Margaret Hunt. She told her story of coming to the New World from England with her family. I skimmed the diary for almost an hour before something caught my eye. An entry dated May 18, 1677. I took the liberty of modernizing the language. The original text had odd spelling of words and unique phrasing. This is more of a summary of what Margaret wrote.

***

They found another dead child today. Everyone thinks the Abenaki are responsible. Every death that can't be explained they blame on the war. Part of the moon was red last night. It wasn't a full blood moon. That's what happened the last time they found a dead child. Satan has more power in this New World. I fear my prayers are not enough.

I've told my husband and others these deaths are the work of evil. They say the Abenaki are evil. I say no. There is another evil. I've seen them. There are witches in this New World. Servants of the devil.

Where are these witches, my husband says. But I know not where they lurk. I lack the courage to search. All I can do is watch over my little ones. I know in my heart the killing is not over. When the moon fills with blood, they will kill again.

I see them in town. Many don't but I see them.

I see how men covet them. Being in the presence allows Satan to reach you soul. They make you sin without knowing. Without control. I've never heard anyone speak their names. But I swear to the Great Lord above I heard one introduce herself to a shopkeeper as Malice. Only a witch would admit her evil ways in her name. They are the ones who kill these children. I feel it in my bones.

No one listens except for Pastor John and Sister Marie. I had them twice now come bless my home to keep Satan and his instruments of evil away. My poor little ones are so frightened. We say a prayer every night before we sleep. Then we say another in the morning for breakfast and one for supper. Those women don't pray unless it's to Satan. I've never seen them attend church thank the heavens. The blood moon is an omen. It's the lord telling us evil is among us.

It's those witches causing this war. Taking children isn't enough. They must take our men as well. They live for death. The Lord will see them punished. Then this war will end, and our children will be safe. I have faith in the Lord and those who carry out his work.

***

Margaret never mentions witches or the moon again. Later that year, her family moved to the Connecticut Colony. Noreen didn't find anything. I didn't find enough of anything.

"Do you have anything about the blood moon?" I said.

"We should have one or two astronomy books in the science section." Noreen said.

"I'll look into that tomorrow. I need to get away from these books for a while."

"Take some time to relax. Why are you working yourself so hard?"

"I have to pay my mother's medical bills. She's at the Mental Health Institute in Augusta."

"I'm so sorry, dear. I didn't mean to…"

"It's okay. No harm done."

"May I ask why she's there?"

"You've heard about my father. And what he did. She never recovered."

"I'm sorry. I didn't know."

"She's doing well with her treatment. But it's so expensive."

"If you need anything, all you have to do is ask."

"Thank you, Noreen. Right now, all I need is a glass of wine and a shower. I'll see you tomorrow."

"Okay dear. Take care of yourself."

I didn't know much about blood moons or how often they happen. My astronomy professor from college would claim I didn't pay attention in his class. I didn't. I only took the class because my only friend at the University of Maine asked me to take it with her. I never would have guessed I'd need that information for my job. I should have paid attention.

Twenty-Five
March 1, 1977

Ernest sat in a diner booth sipping coffee. On the table were various jelly flavors, salt and pepper shakers, a sugar shaker, and napkins. In front of him was a glass of water and silverware wrapped in a napkin next to his coffee mug. The server topped off his coffee.

"Gettin' any food this mornin' Hun?" The server said.

"Only coffee. Thanks." Ernest said.

"Let me know if you need anything."

There were three other people in the diner. They all sat at the counter. Two of them spoke with the other server. The other read the newspaper. Ernest faced the door and kept an eye on the parking lot. He sat far away from everyone else. He picked at his cuticles while he waited. Samantha rushed in carrying her bag and notebooks with frizzy hair pulled back in a ponytail. She looked around, saw Ernest, and hurried to the booth.

"Hey! Good choice on the meeting place. The coffee is great here. How are you?" She said.

"Surviving. Why the hurry?" Ernest said.

"I've been so busy. Work has been crazy. I have little time to myself."

"What are ya havin' Hun?" The server said.

"Coffee please." Samantha said.

"Any cream?"

"Yes please."

"Would you like a menu?"

"Oh. I'm not hungry. Are you?"

"No." Ernest said.

"No. Thank you."

"Be right back with that coffee and cream."

"How are things with the family?" Samantha said.

"Good. We're getting reacquainted." Ernest said.

"That's great!"

"Here you are." The server said.

"Thank you." Samantha said.

The server walked away. Samantha poured some cream into her coffee, then sugar, as Ernest spoke. She unwrapped her silverware to stir her coffee with the spoon.

"It is, but I found out our families lied to me about why she left. Linda is afraid someone will take the baby from us. I told her I won't let anyone take Amy. She acts like she's uncomfortable around me. It's awkward. We're figuring things out, I guess." Ernest said.

"Why does she think someone will take your baby?" Samantha said.

"When they all thought I died, my father said he would raise the child as his own. They were all upset at the time. I guess he planned to even when they heard I was alive. Anyway, we're considering getting a place out here in Maine."

"You plan to keep working with Joe?"

"No. I'll look for something in a nearby hospital. Or maybe the coroner's office."

"The coroner could use the help."

"Did you learn anything about the house we found in the woods?"

"Oh, I've done a lot of digging. And that's on top of my heavy workload. I've learned a lot but there are still some pieces missing. There's a creepy journal that might have answers. It might not. I don't know."

"Okay, slow down. You're talking a mile a minute." Ernest said.

"Sorry." Samantha said.

"It's okay. Start at the beginning."

"Okay. I told you the house is owned by the state and the previous owners were the Skov Sisters. I told you about the newspaper article from 1877 where they were accused of witchcraft. I didn't tell you the paper had sketches of their portraits. They look like the three women we saw in the store. I think they're the great-great grandchildren of these Skov Sisters."

"Are you saying they were witches? That's as crazy as Joe's werewolf story."

"Back then, any women who pissed off a man was accused of being a witch. I don't think they were witches. But I do think they changed their name and moved to another town."

"Changed their name to what?"

"I'm hoping to learn that from the creepy journal."

"What creepy journal?"

"It belonged to one of the sisters. What I've read so far is normal 19th Century stuff."

"Then why's it creepy?"

"I don't know. That's the weird thing. Looking at and holding it makes me feel awful. It makes me feel nervous."

"Weird. Was that all?"

"No! There's more."

"More coffee?" The server said.

"Yes please." Ernest said.

Ernest sipped his refreshed coffee. Samantha sipped then added more cream and sugar.

"There's another journal from 1677." Samantha said.

"From the Skov Sisters?" Ernest said.

"No. This is someone else's. In one entry, she said children were killed by witches."

"Please tell me you're joking."

"I wish I was. She said a child was always killed during a blood moon."

"Okay."

"That's just another name for a total lunar eclipse."

"You've lost me."

"The child they accused you of killing died the night of the eclipse."

"But that wasn't a blood moon, was it?"

"Maybe it only has to be an eclipse not a total eclipse."

"Okay…"

"Look. Three hundred years ago this same thing happened. Everyone assumed it was a war with Native Americans. But people believed in witches back then. This woman, Margaret Hunt, said two children were killed during a lunar eclipse. She described the witches as getting a lot of attention from men and making people uncomfortable. Like the women we saw." Samantha said.

"So, you think it's some ritual sacrifice?" Ernest said.

"Maybe. What past records I could find of missing or killed children usually had an explanation. Abusive parents or a high fall. They didn't have too many records a hundred years ago. But what if this happens all the time? What if kids are sacrificed every eclipse? How many generations has this family practiced this?"

"And what happened to the Skov Sisters a century ago?"

"I hope the creepy journal will answer that."

"If we find out where they went, then we can find their family now."

"Exactly."

"I told you it looked like someone had been in that house in the woods."

"Maybe they use it in secret. Maybe they had things buried around the house. Or in the house. There are too many things we don't know."

"We should take what we have to the police. Let them figure this out."

"They won't believe any of this. They'll call us crackpots claiming witches are killing children. They won't take us seriously. I've tried before with legitimate evidence, and they called me another hysterical woman." Samantha said.

"What about your friend, Jed?" Ernest said.

"He might help but it won't be official. He'd have to do it during his personal time."

"So, what's our next move? Sit tight and wait for someone else to lose their child?"

"I say we try to catch them ourselves."

"Neither of us has the training to hunt down psychopaths."

"I'm an investigative journalist and a damn good one. You have military training and medical training. Jed is one hell of a cop. With his help, all three of us can find who's doing this and stop them. Then we give the police everything we found and tell them these people are crazy and think they need to sacrifice children. They'll believe the killers are crazy."

"I don't like this. Something about it feels too dangerous."

"You were in a war overseas. This should be a walk in the park for you."

"And from that I learned things can go wrong at a moment's notice. A walk in the park turns into a firefight."

"Another reason you should come with me. You're prepared for stuff like that."

"Top off?" The server said.

"Yes. Thank you. I don't know. We have no idea what we're getting in to." Ernest said.

"We're keeping people safe. What if it was your daughter they kidnapped next?" Samantha said.

"Don't say that! Don't even think about that."

"I'm only making a point. No one should experience losing a young child."

"Okay. What's the plan?"

"First we need to know when the next lunar eclipse will happen."

"How do we do that?"

"I'll pay my old astronomy professor a visit and find out what he knows."

"How long will you be gone?"

"It's just a couple hours North. It'll take half a day. I'll call his TA tomorrow to schedule a time to see him. I'll have to plan it around work. It's in another county. My boss wouldn't send me there for anything."

"Okay. We learn when the next eclipse happens, then what? We don't know where to look for them."

"I'm hoping the journal at the library will tell us."

"Why don't you check out the book and read it at home?"

"Because it makes me feel anxious and uncomfortable."

"Oh yeah. Sorry."

"I don't want that thing in my house. Besides, it's part of the rare books collection. Noreen doesn't let anyone check those out." Samantha said.

"What am I supposed to do?" Ernest said.

"You could always go to the library for me."

"It's probably best if I avoid the librarian."

"You're right. I don't know. Have you seen those women again?"

"Not since we saw the house. I've been catching up with Linda. We looked at some of the old houses a couple weeks ago. We have to get to know each other all over again. I think she's changed a lot. I've definitely changed a lot."

"That must be hard."

"It's not so bad."

"How's the baby?"

"She's great. She loves making noise."

"I don't know any babies who don't."

"More coffee?" The server said.

"Not for me. I should get back to work." Samantha said.

"I'll take another cup." Ernest said.

"How much do I owe you?"

"Seventy cents." The server said.

Samantha gave the server a dollar.

"Keep the change."

"Thanks, Hun."

"Listen Ernie. We'll figure this thing out. But we have to take it one step at a time. We can't rush into this." Samantha said.

"Yeah. I get it." Ernest said.

"And I want to meet that baby of yours."

Samantha's heels clicked on the tile floor. She left as fast as she entered. Ernest stared at her coffee mug holding his own. He sipped lost in thought. The server put a check at the end of the table and picked up the used mug and silverware.

"There's no rush. Stay as long as you like. Gimme a holler when you're ready." The server said.

"Thank you."

He sipped his coffee and picked at his cuticles again. A raven stood on the roof of a car squawking at something. Ernest stood and saw a couple bullfrogs hopping around the parking lot. The raven jumped down squawking at the croakers.

Twenty-Six
March 19, 1977

"It warmed up a lot today." Ernest said.

"Yeah." Linda said.

"There's a chill in the air. Should we put her little hat on?"

"It's warm enough. She's okay."

"Spring is almost here."

"Yeah."

"This feels like weather back home."

"It's a nice day for a walk."

Ernest and Linda sat on a bench facing the river. Amy sat in the grass playing with some hand puppets. Ernest watched the river flow South. Linda stared at the ground. They didn't speak for a few awkward minutes. A small boat drifted towards the river's hook. Other boats farther upriver rested on the peaceful water.

"It looks calm, doesn't it?" Ernest said.

"What?" Linda said.

"The water and the sailboats. They're floating along without a care in the world. I haven't felt that calm in a long time."

"Yeah. Me too."

"We should get a boat and go out there sometime. Spend the day sailing up and down the river. Forget about everything for a while. What do you think?"

"I don't know."

"I'm not sure what other things we can do together. We can go see a film."

"Amy doesn't do well in theaters. She doesn't like the

dark."

"I'm only throwing out ideas."

"Okay."

"Do you have any ideas?"

"No."

"You want to keep walking around to different places?"

"I don't know."

"Is something wrong?" He said.

"No." She said.

"Are you sure?"

"I'm fine."

"Okay."

"I'm sorry. I'm just tired."

"It's okay. We can leave if you want."

"We can keep sitting here for a while."

"Okay."

Linda busied herself looking through her bag. She removed the cap from her lip balm. Ernest watched the river. Amy paid no attention to her parents. She made noises and bounced the hand puppets through the grass.

"We haven't talked about how to move forward." Ernest said.

"What do you mean?" She said.

"Where will we live? Getting a place of our own. To raise Amy together. I want to know what you think. What you want."

"I don't know."

"Do you want to stay here?"

"I don't know! I haven't thought about it. I don't want to think about it right now."

"Okay. So, we keep doing what we're doing for now. Is that what you're saying?"

"I guess so."

"What does that mean?"

"It means I can't think of anything else to do. I'm scared. Not only that someone wants to take my baby girl, but also, of raising her. I feel like I've already ruined her life and it just started. It's overwhelming. I don't know what to do. I don't want to think about it."

"We have to do something. We can't sit around here waiting for things to fix themselves."

"I know."

"We don't have to decide anything today. I want some options to look into. I need a goal to pursue." He said.

"Are you going to keep working at that store?" She said.

"No. I've made a couple phone calls to local hospitals. None of them are hiring."

"We can't live in your tiny place. And Ed doesn't have room for us as it is."

"I thought that's why we went looking at houses a few weeks ago."

"You're not making enough money at the store to afford a decent place."

"I have a lot of money saved up from my deployment. We can get a place right now. I don't care where we live as long as I'm with you. If you don't want to stay in Maine, say the word. We can go wherever you want."

"I don't know. I'm not sure about any of this."

"About what?"

"All of it! Wherever we go your father will find us and take her. I can't let that happen. He will never lay a hand on her."

"He won't take her from us. I won't let that happen. He has no right."

"You think that will stop him? You don't know what he's capable of."

"And you don't know what I'm capable of. Is that what this is about? Do you not trust me?" He said.

"It's not that. I just…I think we should consider giving her up for adoption." She said.

"What!? Where the hell is this coming from?"

"It would be better for her. I've screwed up. I dragged her across the country. She'd be better off if I didn't raise her. And your father will never get to her."

"You haven't done anything wrong. Look at her. She's happy. I've seen you with her. You're a wonderful mother. I will never agree to adoption. I waited almost two years to see my baby girl. You two are the only things I care about."

"What if we can't get away from him? What if he finds us no matter where we go? I'll die before he puts his hands on her."

Ernest watched Linda. She covered her mouth fighting to hold back the tears rolling down her cheeks. He put his arms around her and held her. He watched the boats and rubbed Linda's shoulder.

"Everything will be okay." He said.

"I'm afraid it won't be." She said.

"Sure, it will."

"I'm not sure about living with you."

"What?"

"I don't think I can do it."

"We've known each other for years. Why would you think you can't do it?"

"I'm sorry."

"Why can't you do it?"

Linda shook her head.

"First you want to get rid of your child. Then you want to get rid of me." He said.

"I'm trying to keep Amy safe." She said.

"From me?"

"From our families."

"Then I'll stop talking to them. All of them. We can move and never tell them where we go. They'll never hear from us again."

"And we'll live in fear wondering if they found us. I can't do that."

"What else can we do?"

"I don't know! I told you that."

He moved away from her on the bench. He took deep, long breaths. Linda sat with her legs and arms crossed looking away from him. Ernest rested his chin on his hands, elbow on his knees. He stared at the ground tapping both his heels.

"You haven't told me everything, have you? What else is going on?" He said.

"I want her to be safe. That's all. I don't think we can give her the kind of life she needs. The kind she deserves." She said.

"And you want to give her up before we ever have a chance to try."

Ernest looked at Amy. She shook the puppets up and down making beeping noises unaware of the adults' conversation. He envied her. He envied her carefree view of the world.

"I'll never agree to adoption." He said.

"I can do it without you." She said.

"How?"

"I'll tell them you died serving your country. They won't question that."

"And what happens when they see I'm alive and try to get my daughter back?"

Linda sat rigid, still looking away from him.

"Is this what we're gonna do? Are we going to fight for custody of our child? You think that's what's best for her?" He said.

She looked at him, tears welling in her eyes again.

"I don't want to fight with you. I'm so scared something bad will happen to her. And it'll be my fault if something does." She said.

"Nothing will happen. We can handle anything that comes our way if we face it together." He said.

"You father will come for her. I know he will. We can't let him have her."

"Why would he take his only granddaughter from his only son?"

"I can't explain it. But I know that's what he wants. That's why I suggested adoption. Then he would never be able to find her."

"Why are you so afraid of him? I know he's a bastard, but you're acting like he wants to kill you."

"He might. He never threatened to kill me, but I think he would. You don't know how he was while you were away. He acts different around you."

"Why would he act different with me?"

"I don't know. You're his only son. You're a man, not a woman. Whatever his reason, that's how he is. I hate him. I hate your father. Keep him away from me. Keep him away from my daughter."

She wiped the tears from her face and looked away. She took long, heavy breaths.

"Will you tell me why you hate him so much?" He said.

Linda didn't move or speak. She stared at the water. A bullfrog hopped along the riverbank.

"What if we run off somewhere and don't tell anyone? My father won't find us. We can raise Amy together." He said.

They sat in silence. Amy stopped playing. She looked at her mother. Ernest sat back watching the river. A raven squawked in a tree then dropped to the grass. It watched the bullfrog. Ernest looked at the raven.

"I wonder if that's the same bird from Ed's place?"

The raven hopped towards the bank. The bullfrog paid no attention to the bird. Amy returned to her puppets. Linda remained still.

"For the sake of argument, what would we do after giving her up for adoption?" He said.

"I don't know." She said.

"You feel confident about something you haven't thought through."

"I haven't decided anything. I don't know what to do. Part of me wants to run away. Another part wants to give up Amy and then rub that in your father's face."

"What about me?"

"What?"

"Do you want me to run away with you? Do you want to run away from me?"

"I'm not running from you. I want to keep Amy safe."

"Why do you feel she's not safe with both of us?"

"She's not safe from your father."

"You think I can't protect my family?"

"This isn't about you."

"Then what's it about!?"

"I've told you!"

"You haven't told me everything."

"Your father is the problem, and my family thinks I'm crazy and belong in a hospital. Your family and my family want to take Amy from me. I won't let them have her. I'll do whatever it takes. I have to keep her safe." She said.

"All I want is to keep you both safe. But you're not giving me a chance. You're acting like the war is over before it's even started. We can keep her safe if we work together. If it turns out the only way to keep her safe is to give her up, I'll do it. But only as a last resort. So, what are we going to do?" He said.

"I don't know if there's anything we can do. I don't know if adoption would keep her safe. I'm afraid he'd still find a way to track her down. I don't know what's best. What kind of mother doesn't know what's best for her child?"

"You think every new mother has all the answers? All we can do is what we think is best and hope. Hope that we make the right choices. I still question some of my choices."

"I think adoption is best. And I think…I think we should consider – consider separating for a while."

"Are you asking for a divorce?"

"No. At least, I don't think I am. Maybe if she's somewhere safe and we're not together for a while, everyone will leave us alone. Maybe after a while, we can see how things go. Maybe we'll work things out. Maybe we'll divorce. I don't know."

"That's a lot of maybes. Do you hate me? Or resent me?"

"No. I feel abandoned. You left me alone for so long. I know you didn't have any choice. I know if you could, you would have come home. But you didn't. And that's when everything fell apart."

"I'm here now. I can make things right."

"No. You can't."

"I'm sorry I wasn't there. We don't have to divorce because of it." He said.

"I forgive you for going away. I think we'll all be safer if we separate for a while." She said.

"That's it then? You've made up your mind. You don't want

your daughter or your husband in your life anymore? You're going to throw us away like trash?"

"I'm not trying to hurt you."

"Well, it does hurt. I'm sorry it hurt you when I left. But you're going to hurt me if you leave. Is that why you're doing this? Is this revenge? Are you getting back at me?"

"No. That's not what this is about."

"Okay. What's it about?"

Linda looked away. She started crying again.

"No answer? I'm not surprised." He said.

Ernest marched away. He fought back tears. Linda didn't call to him. She sat on the bench crying. Amy made whooshing sounds spinning the puppets in the air. The raven hopped along following the bullfrog.

Twenty-Seven
March 31, 1977

"Hiya Joe!"

"Hey Bob. How are ya?" Joe said.

"I'm doin' alright. How 'bout you?" Bob said.

"Can't complain."

"You still got copies of the Observer?"

"Over on the rack with the other papers."

"Hey Joe. Hey Bob."

"Hey Dick." Joe said.

"Hiya Dick." Bob said.

"You gettin' a paper?" Dick said.

"Ayuh. Marge likes the crosswords, you know." Bob said.

"Say, d'you hear about the Pan Am flight that crashed?"

"A plane crash?"

"Ayuh. Two 747's hit each other. It was a few days ago. In Europe or someplace."

"You know anyone on the plane?" Joe said.

"Nah. My wife's sister says she knows a guy whose cousin was on the plane. He didn't make it." Dick said.

"Why are you comin' in here givin' us sad news on a beautiful day?" Bob said.

"I'm only makin' conversation. Joe, you still got that kid who's all messed up from the war workin' here?" Dick said.

"Ayuh. He ain't messed up. He's a good kid. He's stockin' stuff in the back, so don't talk like that." Joe said.

"Talk like what? War messes with people. It's harsh stuff."

"Talk about somethin' else."

"Nobody likes what I talk about today. Maybe I'll get a newspaper and find somethin' you guys wanna talk about."

"How's business?" Bob said.

"Not bad. Steady." Joe said.

"Watch out boys! Nancy Drew is here. She's gonna squeeze us for information." Dick said.

"I didn't know you allowed goons in your store, Joe." Samantha said.

"Dick, will you read your paper and let people alone?" Joe said.

"Is Ernie here?" Samantha said.

"He's in back. You need him for somethin'?" Joe said.

"Yeah. It's urgent."

Joe disappeared into the backroom. Dick sat at a table reading with Bob.

"Why do you talk to that guy?" Bob said.

"He's a friend. You know what friends are, right?" Samantha said.

"He's bad news girlie. Run while you can."

"The only thing that's bad news around here is your body odor."

Dick laughed behind the newspaper.

"Shut up, Dick." Bob said.

Ernest and Joe returned from the backroom. Samantha motioned for Ernest to follow her to the other end of the counter away from the others.

"Hey. What's goin' on?" Ernest said.

"I've got bad news and worse news." Samantha said.

"Okay."

"A child is missing. A little girl."

"Shit. When's the next eclipse?"

"I don't know. I haven't met with the astronomy professor yet."

"Do we know when and where she was taken?"

"That's the worse news. Someone said they saw her talking to you before she went missing."

"Are you serious? I don't remember talking to any kids. Where'd you hear this?"

"I got a tip from someone in the Hallowell Police Department. They thought I'd want the story. They're on their way to come arrest you. What did you and the little girl talk about?"

"The only kids I talk to come in the store. Most of them are with their parents except a group of boys always playing hooky." Ernest said.

"I'll find out who saw you. Maybe they mixed you up with someone else or saw you with her family but didn't say that." Samantha said.

"Everyone's tried to get rid of me since I got to this town. I'm sure they never saw me with anyone."

"The police are on their way. You need to get out of here. Lay low until we can figure this out."

"That'll make me look more guilty. I didn't do anything wrong. I'm not going anywhere."

"Getting arrested won't make things better for you."

"I was arrested then let go once already. I'll be fine. Find out who saw me. And find that little girl."

"I don't know if I can do all this alone."

"You're one hell of an investigator and a damn good journalist. You said so yourself. And right now, you're the only person I trust."

"What about your wife?"

"She can't trust me. It makes it hard for me to trust her."

"What does that mean?"

"I'll tell you later."

Two police officers walked into the store.

"Ernest Kemp. Can you step outside with us please?" One officer said.

"What's this about?" Ernest said.

"We just want to ask you a few questions."

"You can ask them here."

"Can you tell me where you were yesterday?"

"I was here until about 6 o'clock then I went home."

"You stayed home all night?"

"Yes."

"Was anyone with you or did anyone see you during the time you were home?"

"No."

"Mister Kemp. Can you step out from behind the counter, please?"

Ernest followed the request.

"Ernest Kemp. You are under arrest for the kidnapping of Alice Summers." The officer said.

"Didn't you already clear him of that boy's murder? Why are you arresting him again?" Samantha said.

"You have the right to remain silent."

"Isn't this double jeopardy? Arresting him for the same crime twice?"

"Anything you say can and will be used against you in a court of law."

"Are you even listening to me?"

"You have the right to an attorney."

"Let it go Nancy Drew. I told ya' he was bad news." Bob said.

"If you cannot afford an attorney, one will be provided for you." The officer said.

"He didn't take any children." Samantha said.

"Do you understand these rights I've said to you?"

"Yes." Ernest said.

"Ernie, we're gonna fight this." Samantha said.

"Ma'am, if you want to help him, get a lawyer."

"Do you even care about other people?"

"Ma'am. I'm just doing my job. The detectives will figure this out when they question him. They told us to bring him in and that's all we're doing."

"Don't worry about me. Everything will be fine." Ernest said.

"I'll try to come see you when I have more information." Samantha said.

"I told you you're the only person I trust in this town."

"Guess I have to finish all the stocking." Joe said.

"That's all you have to say." Samantha said.

"He's arrested again for the same thing. That should tell ya' all you need to know." Bob said.

"Here. Here." Dick said.

"You heard the man. If you want to help get him a lawyer." Joe said.

"You think he's guilty?" Samantha said.

"Of course, he does. We all do. That public menace is off the streets." Bob said.

Dick stood and clapped. Bob joined in the applause.

"Will you two idjits sit down?" Joe said.

"We're just happy the child killer is gone." Dick said.

"Haven't you heard of innocent until proven guilty?" Samantha said.

"He got arrested. That proves he's guilty." Dick said.

"Ayuh." Bob said.

"That's not how the system works you morons." Samantha said.

"Everybody calm the hell down or I'll kick the lot of you out." Joe said.

"We're entitled to our opinion." Bob said.

"And I'm entitled to not like or listen to your damn opinion. Read your paper or get out." Joe said.

The men fell silent.

"Sorry Joe." Samantha said.

Screams and squawks echoed from outside. Samantha rushed out. A raven pecked at one of the officers. The other officer held Ernest against the patrol car.

"Owe! Go on! Git! Buzz off!"

The officer slapped the empty air toward the bird. The raven dived and swooped around the officer's head. It slapped his head with its wings. Two more ravens sat on top of the building watching the show.

"Someone get this thing off me!"

"Just get in the car." The other officer said.

They put Ernest in the car, then themselves. The raven landed on the back of the car pecking the window behind Ernest.

"Is that your pet?" The attacked officer said.

"I don't have any pets." Ernest said.

The officer looked at his partner in the passenger seat.

"Am I cut or anything?"

"No. You look okay."

Ernest looked at Samantha. He heard her muffled voice through the car door.

"We'll figure this out. Don't worry."

Ernest nodded. The driving officer spoke on the radio.

"Dispatch. This is Owens. We have the suspect in custody. On our way."

"Ten four Owens. See you soon."

Ernest looked out the window to the other side of the street. The three women stood with a crowd of spectators. The brunette smiled and waved at Ernest. He turned toward Samantha, but she was gone having retreated back inside the store. Ernest returned his gaze to the street. The three women were gone but the crowd remained. Bullfrogs hopped along the sidewalk at people's feet. As the patrol car moved, the raven on the back window flew off and joined the other ravens perched on the roof.

"You guys really think I kidnapped that girl?" Ernest said.

"Buddy, I don't know you or what you're capable of." Owens said.

"Someone identified you and you don't have shit for an alibi. Whether you did it or not, you're the only suspect we got." The other officer said.

"That's how it was last time. How do you know the real kidnapper isn't setting me up as a patsy?" Ernest said.

"We're just beat cops. The detective will figure all that shit out. We just bring you in." Owens said.

The patrol car slowed to a stop at an intersection. Across the street, a group of children were poking a small army of bullfrogs with sticks. A raven landed on the stop sign next to the patrol car.

"What the hell is going on with the animals in this town?" The other officer said.

The driver pushed the patrol car through the intersection

towards the Hallowell Police Station. The raven watched from the station roof as Ernest was led inside. Owens watched the bird anticipating another attack that never came.

Twenty-Eight
April 1, 1977 - Samantha

With Ernest arrested and another child missing, I felt confident that another eclipse would happen soon. I called the astronomy professor at the University of Maine. His assistant did not offer much help.

"I'm sorry. Professor Minsky isn't available. Would you like to leave a message or schedule an appointment?" The assistant said.

"How soon can I see him if I make an appointment?" I said.

"The next open time he has is about three weeks from now."

"That's not soon enough. Is there any way I could speak to him over the phone?"

"I'm sorry. He's currently lecturing. Then he is attending a symposium all next week. When he returns, he has several meetings along with classes and research studies."

"I understand. Please pencil me in for the next available appointment. Is there someone I can talk to right now to find out when the next lunar eclipse will be?"

"Oh, one of the TA's might be able to help with that. First let's get your appointment written in. Tuesday, April 26th and is 2:30 a good time?"

"Sounds great."

"Wonderful. And could you repeat your name?"

"Samantha Belcher."

"Great. Let me see if I can flag down a TA for you."

I wrote the appointment on my own calendar while I waited on the phone.

"Ms. Belcher? Are you still there?"

"Yes." I said.

"Great. I just spoke to one of the TA's and he said the next lunar eclipse is in a couple days."

"Really?"

"Yes. He said it'll be this Sunday night."

"Wow. Okay. Thank you for your help."

"Was there anything else?"

"No miss. Thank you."

"You're very welcome and we'll see you on the 26th."

"Okay. Thanks again."

"Have a great day."

"You too."

The next eclipse was coming fast. I didn't have enough time to make a case for Ernest. The police would never believe my theory. I grabbed a phonebook and dialed a few lawyers. The first number I called never answered. The second was answered by a paralegal. The lawyer was out to lunch. The third number wasn't promising.

"It doesn't sound like your friend has much of a case." The lawyer said.

"Does that mean you won't represent him?" I said.

"I only take cases I know I'll win."

"Thanks for nothing."

Another lawyer was out for lunch. I suspected he was with the first lawyer out to lunch. The next one sounded more optimistic.

"There's not much to go on. Call me if new evidence comes up." The lawyer said.

"Like what new evidence?" I said.

"Like if someone can verify your friend's alibi. Or if another witness comes forward."

"Any other advice?"

"If your friend is innocent, he'll have to wait it out until they find a more likely suspect."

"And if that doesn't happen?"

"They'll try to press him for a confession. If he doesn't confess, they'll charge him, but they don't have enough for a case. They'll assign him a public defender and that'll be enough. It might take a couple months, but your friend will be fine."

"So, all we can do is sit tight and wait for new evidence?"

"That's the best option. New evidence could lead them to a different suspect, and they'll have to release your friend."

"Okay. Thank you for the help."

"And call me if things change."

"No problem."

I felt the best thing for me to do was try to learn more from the journal at the library. I hoped to find a place or a reason for the killing. If I found the girl, that would help prove Ernest's innocence. I was reluctant because of how I felt around the book. I didn't want to hold if for a long time. There wasn't anything else for me to do. I welcomed the warmth of the library.

"Tell me something Noreen. Do you get a weird feeling from this journal?" I said.

"How do you mean?" She said.

"Do you feel uncomfortable when you pick it up? Do you feel anxious for no reason?"

"Are you feeling okay, Samantha?"

"Yes. But I feel weird around that book. I wanted to know if anyone else did or if it was my imagination."

"You are under a lot of stress. I'm sure that's all it is. To be honest, this is the most I've ever seen this book. No one's touched it in years. I've never had much desire to look at all those old journals."

"Why not?"

"I'm not sure. You'd think I would with all the history they hold. Sometimes I avoid walking by that shelf if I can. I have no idea why."

"Well, I'll get to work then."

"Oh yes. I also have some things to attend to."

I sat down with the journal. My heart pounded. My stomach quivered. I inhaled long and slow. Wanting to spend as little time with the book as possible, I skimmed through looking for anything about the lunar eclipse. Pages and pages turned but I found nothing mentioning the eclipse. Then I thought she maybe didn't know the word. Maybe she called it something else or just referenced the moon. I returned to the beginning searching for moon.

One passage described a half moon that was bright that night. Most of the passage was about stargazing. I continued my search. I found a mention of the moon only one more time in the whole journal. The entry was vague.

***

"I have grown tired of this long life. I don't want to live through another unnatural blood moon. I want this curse to end."

***

The rest of the passage detailed an argument between the sisters about Malla's friendships. I wanted answers but found more questions. I collected my notes and realized the awkward feeling had passed. I only needed time to read the book.

"Noreen, have you ever heard of an unnatural blood moon?" I said.

"No. I've seen a few blood moons. That's something that makes me uneasy." She said.

"Thanks again."

The only other lead I had was Ernest's accuser. I had to find out who that was. My source was less than helpful.

"Hallowell Police. Smith."

"Hey Francis." I said.

"I told you not to call me that. And I don't have anything for you." He said.

"How do you know I'm not calling to see how my cousin is doing?"

"Look. Someone told the chief you were there when your guy was arrested. He doesn't want anyone talking to the press. He'd have my ass if he knew we were talking. I'd probably lose my job if he knew we were related."

"Stop whispering. Talk normal. Act like your cousin called

to make dinner plans or something."

"Okay."

"Do you know who accused Ernest?"

"Ayuh."

"Can you get me their name and address?"

"No. I don't think I can do that."

"What about where they saw him with the girl?"

"No. That won't work either."

"Can you give me any clue? Anything?" I said.

"Probably not. What was that Owens? No, just my cousin. Trying to make dinner plans sometime this week." He said.

"Shit. I'm running out of options here. I don't know what else to do."

"Let me check with a buddy of mine and I'll let you know about dinner. I need to get back to work."

"Yeah. Okay. I don't want you to get into trouble. Do what you gotta do. Bye."

"Bye."

Another dead end. I had played all my cards and still had to fold. I didn't know what else to do. I couldn't help Ernest. I couldn't find or help the little girl. I couldn't find whoever was doing this. I started getting that same feeling I got from the Malla Skov journal. I had to go home and relax. Try to clear my head. Sometimes the ideas come when you stop thinking about everything.

I sat on my couch and kicked off my shoes. I considered sleeping. I couldn't think of any ways to take my mind off things. I don't know if I dozed off or not. A knock at my door started me. I crept towards the door. Part of me didn't want to answer. They knocked again.

"Sam? Sam, are you home?"

"Dammit Jed! You scared the hell out of me." I said.

"Sorry. Can I come in?" Jed said.

"Yeah. You want a drink?"

"No. Thank you."

"Mind if I have one?"

"It's your house. Do what you want?"

We stared at each other in my kitchen.

"Well?" I said.

"How've you been?" He said.

"Busy. You could have called to ask me that."

"That's not why I'm here. But I do hope you're doing well. And your mom."

"Momma's okay. That's why I'm busy. Working to pay for her care."

"I'm glad she's getting the care she needs. I can't imagine what that's like."

"Jed. Why'd you come over?"

"Frank called me after you talked to him."

"You mean Francis."

"Damn Sam. Even his mother doesn't call him Francis anymore."

"I only call him that because it pisses him off so much."

"Well, he's really worried about losing his job this time."

"He told me. That's why I didn't push him."

"I know. But he still wants to help. That's why he told me the name of the witness."

"What?"

"The guy doesn't want to talk to the press. That's why he asked to be kept anonymous. I will set up a meeting. I'll take you, but you can't tell him you're a reporter and you can't write about him." He said.

"I just want to help get Ernest out of jail." I said.

"You, um, you really like this, uh, this guy?"

"What? He's married. I'm not trying to hook up with him. He's a friend that's been falsely accused. I'm trying to help him."

"Okay. I just, um, didn't want to get in the way if…"

"What are you saying, Jed?"

"Well, I mean, you said, or, um, you made it sound like you didn't want things between us…"

"You're the one who said you didn't want things to get too serious. You didn't want to ruin the friendship."

"Maybe I was wrong. Maybe that was the biggest mistake of my life."

We stared at each other. Neither of us knowing what to say next. Not knowing what to feel.

"It's been five years. A lot's changed. We're not the same people anymore." I said.

"I know. And maybe that's why it would work." He said.

"I want to have this talk. I really do."

"But?"

"But we need to help Ernest. We don't have much time. And whoever took the little girl is gonna kill her in a couple days."

"How do you know that?"

"I don't have any solid proof. The boy they found in the river; he was killed during the lunar eclipse. The next eclipse is this weekend."

"And the little girl just went missing. Okay. I'll try to contact the guy tonight and maybe meet him tomorrow. I'll call you when I have a place and time."

"What if you can't get ahold of him?"

"Then I'll get his address and pay him a visit tomorrow."

"He's the only lead we've got to finding that little girl. If he's a fraud, we'll have no chance of saving her."

"We can't save everyone. I learned that the hard way. All we can do is try our best. And hope we don't repeat our mistakes."

"You won't. I know you won't.

"I'll call when I have something."

"Call anytime. No matter how late or early."

I felt overwhelmed with confusion. My heart pounded. My stomach quivered. I inhaled long and slow. I had too much going on to start thinking about romance.

Twenty-Nine
April 3, 1977

Ernest sat under brutal fluorescent lighting. The pea soup-colored walls were even more brutal. He leaned his arms on the brown table staring at the long mirror across from him. He had only been in two places since his arrest a couple days before. The room he sat in and the cell where he slept. The police hoped to break his resolve and confess. He repeated the same story each time.

"Just tell us where the girl is. They'll give you ten years max. You'll be out in five. That's the best deal you're gonna get." The interrogator said.

"I haven't kidnapped anyone. I haven't murdered anyone." Ernest said.

"Did I say anything about murder? Ted, you say anything about murder?"

"I didn't say nothin'." Ted said.

"Are you sayin' you killed that little girl?"

"I didn't do anything to or with that little girl. Someone is out there killing children. And while you're in here wasting your time and mine, they're gonna do it again."

"Who's gonna do it? You know somethin'. Don't hold out on us."

"There's three strange women in town. A redhead, brunette, and a blonde. They're always together. Everyone gets weird vibes from them."

"You think these three women are doin' this? Got any proof

for these accusations?"

"No."

"These women got a name?"

"Skov, I think. They're sisters."

The interrogator looked back at Ted. Ted shrugged his shoulders and shook his head.

"We ain't heard a nobody with that name. So, where do we find these three sisters with the funny name? You got their number? Maybe they like to party." The interrogator said.

"I don't know." Ernest said.

"Now you're just jerkin' us around and it's pissin' me off."

"That's the truth."

"Bullshit! You think anyone cares about you in this town? You're a nobody! If you're gonna lie, come up with a better story."

"Come on, Bill. Let's get a coffee." Ted said.

"You better have your shit straight when we come back." Bill said.

Every conversation Ernest had with the detectives since his arrest were similar. One day they'd say he was nothing and worthless. The next day they praised him for all his achievements. Once, Bill tried sitting in the room with Ernest in silence. Some people feel uncomfortable in silence. Ernest enjoyed it.

"I'm surprised they let me see you. They thought I was here for work. I spent ten minutes trying to explain to the detectives that we knew each other." Samantha said.

"It's nice to see a friendly face. I'm guessing you haven't had much luck with a lawyer." Ernest said.

"Most of them wouldn't answer or refused the case because there wasn't enough evidence. I think some of them believe you're guilty and were afraid of losing."

"Are you saying people in this town don't like me? I'm shocked."

"One guy did say they don't have enough to convict you. They'll try to force a confession from you."

"They've been trying since they arrested me. There's nothing to confess so that'll never happen."

"When you go to court, you'll get a public defender.

Everything will work out unless new evidence is found."

"I don't think anyone is trying to find new evidence."

"There has to be something to help your alibi."

"I listened to the radio all night. No one saw me past 6:15. They won't tell me what the witness saw or when. It's like they decided I was guilty before arresting me."

"Maybe. Have you told them about the women?"

"Many times. They think I'm making it up. They've never heard the name Skov."

"I'm sure their family changed the name to something else."

"It doesn't say anything in that journal?"

"No. I haven't found anything helpful in that book. Have you ever heard of an unnatural blood moon?" She said.

"No. I've never heard of a natural one either. What is it?" He said.

"I don't know. It was part of a vague passage in the journal."

"Have you talked to that astronomy teacher?"

"No. I won't get to meet with him for a couple more weeks. But I did talk to one of his TA's."

"What's a TA?"

"Teacher's Assistant. Grad students. He told me the next lunar eclipse is tonight."

"Shit."

"I know."

"What are we gonna do? Well, I can't do anything in here."

"I'm supposed to meet the witness later today. I'll find out what they saw."

"That won't be enough to get me out of here in time."

"No, but maybe it'll help me find who took Alice Summers. Maybe I can find her before…" She said.

"…they kill her." He said.

"That will be enough to get you out."

"And what if you don't get anything from the witness? What if their memory was erased like all the other people used by these women?"

"I don't know if that's true, but if it is, then I'll have to find the women. But I don't know where to start."

"Did you see them the day I was arrested?

"No. Did you?"

"Yes. They stared at me in the police car. One of them waved at me."

"Are you sure?"

"Pretty damn sure. She looked happy I was arrested."

"That's weird."

"I turned to tell you, but you were inside the store. When I looked back, they were gone. But the crowd had a bunch of bullfrogs running around. Or hopping. I don't understand how or why, but I think the frogs have something to do with these women."

"There were bullfrogs all over that accident a few months ago. And there've been a ton all over town ever since. They usually hibernate in the Winter, but they never left. Why would bullfrogs follow them around?"

"I don't know. It may not have anything to do with them. I'm running out of ideas."

"So am I. And things keep getting weirder. You think that raven attacking the police was them too?" She said.

"I don't think so. Why would they want to stop me getting arrested if they were happy about it?" He said.

"Why else would the bird attack someone?"

"I don't know. But I think that's the same one I saw when I found my wife. I think it's following me."

"Ravens will follow people. They have good memories."

"Can you tell my wife what's going on? I don't think she's tried to call. She probably thinks I'm avoiding her."

"Why would you avoid her after trying so hard to find her?"

"We had an argument last time we spoke. There's something bothering her, and she won't talk about it. She doesn't trust me anymore."

"Maybe she doesn't know how to tell you. Or she doesn't know how to say it in a way that makes sense because it doesn't make sense to her."

"I never thought about it like that."

"She'll tell you when she's ready. Give her some time."

"We may not get that time if I don't get out of here."

"Is there anything else you want me to tell her? Anything specific?"

"Tell her I didn't do what everyone else thinks I did. Tell her to keep Amy safe. Tell her I love them both and I'll do anything to keep them safe." He said.

"We'll get you out of here and you can tell her all that yourself." She said.

"Tell her about the women. If they wanted me arrested, they might go after her. Or Amy. What if that's their plan? Get me out of the way so they can take Amy. You have to tell her! You have to go now!"

"Slow down. We don't know that. We don't even know they wanted you arrested."

"It's obvious! We were close to finding them at their house. Of course, they'd come after us."

"Nothing's happened to me. I'm sure your wife and daughter are safe. I will call her first thing after I leave. I promise."

Ernest stared at the table picking his cuticles. He tapped both his heels.

"I have to go. You keep trying to convince the detectives to search for the girl. It's the only thing you can do to help." She said.

"Call my wife. I'll be fine." He said.

"Okay. I'll see you later."

Ernest lost control of his energy. He stood up and paced around the small pea soup room. He took a deep breath and exhaled. Then another. He looked at his reflection in the mirror. He knew the detectives watched him from behind the glass.

"Did they hear the conversation with Samantha?"

He inhaled again and exhaled as he returned to the brown chair. He put his hands on the table interlocking his fingers. He closed his eyes. He called for the detectives. They walked in and he opened his eyes.

"Did your friend knock some sense into ya?" Bill said.

"There isn't much time. You should be out there looking for

that girl." Ernest said.

"So, you want us to let you go and forget all about ya?"

"Keep me locked up. But you won't find her sitting in here with me."

"We will if you tell us where she is."

"I don't know where she is. And if you don't look for her, she will die. Tonight."

"How do you know that? You got an accomplice? Maybe it's that cute brunette bunny who just saw you."

"I can't explain how I know. I just do."

"You gotta give us more to go on, kid. Vague statements won't help you." Ted said.

"You won't believe me."

"Try me, slick." Bill said.

"I think whoever took the girl will kill her tonight during the lunar eclipse."

"The what?"

"The full moon. Maybe it's a sacrifice or something. I don't know."

"And this sacrifice? Will it give you superpowers like the guys in the funny pages?"

"I knew you wouldn't believe me."

"You had me for a minute there. I told Ted you were finished. You were ready to confess. Didn't I say that?"

"Ayuh." Ted said.

"You're jerkin' us around again. And I lost a bet. Ted said you wouldn't confess. I lost five bucks cuz a your jerkin' around."

Ernest didn't move. He looked at the wall. He listened to the hum of the fluorescent lights.

"He ain't talkin' anymore, Bill. Let's give him some time to think things over." Ted said.

Ernest sat lost in the humming lights and pea soup walls.

"Why is war easier than civilian life?"

Thirty
April 4, 1977, 2:00 am

On the night of the eclipse, there was a 911 call made at 2:13 a.m.

"911. What is your emergency?"

"Someone is shouting loud as can be out by Kennebec River." The caller said.

"Stay on the line for Hallowell Police."

"Okay. Thank you."

"Hallowell Police. Clemens."

"Someone is shouting out by the Kennebec River. They woke me up and probably other folks." The caller said.

"Where are you located?"

"I live on Water Street above my antique shop."

"Okay. Is the person shouting a man or a woman?"

"A man. He looks like a drunkard. Oh, but I don't hear him anymore. I can't see him either."

"Okay. I'll send an officer to look around. If you hear him again, give us a call back."

"Oh, I will. Thank you."

"Have a good night, ma'am."

"Goodnight."

***

Officer Abbot arrived on Water Street at 2:50 a.m.

"Abbot to Dispatch."

"Hey Abbot. How's it look out there?" Clemens said.

"Which antique shop am I lookin' for?" Abbot said.

"I never asked. I wasn't thinkin' about it."

"Well, there's at least four. I don't see any drunks around."

"The caller said the guy was by the river."

"He probably passed out somewhere. This feels like a duck hunt."

"See if you can find him and bring him in. The Mayor won't be happy if he keeps wakin' folks up and we ignore it."

"Dammit. Alright. I hate being the only one patrollin' tonight."

Officer Abbot walked down to the bank of the river. With a flashlight in hand, he walked South downriver. The chill wind cut his face. His footsteps were all he could hear over the gentle hum of the river flow. His light beam bounced to-and-fro searching for something worthy of its attention. He stopped.

"This is horseshit." He said.

He turned and something caught his eye. He moved farther downriver. Something stuck out the water onto the bank. He moved closer. He had to confirm his suspicions. A body lay headfirst in the river. A bullfrog hopped away from the body's feet. Abbot ran back to his patrol car. The cold air burned his lungs. He wheezed and grabbed his radio.

"Abbot…to…Dispatch."

"Abbot!? What's wrong?" Clemens said.

"There's a body…on the riverbank. Probably the guy that was yellin'."

"I'll get you some Deputies and Augusta PD out there."

"I'll tape off the area."

***

The coroner approximated the death of Stephen Currier to between 2:15 and 2:30am. Another resident in their statement told police what they heard Currier shout before he died.

"Well, he shouted hey a bunch of times. That's what woke me up. I looked out my window. He was standin' down at the river. He jumped up and down wavin' his arms. Like he was hollerin' at someone. I didn't see anyone else. It was dark. Then he said, 'I knew it. I knew you was real. They didn't believe me.' He quieted a bit, so I went back to bed. Then he said somethin' I couldn't make out. After that he said, 'Wait, don't go. Why was you in the cold water?' I almost got up again, but he didn't say anythin' else. I heard a splash and that was it. I went back to sleep." The witness said.

The coroner's report revealed Currier had died from a heart attack. The police report declared he was delusional from too much alcohol in his system. He saw something that, combined with the alcohol, was too much for his heart.

It was several months later when someone noticed his statement from November about three women in the river. There were no other reports confirming whether he did or didn't see anything the night he died. Only two people attended the funeral service for Stephen Currier a week later, Ernest and Joe from the general store.

His death went unnoticed by most of the town. They were more concerned about the death of Alice Summers.

Thirty-One
April 4, 1977, 8:00 am

Ernest sat in the pea soup room. He held his head in his hands, his elbows on the brown table. The detectives walked in and placed a Styrofoam cup on the table. They returned to their usual places. Bill sat across from Ernest. Ted stood behind them next to the mirror. Ernest held the cup up to his face. The steam from the coffee filled his nostrils. He cherished the warmth on his face. He sipped almost burning his mouth. The heat fell down his throat.

"You sleep okay?" Bill said.

"About as good as sleeping under a tree in Cambodia." Ernest said.

"Ayuh. I bet. The cots in this place are shit."

"I've slept on worse."

The room fell silent. Bill slurped his steaming coffee. Ted lit a cigarette.

"Cigarette?" Ted said.

"Please." Ernest said.

Ted shook one out of the pack. He held out his lighter. Ernest inhaled with the end near the fire. The room filled with smoke sauntering with the steam from the coffee. The flavor of the cigarette helped Ernest ignore the stale air in the pea soup room.

"Okay. Walk us through this whole thing one more time." Bill said.

"I told you. I was in my room all night. No one saw me." Ernest said.

"Not that part. The people you think kidnapped the little

girl."

"What?"

"Tell us about them."

"You didn't believe me the first time I told you."

"Maybe you'll convince us this time."

Ernest looked from one detective to the other. He took a long drag off the cigarette. Ted held an ashtray near Ernest. He flicked his ashes. Ted returned to his spot by the mirror. Ernest sipped his coffee.

"Three women. I don't know their names. I've seen them at the store and around town on the street. I see them one second and they're gone the next." Ernest said.

"You said something about a sacrifice." Bill said.

"I don't know if that's what it is. Or why they do it. I don't have any proof. Samantha and I…"

"The reporter?"

"Yes. She and I have been looking for them but keep hitting dead ends."

"What would you do if you found them?" Ted said.

"I haven't planned that far ahead, to be honest."

"Anything else?" Bill said.

"I don't know anything else. Samantha thinks they brought all the bullfrogs into town."

"The three women? Why would they bring an army of bullfrogs with 'em?"

"I don't know. She said she started seeing a bunch of them after a car accident a few months ago. It was a few days before I got to town."

The two detectives stared at Ernest. Bill sipped his coffee. Ted sucked his cigarette. No one spoke. The stale pea soup room felt heavier.

"Well, Mister Kemp, in light of recent developments, you are free to go." Bill said.

Ernest sat still. The cigarette smoldering in his hand.

"Who's being jerked around now?" Ernest said.

"No jerkin' around, kid. You're no longer a suspect in this case. You can pick up your personal items and go home." Bill said.

"You're serious?"

"Ayuh."

"What changed?"

"Well, for one it's no longer a kidnapping case. And there's new evidence."

"I don't understand."

"You don't need to understand. You get to go home. Just go."

"They found her, didn't they?"

"They found her body out in the woods. She died last night. They found three sets of footprints around the body. All about the size of an adult female." Ted said.

"Shit."

Ernest leaned back in his chair. He took the last drag off his cigarette. Ted held the ashtray out to him.

"So, what are you guys gonna do?" Ernest said.

"Us? Pick up another case. This one's goin' to homicide. It's not our case anymore." Bill said.

"Should I talk to them?"

"They'll come to you if they need to." Ted said.

"Your statements from our little visits here are in the file. But they may have more questions." Bill said.

"Okay. Thanks, I guess. Thanks for the coffee and the cigarette."

Ernest was escorted towards the front of the building. They returned his personal items. He signed the form stating nothing was missing or damaged. He signed several more forms. The escorting officer told him he was free to go. He went straight to the bathroom. His hygiene made him feel repulsive. He hadn't showered, shaved, or brushed anything in a few days. He washed his hands and face. He felt clean enough to travel back to his room. He looked at his reflection.

"Life never goes the way you want it to. What the fuck is the point?" He said.

He dried his hands and face with the harsh, brown paper towels. He looked at his face rubbed raw and dry. He lit a cigarette and sighed. He walked out of the police station. He saw Samantha waiting by her car across the street.

"There you are. I've been waiting for almost an hour." She said.

"Who told you they were letting me go?" Ernest said.

"They didn't tell you about the girl?"

"They did."

"When I heard this morning, I figured they'd release you."

"Did you hear there were three sets of women's footprints around the girl's body?"

"What? So, the police are looking for them?"

"I don't know. They said homicide will look into it and they have my statements about the women."

"At least you won't get accused again."

"Maybe. Did you call Linda?"

"Yes. I left a message with someone named Ed. He said he knows you and he'd pass on the message."

"Did he say if she was okay?"

"He didn't say she wasn't okay. Who is he?"

"The guy she's staying with."

"Are they, I mean, does he know you guys are married?"

"Yeah. Why?"

"You said you guys are having a hard time. You think she's keeping something from you."

"What? Oh! No. No, they're not together. He looked relieved the first night I showed up."

"Sorry. I didn't mean to assume anything."

"It's okay. He's a relative of one of Linda's childhood friends."

"Oh, okay. What are you gonna do now?" She said.

"I'll wait a few days for things to cool down. Then I'll go talk to her. Try to explain things. I don't know how to tell her anything without sounding crazy. It all keeps getting weirder." He said.

"It does. I met with the witness yesterday. They guy who accused you?"

"Yeah."

"He had no memory of seeing you."

"I'm not surprised."

"That's not the weird part. He didn't even remember talking to the police."

"What?"

"Jed said the guy didn't want to talk to the press. Some people are like that. So, I pretended I was helping Jed. The guy told us an officer called to follow up on his statement. He didn't remember giving one. He saw and confirmed his signature on the police documents. That's why he didn't want to speak to the press. He thought people would hate him or say he made it up. He's worried about his health."

"I guess his statement doesn't matter now anyway."

"Well, what spooked him, was something he found in his jacket. He wore it the day he went to the police station. He found a small leather pouch. He'd never seen it before. It was filled with sand or something. And it smelled weird."

"What's that got to do with anything?"

"The last thing he remembers from that day is bumping into three women. One of them said something weird he didn't understand. It was another language. The next thing he remembers is being at home that evening. The rest of the day was gone."

"I still don't understand what the pouch is for."

"I don't either. I asked to see it, but he said he threw it away. He thought it was black magic or something."

"He could be lying." He said.

"Maybe. But he looked too scared to be making up things. And I'm starting to think black magic would explain all this." She said.

"We don't know enough to explain anything. But we have to do something before more kids are taken and killed. What's the plan? How do we find them?"

"I don't know. I meet the astronomy professor at the end of the month. I'll learn what I can from him. I hope it gives us another lead. What are you gonna do?"

"Get my wife and daughter out of harm's way. If they are targeting me, I can't have any distractions. You should check on your loved ones too. Make sure they're safe."

"That's already taken care of. There's something else. Joe said you'd want to know. That homeless drunk kids are always trying to get beer from?"

"What about him?"

"He died last night."

"Damn. How?"

"Heart attack. Then he fell into the river."

"He was always happy as long as he had a bottle of vodka. I'd bought him some a few times so the kids would leave him alone. He put up with them because they gave him money for booze. After the first time, he's always come in to say hi. It felt like I was his only friend."

"You're a nice guy. He recognized that."

"It wasn't only that. He reminded me of someone from when I was in the service. Liked to drink but had a heart of gold. Dale Foster. I'd never seen anyone drink so much whiskey." He said.

"What happened to him?" She said.

"When my ship sank, he went down with it along with everyone I had worked with for months."

"I'm sorry."

"When's the funeral?"

"What?"

"For Stephen."

"Oh. Later this week, I think. His body is going to the funeral home later today. Joe's paying for the casket."

"That's nice of Joe."

"Joe was his friend too. He always stood up for him."

They stood by Samantha's car a moment longer before leaving. The raven perched on the roof of the police station watched them drive away. It followed, gliding through the air. It rested on a stop sign at the intersection where the car had stopped.

"What the hell? Is that the one you were talking about?" Samantha said.

"Yep. I think so." Ernest said.

Thirty-Two
April 6, 1977

"Hey Harold. How are you?" Ernest said.

"No complaints. Work's been good. How about you?" Harold said.

"I've had better weeks. Can you take me up to Shady Lane?"

"Gonna visit the wife after a rough week? You two moving into a place of your own yet?"

"We gotta work through some things before we do that. We're not sure if we want to stay in Maine or not."

"Well I won't force ya ta stay here, but I won't complain if you do stay neither."

"I'll take that as a compliment."

"After the night we met, I've appreciated all your business. Wasn't that the night you found your wife?"

"That was it. You're the only cab driver I've used since."

"Thank you. Glad I can be useful."

The rest of the drive involved a lot of small talk. Harold described his favorite movie he saw in December about a boxer. Ernest remembered hearing about it, but didn't find many opportunities to add to the conversation. The ride felt shorter than the first time.

"You need me to wait?" Harold said.

"You probably should, just in case." Ernest said.

"No problem."

Ernest approached the trailer. He heard a squawk overhead.

Two ravens landed on tree branches and watched him.

"Why are you following me!?"

One raven croaked an answer.

Ernest knocked on the door. He looked over his shoulder at the two ravens still watching.

"Hey Ernie! They let you go. Everything turn out okay?" Ed said.

"I guess so. They figured out I wasn't involved." Ernest said.

"Well, I'm glad to hear it. You here to pick up the rest of Linda's stuff?"

"What? She's not here?"

"Sorry. I thought you knew."

"You gave her my message, right?"

"Ayuh. She got spooked and went to a motel. Said she'd get the rest of her stuff when you guys figured everything out."

"What motel did she go to?"

"The Eight Rod Motel. It's up in Augusta off the Interstate. Exit 113. I thought this was somethin' you planned for, to avoid your families and what not."

"It's okay. She and Amy are safe and that's what's important. Thank you. For everything."

"Ah, it wasn't nothin'."

"We'll figure something out to get the rest of her things."

"No worries. Just let me know."

"Okay. Thanks again."

Ernest looked at the ravens while walking back to the taxi. They tilted their heads in silence.

"You feel like making another twenty bucks, Harold?" Ernest said.

"Ayuh."

"My wife went to a motel in Augusta. I-95. Exit 113."

"Sounds good to me."

"Can you stop at a bank on the way? I don't have enough money on me."

"You got it."

The drive took about 15 minutes after they left the bank.

"This is easy money. You gotta stop treatin' me so good." Harold said.

"Wait here. I'll need a ride back to town." Ernest said.

"Imma get a coffee at the diner. Come over if you're done before I get back."

Ernest gave a thumbs up and entered the motel office.

"Can I help you?" The receptionist said.

She turned the page of a magazine never looking at Ernest.

"Yes. Can you tell me which room Linda Kemp is staying in?"

She slowly looked over her glasses at him.

"You the husband?"

"Yes ma'am."

She sucked on a cigarette and turned another page.

"Room 27."

"Thank you."

He walked out to the closest room. Number 15. The room above it was 30. 27 was on the second floor. The stairs were behind the office. He walked up and around and knocked on the door. He heard nothing. He lifted his arm to knock again when he heard the bold and chain unlatch. Without a word, Linda embraced him.

"Hi honey." Ernest said.

"I'm sorry. When Ed told me everything I freaked out. I didn't know what was going on. I wasn't trying to run away again. I didn't know what to do. I thought your father may have…" Linda said.

"Whoa! Slow down. It's okay. I'm happy you're safe."

"Well what's going on?"

"Someone said I did something I didn't do. I was in jail for a couple days while they questioned me."

"They thought you kidnapped that little girl. What happened? Did they find her?"

"She was killed while I was in jail. They found evidence pointing to someone else."

"Then what was with the cryptic message I got from Ed?"

"I thought whoever accused me was someone trying to make things difficult for us. I thought they might do something to you. That's all."

"Well, either way, I think Ed was happy to see me go."

"Yeah, I noticed that too."

"I got some leftover chicken from the diner across the way if you're hungry. I was getting ready to take a shower. I haven't washed my hair in a couple days."

"Oh. Go ahead. I can spend some quality time with my little girl."

"Yeah. I'll just be a few minutes."

"Take all the time you need."

Ernest watched Amy gnaw on some toy keys. She stopped and looked at him a few times and smiled a giant smile, then returned to her chewing. The phone rang. He lifted the receiver and heard the water in the bathroom stop.

"Hello?" Ernest said.

"May I speak to Misses Linda Kemp?"

"She's in the shower. Can I take a message?"

"This is Susan from the adoption agency. I was calling with some follow up questions for her application. Could you have her call me at her earliest convenience?"

Ernest's grip tightened around the receiver.

"Yes. I'll give her the message."

Linda stepped out in a towel, twisting another around her hair.

"Thank you. Have a nice day." Susan said.

"Thank you. You too." Ernest said.

"Who was that?" Linda said.

"That was Susan from the adoption agency. She has some follow up questions for your application."

"Shit. I can explain."

"You went behind my back."

"Let me explain."

"You couldn't even tell me before you did it?"

"You were in jail."

"I've been out since Monday."

"I didn't know that."

"You could have called the police station!"

"I didn't know what was going on. I was scared. I didn't know if you're father had shown up. And then I hear about children getting kidnapped and murdered. I told you that was the only way I could think of to keep her safe."

"So, you just came to this motel and then went straight to the adoption place?"

"No. I hadn't heard from you. I was worried. I went by there yesterday to learn more about it. I had some questions. That was it. They got excited and started the application. But I never finished it. That's why Susan called."

"I still don't understand why you considered that option at all."

"I've told you!"

The wall vibrated from pounding in the next room.

"Goddammit." Linda said.

"What was that?" Ernest said.

"The people in the other room. This place has thin walls."

"You never told me why you think adoption is the best choice."

"I said so your father can't find her. And now there are child killers running around. This is the only way to protect her. To keep her safe."

"I can keep her safe. I can keep you safe. Or don't you believe that anymore?"

"I wasn't safe before. When you left. And I don't feel safe now."

"What is it you're not telling me?"

"It doesn't matter."

"It does matter."

"No, it doesn't!"

The wall shook with angry pounding again.

"Oh, fuck off!" Linda said.

Linda stood looking at the ground. She had one arm crossed in front of her. Her other hand rested on her chest below her neck. Ernest stood awkward and confused. He didn't recognize his wife.

"You're right. I left. I didn't protect you from whatever happened. I wish you would tell me. But things are different now."

He said.

"How are they different?"

Her voice was small and quiet.

"I'm here. That's what's different. I'm here now and I will protect you. Both of you."

She said nothing. She grabbed a change of clothes and stomped into the bathroom. The room shook when the door slammed.

"We're not done talking about this."

"Let me get dressed!"

Ernest rubbed the bridge of his nose. He wanted a cigarette but didn't want to smoke near Amy. Linda sat on the bed to put on her shoes.

"What's going on with you?" He said.

"What?" She said.

"Something's bothering you. You won't tell me about it. And every time I bring it up, you get pissed off and push me away."

"Did you ever think maybe I was doing that on purpose?"

"Why?"

"Because I don't want to talk about it. And every time you bring it up, I tell you that. But you keep asking and that pisses me off."

"Okay. Why don't you want to talk about it?"

"Goddammit Ernie! I just don't. Why isn't that good enough for you?"

"Because whatever it is, it's making you consider giving up your child. It's making you angry and irritable."

"You're the one making me angry and irritable!"

A loud knock at the door held their attention.

"Augusta Police. Open the door please."

Ernest opened the door. Two uniformed officers stared back at them.

"Can we help you?" Ernest said.

"We've gotten several complaints of shouting and door slamming." The officer said.

"Really!? You can pound on the wall and call the police,

but you can't come over here yourself. You chickenshit!" Linda said.

"Ma'am, you need to calm down."

"Don't tell me to calm down!"

"Linda stop!" Ernest said.

"No! Fuck them and fuck you too!"

"Ma'am, if you don't calm down, I will place you under arrest for disorderly conduct."

"Then do it! And while you're at it, arrest the shit bags in the next room who I hear fucking every night!"

Ernest moved away from the door. The officers moved towards Linda.

"Don't touch me!"

"You're under arrest."

"Fuck you!"

Linda spit at the officers. They pushed her against the wall. Ernest picked up Amy attempting to quiet her crying. The officers handcuffed Linda and explained her rights. Linda's cheeks glistened from her tears.

"It's okay, sweet pea. Mommy's okay. Don't cry." She said.

Ernest watched the officers put Linda in the back of their car. Amy cried in his ear. He held back his own tears trying to comfort her.

"Shh. It's okay. Everything's okay."

He walked out the door and saw Harold walking to his cab. He looked at the patrol car then up to Ernest. Confusion painted his face.

"It'll be a while before we leave." Ernest said.

He turned towards the room. A pair of eyes watched him through the curtains of the room next door. He stared back at them until the curtain closed.

"Fucking civilians."

Thirty-Three
April 26, 1977 - Samantha

The drive North to the University of Maine took a couple hours. I lied to my editor and told him I needed time off to meet with my mother's doctors. He was so nervous you'd think I told him I was going to the bathroom to change a tampon. He avoided me the rest of that day. I had stopped by to visit my mother on the way to the university. The nurse escorted me to her room.

"She's been having nightmares. We upped the dosage of her medication so she could sleep. She may not be coherent." The nurse said.

"Did it help with the nightmares?" I said.

"Been sleepin' like a baby since."

"Hey momma. I'm just stopping by for a quick visit."

I waved my hand in front of her face.

"I said she may not be coherent."

"Not coherent? She looks catatonic. Can't you reduce the dosage? Or give her something that doesn't make her a vegetable?"

"The doctors have been gradually lowering the dosage. They're trying to find the right amount to stop the nightmares while allowing her to function throughout the day."

"They better be. If she's like this this weekend, I'm having a word with the administrator."

"I will inform the doctors."

"Thank you. I'm sorry. I know you're trying to do what's best for her."

"It's okay. I'd be worried if you weren't upset."

"Okay momma. I have to go. Maybe I'll stop by on my way back home. I'll come see you on Saturday. I love you."

My mother's glazed over eyes stared passed me. I left before losing myself. I used the radio to distract me as I got back on the interstate.

Thanks for tuning in to WABK 1280. Next up we have ABBA with 'Dancing Queen.'

I listened to the song and all I could think was how I never got to be that girl. The dancing queen. My father never let me go to a dance. I shut off the radio and cried for several miles.

I went over some of my questions for the professor. After an hour, I gave the radio another try. I turned the knob to find anything. Nothing interested me. I shut the radio off again. My thoughts kept circling back to childhood. I read billboards aloud to help distract myself.

I spent more time than I wanted searching for Professor Minsky's office. It had moved since I was in college. I met his assistant with ten minutes to spare.

"Hello. I'm Samantha Belcher. I have a 2:30 appointment with Professor Minsky."

"Yes. The professor just finished a lecture and should be here in a few minutes. Please have a seat. Help yourself to some water if you'd like." The assistant said.

"Thank you."

I waited about five minutes in the quiet. The water cooler gurgled. The assistant read a book and snacked on some baby carrots. She couldn't have been more than 19 or 20-years-old. An older man walked in carrying books and notebook papers. He wore a gray tweed suit and large glasses making his eyes look twice their size. He was clean shaven but with wild white hair and a bald spot on his crown.

"Professor? Your 2:30 appointment is here." The assistant said.

"What's that?" Professor Minsky said.

"Your appointment with Miss Belcher."

"Who?"

"Hello. I'm Samantha Belcher."

I stood to shake his hand.

"Oh. How do you do? Uh. Come. Come in. Pardon the mess. Have a seat please."

"Thank you for seeing me. I know you're very busy."

"Hmm. Yes. Yes. Uh, what can I do for you?"

"I wanted to learn more about lunar eclipses."

"You can learn quite a lot from books. It's a common phenomenon."

"Excuse me?"

"My apologies. Eclipses are a common phenomenon."

"Of course. But I wondered if there are any rituals involving the lunar eclipse."

"Well, that is a history or theology question. I'm not aware of any modern-day religions that practice such rituals. Why do you have an interest in eclipses and rituals if you don't mind my asking?"

"I don't have any concrete proof. But I think some murders down in Hallowell involve a ritual with the lunar eclipse."

"You suspect this without any evidence?"

"During the last two eclipses, a child was killed each night."

"That's terrible. There was one earlier this month."

"Yes. They found a little girl in a clearing in the woods with footprints surrounding her body."

"And the murder before that?

"They found a boy in the river. He died from similar injuries."

"Do, uh, do you work with the police?"

"Not directly. I'm conducting my own investigation. When I find solid evidence, I'll turn it over to the police." I said.

"Did you know any of the victims?" The professor said.

"Not personally."

"Why not let the police handle things?"

"I'm covering the story for the Kennebec Journal."

"Eh, a reporter. That explains it."

"Professor, please, another child could die during the next eclipse. But I don't know when."

He stood and surveyed a bookshelf.

"An eclipse is very simple. One celestial object casts a shadow over another. In the case of a lunar eclipse, the Earth blocks the light from the sun to the moon."

He removed a book and returned to his desk. He searched through the pages.

"Here we are. The next eclipse is at the end of September. A penumbral according to this." He said.

"What is that?" I said.

"A type of eclipse that casts a shadow but doesn't completely block out the entire moon."

"What were the last two eclipses? Were they penumbral?"

"Hmm, the one we just had was a partial eclipse. And before that was another penumbral."

"Would those be considered an unnatural blood moon?"

"I'm not familiar with the term. A total lunar eclipse is called a blood moon because the light reflecting off the Earth's atmosphere gives the moon a red hue. I suppose one could call that a natural blood moon. But all of this is perfectly natural. There's nothing unnatural or supernatural about these events."

"How would a superstitious person view a blood moon?"

"I can't say, for certain. Ancient cultures believed it to be an omen. They felt some evil was attacking the moon or attacking them."

"Do you suppose they might have thought it was something unnatural?"

"Perhaps. Where did you hear of this term?"

"I saw it in a hundred-year-old journal. A young woman said she was tired of a long life. She didn't want to be cursed anymore. She didn't want to live through another unnatural blood moon." I said.

"Is that the only time it was mentioned in the journal?" He said.

"Yes."

"Hmm. It could be a coded message. It may have nothing to do with the moon or an eclipse. I don't see how an old journal fits with the murders you're investigating."

"The suspects in the murders, no one knows who they are, but they've been seen around town. These women look exactly like three women in a newspaper clipping from a hundred years ago. They were sisters. The journal belonged to one of them."

"How does that relate to the present day?"

"I think they're descendants of the sisters from the newspaper article. There wasn't anything in the journal to prove that."

"Sounds like Apophenia."

"Excuse me?"

"Apophenia. Seeing meaning between two unrelated things. A term developed by a psychiatrist some 20 years ago. You're seeing connections between today and a century ago because you want to. I mean no disrespect. But I don't think this is what you would call a solid lead."

"Maybe not. For the moment, it's the only one I have."

"I understand. Was there anything else?"

"No. Thank you again for your time."

"I'm sorry I wasn't much help."

"You were most helpful. Thank you."

"I do hope someone finds whoever is committing those terrible crimes. A parent should never have to bury a child. It should always be the other way around."

I smiled feeling awkward.

"Yes. Well. Thank you for your time." I said.

"It was a pleasure my dear. Good luck with the investigation." He said.

"Thank you."

I sat in my car before leaving. I didn't want to think about burying my mother, but that wasn't what bothered me. Apophenia. Is that what I was doing? I reviewed all my research. I'd forgotten about the house Ernest and I found. That was another link to the Skov Sisters. Despite my own reassurance, I felt I moved in the wrong direction. If the professor was right about the next eclipse, I had five months to figure everything out. Plenty of time. Unless I kept hitting dead ends. I'm certain I never had this many dead ends for a story. But none of those stories were about the deaths of children.

I drove home feeling unsatisfied. The only thing on my mind was returning to the house in the woods. I wanted to do a thorough search. Maybe Jed would help. I knew Ernest would. My thoughts were so focused, I almost missed my exit to see my mother again. I never got to see her twice in one week. I wanted to take advantage of the extra time. Even though she wouldn't comprehend I was there until her medication wore off. I wasn't sure I wanted to see her like that again. What if that was the only way to stop her nightmares? I felt I was losing her. I almost lost her once before. I sat in the institute's parking lot feeling selfish and sorry for myself.

Thirty-Four
May 1, 1977

"Mom? Can you hold on a sec? Amy's being fussy again." Ernest said.

He cradled the phone receiver between his ear and shoulder to pick up Amy. She cried in his ear while his free hand reclaimed the receiver. She rested her head on his shoulder mumbling and sniffling.

"Shh. It's okay. I'm sorry, mom. What were you saying?"

"Nothing important. Has Amy been like this for a while?" Gail said.

"Yeah. She's not hungry and has a clean diaper. I think she misses Linda."

"She might be teething. When you were fussy like that, I'd rub a little whiskey on your gums, and you'd calm right down."

"She does have some bottom teeth already, but are you saying you want me to get her drunk so she'll fall asleep?"

"Don't be ridiculous. You dip your finger in some whiskey, then rub it on her gums. It'll numb the pain. It's medicinal."

"And if that doesn't work?"

"You'll have to keep holding her until she falls asleep. This is important bonding time. Your father never understood that."

"You think we don't get along because he didn't hug me enough as a child. I don't think it would help us much."

"Maybe not but it wouldn't hurt you either."

"Okay. I have to put the phone down. I've got some whiskey in the freezer."

"You're not drinking too much, are you?"

"No ma'am. I got this bottle around Christmas and haven't finished it."

"Alright. I'll wait."

With Amy in his arms, Ernest pulled one of three bottles of Jameson Irish Whiskey from his freezer. He emptied the last of the bottle into a glass. It wasn't enough for one drink. He put the empty bottle into a bag with several empty Jameson bottles. He shifted Amy into his other arm. He dipped his finger in the amber liquid. Amy tried to push his hand away. Ernest wiggled his finger into her mouth rubbing it all over. She protested even after he pulled out his finger wiping it dry on his pants. He drank the remaining whiskey. Amy returned her head to his shoulder.

"Okay. I'm back." He said.

"How'd it go?" Gail said.

"She wasn't happy about it. Seems like she's calmed down a bit though."

"There you have it. She'll be asleep in no time. When will Linda get back. I'd like to speak with her."

"Not for a while. She, uh, she got arrested."

"What!? When!? Why!?"

Ernest told her about the police questioning him. Then about finding Linda in Augusta. He told her about the argument and the police.

"So, I'm taking care of Amy until everything is worked out." He said.

"Well, this is ridiculous. I said she was trouble." Gail said.

"Mom, she's not herself. Something's bothering her and she won't tell me."

"First, she runs off with my grandbaby. Then she hides from everyone. Then she tries to give up my grandbaby without telling anyone. Then she gets herself arrested..."

"Are you listening to me?"

"She gives no thought to other people. Not even her own child."

"She thought she was keeping Amy safe. The arrest was a misunderstanding."

"You said she spat on the police. That's resisting arrest and assaulting an officer."

"How do you know so much about the law?"

"I wasn't always a housewife Ernest James Kemp. Don't sass your mother."

"Yes ma'am."

Amy had fallen asleep in his arms. The room was quiet.

"All I'm saying is Linda has a lot to answer for." She said.

"I know. But something's got her scared. Even if she wasn't in jail, I'd still be worried about her. She's not herself." He said.

"That's not an excuse for her behavior."

"No, but if I knew what was going on, I'd understand her behavior."

"You'll have to ask her. I don't think she even knows what's going on with her. I know I don't."

"Every time I try to ask, she gets defensive. I don't know if she's afraid to tell me or if she just doesn't want me to know. I know I was gone a long time but it's like we don't trust each other anymore."

"Time apart will do that. People change Ernie. Whether you want them to or not. And you'll change too."

"Yeah. I know."

No one spoke for a moment. Ernest laid Amy on his bed. She didn't stir.

"Why don't I come out to visit? I can help with Amy." She said.

"No mom. I'll get things figured out." He said.

"It's no trouble. I can be there in a couple days."

"You don't need to go out of your way for me."

"I'm your mother, Ernest. I've gone out of my way for you since you were born."

"I understand mother. But Linda doesn't want you or her parents getting involved in our lives. And I agree with her."

"This is absurd. You're going to listen to a woman who tried to get rid of your child without you knowing?"

"We both want what's best for Amy."

"So do I, and that's why I'm coming to Maine."

"No, you're not."

"You will not speak to me that way."

"I'm an adult and I'll speak however I wish. I'm telling you to stay out of this."

"You wouldn't talk to your father this way."

"You're right. I'd use more swear words then tell him where he should go."

"This – this is some kind of prank, isn't it? Well, it's not funny."

"No, it isn't."

"We're coming out there. All of us. Your father and Linda's family too."

"Stay home. I'll call you when I know more."

"No, we are not done talking about this."

"Bye mom."

"Ernest…"

Amy's chest rose and fell in silence. Ernest looked at her taking a deep breath. He rubbed his face.

"What am I gonna do with you?"

He gathered the bag of bottles and other garbage. He looked back at Amy still sleeping before walking out the door. He met the antique shop owner's wife coming back from the dumpster. She was an older woman wearing a long brown dress. She carried a large ring of keys. Ernest remembered when he first moved in and had locked his key in his room. She spent almost five minutes searching her key ring. To her credit, the door opened with the first key she used.

"Excuse me, Lorraine?" Ernest said.

"Yes. Who is it?" Lorraine said.

"It's Ernest Kemp. I'm renting a room over your shop."

"Yes. What is it? Is it that toilet again? I'll call Patrick."

"No. No ma'am. The toilet's fine."

"Need more light bulbs, is it? I'll call Patrick."

"No ma'am. Everything with the room is fine."

"Oh. Moving out. The room'll need cleaned. I'll call Patrick."

"I'm not moving out. I have a favor to ask."

"What's that now?"

"A favor? I have to work soon, and I need someone to watch my baby girl."

"Why you talkin' ta me?"

"I don't have anyone else. Look, I'll even pay you 10 dollars."

"That's more than one night in the room. You must be desperate."

"It's only for today."

"Ha! I've heard that one before."

"You have my word. I'll call around for a regular babysitter tomorrow."

"Where's the mother?"

"She's out of town for a few days."

"And she left the baby with you? Hmph."

"I know I'm asking a lot but…"

"Hold it right there."

She stared at Ernest with her hand held up between them.

"I love children. I don't mind watchin' her for a few hours." She said.

"Thank you so much Lorraine." He said.

"This one time! I won't do this a second time."

"Yes ma'am. I won't ask again."

"Well don't just stand there. Get all her things and bring them to the office."

"Yes ma'am."

Ernest managed to get Amy downstairs without waking her. Lorraine had a couch in a back room where the child could sleep.

"Well, if she stays like that, I won't have any trouble 'tall." Lorraine said.

"Thank you again."

"You go on to work. Oh! I forgot I need to call Patrick."

Ernest arrived at the general store with a few minutes to spare. Samantha caught up with him on the sidewalk.

"Hey! How are things?" She said.

"I've been better." He said.

"Is everything okay?"

Ernest explained why he had Lorraine watch Amy. He told her about his wife and talking with his mother.

"I'm so sorry. That's a lot to deal with." Samantha said.

"I'll manage. I need to find a full-time babysitter. I can't rely on Lorraine all the time." Ernest said.

"I might be able to help with that. Jed has a niece who already does some babysitting for family and neighbors."

"If you don't mind introducing me, I'd appreciate it. I love spending time with Amy, but I can't watch her while I'm working."

"I get it. You're braver than I am. I've never been good with kids. I can't handle the screaming and crying."

"I can't handle it either. But it's better than sitting in my room alone. At least crying gives me something else to think about."

"Other than what?"

"Nothing. I wish my mother would stop trying to but in on my life. I guess that's what mother's do. Is your mother like that?"

"Um, no. She, uh, doesn't tell me what to do or anything. I visit her once a week."

"Sounds like you have a better relationship with your mother than I do."

"So, what are we gonna do about those women? The Skov Sisters."

"Shit. I haven't been thinking about it. A lot happened recently." He said.

"I understand." She said.

"I don't know what to do. Have you learned anything new?"

"The next lunar eclipse is in September. If that is when they take children, we have some time."

"You have a plan?"

"I want to search that house again. We didn't really go through everything the first time. Jed might even give us a hand."

"I gotta talk to him about getting a babysitter anyway."

"Right. We'll plan something then go out there when we all have time."

"I just hope we find something useful this time."

Thirty-Five
May 6, 1977

"We stand a better chance of finding them there if we go at night." Samantha said.

"That's exactly why we shouldn't go there at night." Ernest said.

"We'll have Jed with us. He's a deputy and can call for backup. Besides, you were in the war. Why are you scared?"

"I know what it's like to almost get killed and I don't want to do it again. Have you ever had bullets fly past your head with your face in the dirt? I bet you haven't."

"All I'm saying is I don't think it will get that bad."

"Okay. Then punch the gas and take the next turn without slowing. I don't think it will get that bad."

"What are you talking about? There could be another car."

"But maybe there isn't. You only see the turn. You never see the road ahead. Just because you think things won't get bad doesn't mean they won't. Everything can explode in your face before you know what's happening."

"Did something like that happen to you?"

"Many times."

"Do you wanna talk about it?"

"No."

They drove down the street in silence. Ernest looked out the passenger side window. His gaze was far away. The window reflected the scowl on his face. He turned toward the backseat. Amy slept in a car seat. Drool drippled down on the strap holding her in the seat. The pacifier had escaped into her lap. Ernest's eyes returned to the distant place.

Samantha parked in front of Jed's house on the street. The sun made its escape toward the horizon casting long shadows. Ernest carried Amy, sleeping in the car seat, and a diaper bag.

"All this stuff almost weighs as much as my medical pack in the Navy." Ernest said.

"Looks like you already got the arms for it."

Jed met them on the porch and walked after them through the door.

"That's why you want to meet my niece, I take it." Jed said.

"I need a sitter for when I'm working." Ernest said.

"Joe won't give you any time off?"

"He can't do the heavy lifting. He's hoping to get a high school kid to help him in the Summer."

"What's happening with your wife?"

"She had her arraignment. The judge denied her bail because she assaulted a guard the night before."

"Is she trying to fight everybody?"

"It seems like it. She said she felt safer in lockup anyway. All she told me was to keep Amy away from our families."

"Why would she say that?"

"They threatened to take Amy away from her. Linda doesn't seem to care if Amy's with her or not. As long as Amy's not with our family."

"What are you gonna do?"

"All I can do is wait for Linda's court date next month."

"I know some of the guys at the courthouse, so if you need anything, let me know."

"Thank you. Right now, I just need a babysitter."

"Well, my niece has a way with kids. Almost like she knows what they're thinking. She can speak baby, I guess. I know her parents won't mind if I vouch for you."

"I appreciate that. When can we meet her?"

"I had an idea about that. Whatever plan we make here; we can have your daughter and my niece stay here while we do it. If we're out until Lord knows what time, my sister and brother-in-law won't mind if their daughter's at my place." Jed said.

"What is the plan?" Ernest said.

"We're only searching the place. I expect the drive to take longer than the search." Samantha said.

"What kind of search are we talking about? Just a quick walkthrough of an old shack? Or should I bring a shovel and tools to pull apart walls and floorboards?" Jed said.

"I guess I hadn't thought about it much."

"You said this place is a good walk from the road. We should bring some tools and a couple shovels just in case. We don't have to use them."

"That's a good idea. What if someone's there when we get there?" Ernest said.

"You think the murderers will be there?" Samantha said.

"That or vagrants needing a place to sleep. Or kids wanting a place to party."

"I'll have my badge and my pistol. I hope we won't need it. Remember, I'll be there on my own time. This won't be official Sherriff's business. I can't run around waving my badge at people." Jed said.

"That's just as well because I don't think the police are in the mood to help me out with anything. I'm waiting for everyone in town to get out their pitch forks and torches." Ernest said.

"Folks around here don't like outsiders."

"I've never been to a town that liked outsiders." Samantha said.

"It's more than that. Some people are saying bad things didn't happen before I came to town." Ernest said.

"Trust me, there were murders before you got here." Jed said.

"My wife was up here for a while without much trouble."

"People don't look at a woman with a baby the same way they look at a man who was in the war." Samantha said.

"Maybe they won't feel that way now that they see me with Amy everywhere."

"Not for a while. People are scared and don't know what to do. They don't know who to blame. It's easy for them to hate you because they don't know you."

"She's right. They won't leave you alone until the people doing this are caught." Jed said.

"I still think I brought back some darkness with me." Ernest said.

"What do you mean?" Samantha said.

"Ever since my ship went down, it feels like death follows me. I guess it started before that."

Ernest looked away like he was lost somewhere.

"You're not making any sense." Samantha said.

"I don't know what I'm talking about. All I know is I don't want anyone else around me to die." Ernest said.

"We're gonna stop them. We have plenty of time before they take another kid."

"How do you know that?" Jed said.

"So far, they've only killed during the lunar eclipse."

"That we know of. There could be other bodies waiting to be found."

"All the more reason for us to act sooner than later."

"Well, when's the next eclipse?"

"September."

"Then I hope that is the only time they kidnap kids."

"What if they're the bad omen?" Ernest said.

"I'm sorry, but you're being a bit overdramatic." Samantha said.

"I mean the women. What if they're the bad omen?"

"What are you saying?"

"The last time I was arrested, they were watching across the street. Like they were expecting it. What if they're the ones who tipped off the police?"

"Why would they target you?"

"Maybe they knew I suspected them. Maybe I didn't react the way all the other men did, and they saw me as a threat. I don't know."

"Maybes aren't enough evidence for me. But I'll entertain the idea that someone is targeting you." Jed said.

"We have to find them and ask." Ernest said.

"That's why I want to search the old house." Samantha said.

Amy woke and started crying. After having no luck with the pacifier, Ernest took her into the bathroom to change her.

"You're convinced they'll be there waiting for us. Would you mind explaining why you're so sure?" Jed said.

"The house once belonged to three sisters with the family name Skov. I found a sketch of the sisters in the old newspaper clipping. They look like the three women Ernest, and I have seen around town. The first time we went to the house, it looked like someone had been there."

"How'd you figure that?"

"There was a table covered with candles. The wax had dripped down the side on the floor."

"Those candles could be a hundred years old."

"They didn't have a layer of dust."

"What?"

"Everything was covered with dust except the candles."

"Okay. You have my attention. What's the plan?"

"The plan is to search the place and hope they're not there."

"That's not much of a plan. And if they are there?"

"Maybe we'll overhear their plan. Or find out who they really are."

"No more maybe this or that. Let's focus on what we know. The facts."

Ernest came back with Amy. He put her back in the car seat and ran the dirty diaper to the trashcan outside. Samantha covered her nose. Jed sprayed an aerosol can. The room filled with the scent of evergreens. Amy played with her stuffed animal.

"That's better. What I miss?" Ernest said.

"We were about to go over everything." Samantha said.

"Only the facts we know. No maybes or what-ifs." Jed said.

"Okay."

"We know besides us someone has been in that old house recently." Samantha said.

"Right. But we don't know who. Don't speculate. Wait until we have more evidence." Jed said.

"The county owns the property. The last owners were the Skov Sisters about a century ago. An old sketch from a newspaper around the same time shows the Skov Sisters. They look identical to the women we've seen in town."

"But what does that mean? Who are these women?" Ernest said.

"We're only talking about what we know. No questions. No assumptions." Jed said.

"What else do we know?" Samantha said.

"There've been a lot of deaths the last few months. There's not enough evidence to suggest they're all related."

"What else do we know?"

"There's a lot of bullfrogs around town. And a raven keeps following me." Ernest said.

"Ravens follow people all the time. What's that got to do with anything?" Jed said.

"It's weird."

"I don't see how that's related to what we're talking about."

"I don't know much else other than everybody thinks I'm doing the killing."

They sat in silence. Each looked away from the group rolling around thoughts in their minds.

"Hey Jed? When did you start seeing a lot of bullfrogs?" Samantha said.

"Maybe November. No! It was a couple day before Halloween." Jed said.

"That homicide on Outlet Road. I don't remember seeing any bullfrogs before that. I wish I didn't remember that scene."

"I told you not to look. You never listened to me before. I don't know why I thought you would that time. The local wildlife has nothing to do with this. Can we focus please?"

"When are we going out there? Ernest said.

"How about this weekend?" Samantha said.

"I'm working ten hour shifts this weekend. It'll have to be next weekend." Jed said.

"Next Friday?"

"Sure."

"When can we meet your niece?" Ernest said.

"I'll call you tomorrow and we'll set something up. I'll make sure she's free next Friday too."

"Thank you."

"Let's meet up again before going out there."

"Why?" Samantha said.

"So, we have a plan if one of us gets lost or if we find someone in that old shack. We don't know what we're walking into. We need to be cautious." Jed said.

"That's what I said in the car. Everything can turn to shit in a second." Ernest said.

"Are you boys teaming up against me now?"

"Only if you think we shouldn't be careful." Jed said.

"Okay. We'll be careful."

Thirty-Six
May 13, 1977

The breaks squeaked as the car rolled to a stop.

"Okay. Everyone has their compass?" Jed said.

Everyone nodded.

"And what do we do if we get separated?"

"Meet back at the car." Samantha said.

"Right. Which is West of the cabin. Go West until you hit the road. If we stay together, we should be fine."

They all stepped from the car. The air was chilly but not cold. They crept into the woods, Jed in front, Ernest at the rear, and Samantha between them. Samantha removed her compass verifying they walked East. She glanced back at Ernest and saw something shiny in his hand. He noticed and showed her his revolver.

"Just in case." He said.

She nodded. They continued without speaking. They heard the crunching dirt under their feet and another sound in the distance.

"What's that humming?" Ernest said.

"Bullfrogs." Jed said.

The chorus grew louder as they moved towards the cabin. No one spoke again. Jed held a flashlight with a red cover. The red light lit up their path well enough to see but the color made it less bright. Something moved on the ground across the light. They stopped. No one moved. No one spoke. A humming sound like the bullfrogs floated from behind a tree mixing with the other noises.

"Just a bullfrog." Jed said.

Samantha repeated this in a whisper to Ernest. They skulked closer to the cabin. After a short time, Jed stopped again. Several red colored bullfrogs hopped over each other and hummed in unison. There were too many to step over. Jed panned the flashlight looking for a clear path.

"Have you ever seen so many?" Samantha said.

"Only when we found the bodies of the Evans couple. Never before." Jed said.

Ernest had moved closer to hear what they were saying. He tapped both their shoulders.

"The cabin. There's candlelight in the window." He said.

"Stay quiet. Let's move around these frogs." Jed said.

They followed the edge of the bullfrog barrier. They were still several feet from the cabin but could see through the window. Jed turned off his light and they all watched in darkness. Two women stood in the room, one with her back to them.

"Those are the women we saw in town." Samantha said.

"Shh. They might hear you." Jed said.

The redhead faced them. She was looking at something out of their view. The cacophony of bullfrog hums deafened any other sounds in the forest. The candleflame was still, appearing artificial. Unseen candles cast light throughout the entire room. The brunette had her back to them and moved her arms. She spoke to the redhead and someone else.

"What are they saying?" Ernest said.

His breath was hot on Samantha's ear as he whispered. She mouthed the words 'I don't know' then returned her gaze to the window. The redhead spoke. She was too far away for anyone to read her lips. Their conversation continued for several minutes. The redhead turned away. The brunette pointed her finger like she was scolding a child. The blonde stepped into view, the third sister. Her face held both anger and sadness.

"I don't want to do this anymore!" The blonde said.

Her shout quieted the bullfrogs. The forest fell silent. Jed took Samantha's hand. Her other hand gripped his shoulder. The three women didn't speak for a moment. Through the silence, the words coming from the cabin were clear.

"We can't just walk away from this." Someone said.

"I know." The blonde said.

The redhead's voice was muffled before she stepped into the window's view.

"I know Bella." The blonde said.

"You're being selfish. Consider how we feel about this." The brunette said.

"Selfish? You're one to talk Carla. You've never considered my feelings with any decision you made. Nothing is ever discussed. You're the most selfish of us." The blonde said.

The redhead said something too quiet to hear.

"Quiet Bella! If not for me, you both would have been dead ages ago. Without me pushing you, you'd never have done what was necessary." Carla said.

The redhead, Bella, put up her hands and walked away.

"Everything you've done was for yourself. You don't care about us. You care about power. You only keep us around because the ritual requires three." The blonde said.

"I can perform the ritual with anyone. I chose you two because you're my sisters. Yes, I enjoy the power. But I share that power with my family." Carla said.

The two women stood for a moment not taking their eyes off each other. The blonde covered her face and mumbled something. Carla rubbed the bridge of her nose. The blonde's shoulders bounced up and down. Bella returned.

"Quiet! We're being watched." She said.

The bullfrogs reignited their humming.

"Get down." Jed said.

They each took cover laying on the ground behind a row of trees. The three sisters stepped from the cabin. Bella held a candle. They each looked out into the dark forest.

"I don't see anyone." The blonde said.

"Are you sure someone's here?" Carla said.

"Yes, I can smell them." Bella said.

"Who is it?"

"The man followed by ravens. And others."

A bullfrog hopped onto Ernest's arm. He pushed it away without a sound. Samantha covered her mouth.

"Show yourselves! We know you're out there! Or do you like crawling around with the frogs!?" Carla said.

The hum of the bullfrogs grew as she raised her voice.

"Will you be quiet!?"

The frogs froze. All was quiet. No one spoke or moved. Samantha held her breath afraid the sisters would hear her panting. Carla walked away from them as she spoke again.

"Why do you pursue us? We've done nothing to you."

Ernest looked at the other two and held his finger over his lips. He stood and took careful steps moving away from the cabin, the sisters, and Jed and Samantha. When Samantha lost sight of him in the darkness, they all hard him shout.

"You're killing children! I'm here to stop you!" Ernest said.

"Why do you care? You're not a law man. You have no proof." Carla said.

"You're not denying it. That's enough proof for me."

His voice echoed from somewhere else. He was moving to draw their attention away. Carla whispered but Samantha could still hear.

"You stay here. You take the back path. I'll go this way and keep him talking. Look for the others." She said.

Bella remained by the cabin with her candle. She sniffed the air, taking in large breaths. Samantha looked at Jed. He shook his head. She looked toward the cabin and Bella was gone. Carla shouted from further away.

"We've met many men like you who thought they could stop us. They all died. Just like you will die. We've lived in these woods all our lives. You can't hide from us." Carla said.

"But you still haven't found me." Ernest said.

"We will soon enough."

Samantha looked all around her. Everyone had disappeared into the dark forest except for Jed and the statuesque bullfrogs. The candlelight in the cabin remained still beaming out from the window. They heard dirt crunching under someone's feet. Samantha squeezed Jed's hand. Ernest crept out of the darkness towards them. He held his finger to his lips then mouthed the words 'Go to the car' before sneaking off again. They stared at each other for a moment. They heard more footsteps before they decided to move. The blonde stood near the front of the cabin, waiting.

"Have you found them?" The blonde said.

Bella reappeared with the candle shaking her head.

"I think they're moving around us. I smell them everywhere."

"Where is Carla?"

"Hunting them like she always does."

"We need to leave before we're caught."

"We'll be fine. Go look for Carla."

The blonde walked off frustrated. Samantha watched her leave. When she looked back, Bella had disappeared again. Samantha and Jed waited a few moments. They looked at each other and exchanged nods. They rose clutching the tree in front of them. They looked around. They saw and heard nothing. They stepped away from the cabin making careful and methodical movements. A squawk rang out from the silence. Samantha snapped a twig under her foot. They froze. They listened for footfalls and other noises. None came. They returned to their careful movements.

Samantha jumped when she heard the gunshot. There was a scream resembling a battle cry and another gunshot. Jed pushed Samantha and they started running. Bella appeared in front of them blocking their way. Samantha screamed and they turned the other direction.

"You can't run from me or hide in the trees." Bella said.

They passed the cabin and ran into Bella again. Jed screamed. They turned towards the thickness of the forest. Bella again blocked their path and hit Jed with a branch. He stumbled but didn't fall.

"Keep running!" He said.

Samantha ran alone in the darkness. She stopped behind a tree to catch her breath. Her shaking hand removed the compass from her pocket. She found West and ran again. Twigs and branches smacked her face. She heard another gunshot from a distance. Tears and cuts covered her face. She heard a squawk behind her. She couldn't see the bird flapping around her head. She screamed and ran faster.

"Oh God, what is happening?"

She looked behind her for the bird, for the sisters, for Jed. The darkness hid everything more than a few feet away. Something caught her ankle and jerked her to the ground.

She woke in the car and saw Ernest getting into the passenger seat in front of her as Jed drove. Her head throbbed.

Part Three
Full

"There is something haunting in the light of the Moon. It has all the dispassionateness of a disembodied soul and something of its inconceivable mystery." — Joseph Conrad

Thirty-Seven
1875 - Malla Skov's Journal

Monday, October 4, 1875

I saw a blue jay today outside the cabin. Its colors were so striking against the dirt and the trees. I felt it was filled with joy. It chirped a sweet chirp. That is, until a bulbous bullfrog chased it away. It was one of the older frogs. This one looked more yellow than green. They are such slimy things and I grow weary of seeing them everywhere. Bella loves them. She treats them like pets. Carla tolerates them as long as they hold a purpose but would not shed a tear if they were gone. At least I had a brief moment of something beautiful.

I spent most of the day reading *Frankenstein* by Mary Shelley. Again. I have lost count of the number of times I've read it. Perhaps the lifestyle my sisters and I have has drawn me to this story of resurrection. A true life after death. Or perhaps I'm pleased to read the work of a woman author. I suppose it's both. In either case, it's one of my favorite novels. I've read there is a play based on the novel, but I've never seen it. Perhaps I will one day, if I can leave this life.

I spent a little time in the garden. Carla is the botanist of the family, but I like to sit among the tomatoes, potatoes, elderberries, and milkweeds. Many of them are almost ready for harvest. The three of us don't need much to last the winter. The tomatoes look smaller than last year. Carla says it's only my imagination and they are the same as they've always been. Sometimes I think she disagrees with me on purpose. And even if Bella agrees with me, she will always take Carla's side. She tries to avoid conflict. I don't think she would ever stand up to Carla. She can be kind to me, but I hate Bella sometimes. Carla doesn't have a kind bone in her body.

I once thought Carla would grow kinder with age, but the reverse seems to be true. I don't understand where all her hate comes from. She once yelled at me for playing with a stray dog. She said she couldn't stand the noise and wanted us to stop. If I were able, I would have left her long ago. Everyday living with her is a chore. It's exhausting how awful she is and how she views the world.

I suppose I can't blame her given what we've all been through. I try not to think about that night. It was so long ago but feels so recent. We were so young. And we've faced more struggles since. I think we'd be happier if we left this place. The forest holds some power over us. Maybe that's why we've survived so long.

***

Tuesday, October 5, 1875

Today was an extraordinary day. It started like so many others. My sisters and I went into town. We needed flour and fabric. We traded some fur pelts for the fabric as we always had. Many of the herbs we grew were sold to the drug store. Bella was always the one to get the fabric and Carla always went to the drug store. I often would accompany one or the other but today I was sent to the general store for the flour and any other items we needed.

I always enjoy the days like this. I get a little time away from my sisters and see the other people in town. Though many of them don't care to look at me. A couple of women gave me an awful look before walking away. I was used to this but then someone behind me spoke.

"Don't mind them. They're rude to everyone who doesn't have fancy clothes like them."

He was a young man, tall, dressed in plain clothes. He had dark brown hair and a kind smile with kind brown eyes. He picked up a bag of flour.

"Not everyone is like them." He said.

I smiled but didn't know what to say. Few people ever

speak to me. A young woman with dark brown hair walked over to him.

"Benjamin, please hurry. I still must go to the post office." She said.

She wore a plain dress, but it was a little nicer looking than mine. She looked up at him with big brown eyes.

"Yes, Isabelle. I remember." Benjamin said.

"Who is this?"

Isabelle looked at me and smiled.

"Forgive me for not introducing myself. My name is Benjamin, and this is my younger sister Isabelle."

"Hello."

"Hello. My name is Malla." I said.

"That's such a pretty name." Isabelle said.

"Than – Thank you."

"Would you like to walk with us to the post office?"

"I'm sorry, I must meet my sisters at the drug store."

"That's on the way." Benjamin said.

"Oh, I hope you'll walk with us. I'd love to speak with another girl. I only have brothers." Isabelle said.

"I don't want to impose."

"There's no imposition. We'd love to have your company." Benjamin said.

"That sounds nice." I said.

We paid for our things and began the short walk down the street. I'd forgotten what it was like to chat with other people.

"Do you live in town?" Isabelle said.

"No." I said.

"That's why I've never seen you before. Traveling can be such a pain sometimes. I hope you don't live too far away."

"No, but when we do come to town, we make a day of it since we don't come often."

"I imagine you do your own hunting and fishing." Benjamin said.

"How do you know that?"

"Our father's the butcher. I work for him when I'm not escorting Isabelle. It's only the people who don't hunt that buy meat from us. I've never seen you at our shop, so I guessed that you hunt and fish."

"Oh, yes. We've done it all our lives, my sisters and I. We've been here since before the town."

"Do you mean to say your family has been here since before the town?" Isabelle said.

"Um, yes. I mean to say."

"What does your father do for money?"

"Our father died many years ago. And our mother."

"I'm so very sorry. Our mother passed on about four years ago. This was her dress, in fact. Isn't it lovely?"

"Yes, it's very nice."

"Do you get to read much out in the wilderness?" Benjamin said.

"I have a few books I've read many times. Each of them." I said.

"Which is your favorite?"

"*Frankenstein* by Mary Shelley."

"That's one of Benjamin's favorites." Isabelle said.

"Is it really?" I said.

"I understand the monster's pain. I suppose I should call him Adam."

"That is his name."

"Have you heard about the library? They should finish building it in a few years. Perhaps you can get some new books to read." Isabelle said.

"Perhaps. Um, there are my sisters. Thank you for the conversation. I should be going."

"It was nice meeting you. I do hope we can chat again." Isabelle said.

"As do I. Goodbye."

"Goodbye."

I saw my sisters faces when I entered the drug store. They were not happy with me.

"What was that?" Carla said.

"What?" I said.

"Those people. Why were you talking with them?"

"They were being kind. It's nothing."

"You know why we can't socialize with these people. You know what happens a year from now."

"It was nothing. They saw some women sneering at me and offered to walk with me. That's all."

"She's right, Malla. You must be careful while we're in town. People will try to take advantage." Bella said.

"Please don't speak to me like I'm a child. And for once could you both not team up against me. It was nothing. Let us go home."

But it was something. I've never been treated with so much kindness by strangers. Regardless of my sisters' warnings, meeting Benjamin and Isabelle made this a wonderful day. I do hope I see them again. It's a nice change from my droll, boring life.

Bella came to speak with me after we returned home while Carla looked over the garden.

"I'm sorry for earlier in town. I didn't mean to presume you were childish." She said.

"Thank you but I understand." I said.

"You know we have your best interests at heart. We don't have normal lives. Ours are more complicated. We can't have what normal people have."

"I'm aware. And it's not like I'm going around trying to make friends. It was nice to have a conversation with someone who isn't my sister. That's all."

"I understand. But promise you'll be more careful."

"I will."

Sometimes I don't know how those two are content with this life that was thrust upon us. Perhaps others find a long life to be a blessing. I only see it as a curse. What's the point of a long life if you don't enjoy it?

Thirty-Eight
May 14, 1977

"Okay. Let's see if I got this right. You three go to this cabin thinking the child killer is there or was there. You find more bullfrogs than anyone can count and some women having an argument."

"Sisters, Detective. They're sisters." Samantha said.

Samantha rubbed her face trying to smear away the exhaustion.

"You heard them say they were sisters?" The detective said.

"Yes." Samantha said.

"You have proof they're involved in the murders?"

"Not enough. They didn't deny it when Ernest mentioned it."

"As you said, that isn't enough. Do you know anything that can help us find them? An address or names?"

"They called the redhead Bella. The brunette was called Carla. I never heard the blonde's name."

"When you were alone running back to the car, you said you tripped. That's how you got the bump on your head."

"Yes."

"You weren't pushed or shoved?"

"No. I was looking behind me and didn't see a fallen branch. Next thing I remember is waking in the car."

"What happened after you were in the car?"

"I was still dizzy. Jed was talking into his radio. I missed most of what he said when Ernest spoke to me. He asked me how

I felt. I told him my head hurt. He asked if I was dizzy or felt nauseous. I wasn't dizzy anymore and felt fine. He asked if I could see okay. I said yes. He said he thought I'd be okay but wanted me to see a doctor when I got back to town."

"Thank you, Miss Belcher. I may have more questions after I speak with Mister Kemp and Deputy Wells. You're welcome to some coffee or water. We also have vending machines down the hall near the restrooms."

"Thank you."

***

I sat in the police station drinking their awful coffee. I read the newspaper scrutinizing one of my articles. I wouldn't hear Jed and Ernest's versions of that night for several hours. The following transcriptions are from Jed and Ernest's interviews with the detective. They tell a clearer picture of what happened.

***

Jed

"…I yelled for her to keep running. I stopped the redhead from hitting me again. We struggled with the tree branch. She was strong. I don't know how long we struggled. A bird squawked far off. She looked agitated by the sound. She grunted and I flew back. I must have been disoriented because it looked like I was ten feet away and the redhead was gone. I never heard her make a noise like all the other times she popped up in front of us. She just vanished." Jed said.

"You said she wore dark clothing." The detective said.

"Yes. They all did. She also carried a candle. She didn't have it when she hit me. At least I don't remember seeing it. It was weird. The flame didn't flicker. Like it wasn't a real flame. But I felt the heat and could smell it."

"What did you do after the woman disappeared?"

"I tried to find Samantha. I went to where I last saw her. We had all planned to meet up at the car. I found West on the compass and ran. I'd stop every few feet to look around hoping to see her. After the third or fourth time I stopped. I heard something croaking. Somewhere close. I followed the sound and found a raven perched in a tree. It croaked and looked down. Samantha was

217

laying under the tree. She was beathing but unconscious. I carried her back to the car. I waited for Ernest. I considered looking for him but didn't want to leave Samantha. I had been waiting about five minutes when Ernest ran out of the trees down the road. He ran towards me shouting to start the car. I asked what happened. He said he didn't know. He shot one of them, but it didn't faze her. She was still strong. I turned the car around driving back to town. I reported the incident over the radio. Samantha stirred in the back. She had a big bump on her head. Ernest checked her out. He said she was fine but should see a doctor when we got back. We didn't stop until we got here."

"Is there anything else you remember? Any detail that might seem trivial can be helpful."

"Well, I'm sure it was my imagination, but I thought I saw them in the rearview mirror watching us leave."

***

Ernest

"…I was trying to distract them so we all could get away." Ernest said.

"What brought on this idea?" The detective said.

"It was something I saw a couple Marines do in Cambodia. They drew enemy fire so we could escape. They, uh, they didn't survive."

"Did you expect to survive?"

"I didn't see any weapons, so I didn't believe our lives were in danger."

"What happened when you left the other two?"

"I got far enough to where I couldn't see them and shouted at the women. Then I ran to another place."

"What did you shout?"

"I was there to stop them killing children. They didn't deny it which tells me they're the killers."

"Well, that's not enough for a conviction. Then what happened?"

"I listened for a minute. I didn't hear anything, so I moved to a different spot. One of the women said she would kill me like she's killed others. She said she lived in the woods and would find

218

me."

"Which woman was this?"

"The one with the dark hair, I think. I forget what the others called her."

"What happened next?"

"I joked that she hadn't found me and ran off again. I found Jed and Samantha. I told them to go back to the car. Well, I mouthed the words and hoped they understood. Then I went around the front of the cabin. I didn't see anyone until the blonde ran up. I looked away and when I looked back the redhead and blonde were talking. I was too far away to hear anything. I decided to look for the other woman while she was alone."

"Did you see the blonde and redhead go anywhere before you left?"

"They were still talking when I left. I stopped somewhere to listen. It was dead silent, like an uneasy silence. I would have heard someone approaching me. I heard a bird squawk to my right. It was close. When I turned my head, the dark-haired woman was coming at me with a branch. I caught the branch and we struggled with it for a minute. She was strong. Stronger than any man I've ever fought. She pushed me and I fell back a few feet. I don't know how she did it. I picked myself up and fired my revolver. Somehow, she dodged it and the bullet hit a tree."

"What do you mean somehow she dodged it?"

"I've never seen anyone move that fast. It's like she was a blur and then was several feet away in an instant."

"Okay. She's fast. Then what?"

"She made this yell and charged at me with the branch. When she got closer, I fired again. She wasn't fast enough this time and I hit her shoulder. She dropped the branch and stopped. She was angry. She said guns don't work on her. I said it looked like it hurt. She laughed then said pain is temporary. I said pride is forever. She smiled like she understood what I meant."

"What did you mean?"

"It's something I've heard Marines say to push us to go the extra mile."

"Okay. What did she do after that?"

"When I got to my feet, she was in front of me and had her hand around my neck. She was lifting me off the ground with one arm."

"This was her good arm, not the one you shot?"

"Yes. She choked me so I squeezed her bullet wound as hard as I could. She lowered me to the ground but kept strangling me and I kept squeezing her shoulder. Her grip loosened. She finally let go. I fell to my knees coughing and gasping for air. I looked up and saw the blonde behind the other woman. I don't know how long she had been there. The dark-haired woman leaned against a tree breathing heavy. She said I will die when the moon is full and stumbled away. I picked up my revolver and tried to follow her. The blonde stopped me as I raised my arm to fire. We struggled. She was strong too. She pushed my arm down as I squeezed the trigger. The round went into the ground. She squeezed my wrist until I dropped the revolver. With one arm, she pushed me back into a tree. It knocked the wind out of me. She held me up and said some weird shit."

"Weird how? What did she say?"

"I still don't understand most of it. She said the ravens will guide me and I should trust them and trust my instincts. There was another bird squawk from far off. She looked over her shoulder like she was listening. Then she said she would distract her sisters so me and my friends could escape. I fell to my knees and when I looked up, she was gone. I never heard her leave. She didn't make a sound."

The detective scribbled some notes. A knock at the door interrupted the silence. A uniformed deputy stepped in, handing a file to the detective then left. The detective read the file and looked over a few photographs. He put everything under another file.

"What happened after you were alone?" The detective said.

"I picked up my revolver and moved around the cabin like I had before. I didn't see anyone. The bullfrogs were still there not moving and not making noise. I listened for a minute and didn't hear anything. I started running back to the car. I got turned around at one point and remembered I had a compass. I stopped a few times to listen. It was still dark and still too quiet. I finally made it to the street. I looked around and saw the car further away than I expected. I ran and said start the car. I wanted to get out of there. Jed asked me what happened. I said I didn't really know, but I shot one of them and I still struggled with her. After we hit the road, Jed reported everything on his radio. Samantha woke up in the back seat. She had a bump on her head. I checked her out as best I could making sure she didn't have a concussion. She seemed okay but I told her to see a doctor when we got back. I saw the three women out the back window as we left. Then they disappeared, like they vanished. I don't know if my mind played tricks on me or not. Then we drove back to town."

"Spooky stuff."

"Tell me about it."

"Your story lines up with Deputy Wells and Miss Belcher. This file is from the scene. We found a couple rounds matching your revolver's caliber; one in the ground and one in a tree like you said. The cabin was empty but the smell from the candles was still fresh. No bullfrogs and no women, but there were multiple footprints from people and frogs. I'd like all of you to meet with a sketch artist so we can find these women."

"And that's it?"

"For now, yes. This is a weird case. We have a specialist, one of our other detectives, working on the murders. He might have more questions for you. I recommend you stop trying to play hero and let the Sherriff's Department do their job. The war's over. You can relax now."

"Easier said than done, Detective."

Thirty-Nine
June 2, 1977

Ernest watched Amy in his room. He sipped his coffee while his daughter played with toys on his bed. She made noises at the toys. Amy didn't react to the knock on the door.

"Oh good. I wasn't sure we had the right room. Hello Ernie. How are you? How's our precious granddaughter?"

"Beatrice. Herb. I didn't know you were coming." Ernest said.

"We made arrangements after we heard Linda was in jail. Thank the lord it happened way out here and not back home. What would the neighbors think? Oh, Amy you've gotten so chubby. Hello. Hello there." Beatrice said.

Amy stared at Beatrice then returned her attention to her toys.

"She's very interested in those toys. It's like she doesn't know her own grandmother." She said.

"She's played with them all day. She ignores me too. Don't take it personally." Ernest said.

"Well as long as she's happy and healthy. And what of Linda? Shouldn't she have been out by now? How long's it been? They can't keep her locked up. We better get a lawyer. They can sort this whole mess out by the end of the day."

"Will you shut up and let the man tell us what's going on?" Herbert said.

Beatrice's face held both surprise and resentment.

"I'm sorry, Ernie. Please go on. We'll talk about this later

Herbert." She said.

Ernest rubbed his eyes as there was another knock on his door.

"Well, who could that be? Are you expecting someone?" Beatrice said.

"No."

Ernest opened the door revealing his parents.

"Great. You're all here. Good thing I didn't have any plans today." Ernest said.

"Hello Gail. Bob." Beatrice said.

"Beatrice. Herbert. You know, Ernest you could try giving us a proper hello." Gail said.

"That's not an appropriate way to greet your mother." Bob said.

"Showing up unannounced isn't appropriate either, but here you all are. There's coffee made if you want any." Ernest said.

Gail busied herself preparing two cups of coffee. She gave one to her husband then put one scoop of sugar in the other and stirred. She looked in the small refrigerator. She opened and smelled the carton of milk before pouring some into the coffee. She stirred for some time before sipping. Beatrice broke the brief silence.

"You were about to tell us about Linda." She said.

"Yes, we'd like to know as well." Gail said.

Ernest stared out the window sipping coffee. A beam of sunlight cut through the blinds hitting the wall behind the bed. The two sets of grandparents stood by the door near the small table with the coffee pot; the darker half of the room. They waited for the silhouette of Ernest's form in the sunlight to speak.

"After Linda was arrested, they kept her in a cell until her arraignment for a couple days. The night before she was supposed to post bail, she got into it with another prisoner. The guards had to separate them. In the commotion, Linda assaulted one of the guards. New charges were drawn up. The judge denied her bail believing she was a threat to the public. Her court date was scheduled for a couple weeks ago, but they postponed it until July. They want to assess her mental state before charging her with anything. There's where we're at right now."

Herbert stared at the floor. Beatrice covered her mouth. Shock painted her face. Gail turned away and tidied up the coffee pot. Bob folded his arms never taking his gaze off his son. Amy played never noticing the heaviness in the room.

"Well, that settles it. Linda is our daughter and our responsibility. And if she's mentally unfit to be a mother than we should take care of Amy." Beatrice said.

"Like hell you will."

"Bob."

"No Gail. This is ridiculous. You have no claim on that child."

"I can take care of Amy." Ernest said.

"Oh nonsense. You can't raise a child alone. Ernest and Amy will stay with us." Gail said.

"So, you'll just take our grandchild and leave our daughter to rot out here. Is that it?" Beatrice said.

"Maybe if you had done a better job raising your daughter she wouldn't be rotting in jail."

"Robert!" Gail said.

"How dare you? You – You ogre. Herb, do something!" Beatrice said.

Bob and Beatrice continued shouting insults. Gail tried to calm them down and separate them. Herbert had turned away rubbing his temples. Amy was starting to cry and looked at Ernest. Ernest's booming baritone overpowered everyone else.

"That's enough! Be quiet! Everyone shut up!"

They all stared at him as he picked up Amy to quiet her. They looked away.

"I know. It's okay. They're all a bunch of grumpy old people. They're not mad at you. They just don't have any manners." Ernest said.

Amy's cries faded. She rested her head on Ernest's shoulder. He got a tissue and wiped her face.

"It looks like your nose was crying too. That's nasty let's clean that up."

The room filled with awkwardness. Bob drank his

remaining coffee in one gulp to occupy himself. Herbert continued rubbing his temples. Beatrice hugged herself staring at her husband with contempt. Gail watched her son and granddaughter with a sad smile.

"If you're all going to act like children, don't tell me how to take care of my child. Something happened to Linda that made her leave. She won't tell me everything. But she did tell me about all your nonsense and fighting over Amy. All she wanted was to keep Amy away from all of you. Now I know why. I'm going to sort out this mess with Linda and then we're going to build a life together. I thought about maybe getting a house here in Maine. Maybe we'll go somewhere else. But it'll be just me, Linda, and Amy. No one else." Ernest said.

"Sweetheart. I want you to be happy. But don't do anything rash. You're going through a hard time. Let us help you through it. That's what family is for, and I always say nothing is more important than family." Gail said.

"Then we better make sure Amy is your family before you run off with her." Beatrice said.

"Excuse me?"

"You heard me, Gail. How do we know your son is the father?"

"You're a piece of work. First you want to steal my grandchild then you accuse your own daughter of being a whore. Do you even love your daughter?" Bob said.

"Of course, I love my daughter and I love my granddaughter just as much. I want a paternity test. And if Ernest is not the father, then you have no claim to Amy. None of you do." Beatrice said.

Herbert covered his face. Bob's hands were shaking in fists.

"How could you say that? We used to be friends. You know how long our kids have known each other." Gail said.

"We're not doing this." Bob said.

"It's the only way to settle the matter." Beatrice said.

"Haven't we all been through enough? I see where she gets it from. You're just as disturbed as your daughter."

"You're only capable of shouting insults at people. Have

you ever had an intelligent thought?"

"If you make Amy cry again, I will through you all out. By force if necessary." Ernest said.

"Bob. Dear. Maybe you should go for a walk and cool off." Gail said.

Bob scoffed, glaring at his wife with large eyes.
"Fine!"

He stormed out. Gail caught the door before it slammed and secured the latch with a gentle click.

"Why did you tell Linda you never liked me and didn't want her around my family?" Ernest said.

"Well, you see how your father is. I assumed you would turn out just like him. Linda deserves better than that. Your family drove my baby girl away. Then not long after you find her, she gets arrested. You're all a bad influence on her." Beatrice said.

"She was trying to give Amy up for adoption behind my back. When I found out, we had an argument."

"What?"

"Some of her neighbors didn't like us shouting. Linda shouted at them, and they called the police. It wouldn't have been much of an issue. But then she fought the guard in jail and made everything worse for herself."

"I still think she wouldn't be in this mess if it wasn't for you. And I will get a paternity test."

"We will never agree to that." Gail said.

"Then I'll get a court order. There has to be one descent lawyer in this town."

"Go ahead. Take me to court. I'll see you there." Ernest said.

"Don't you worry, Ernest. I'll get your father and we'll make a plan. They will never get our grandchild." Gail said.

She left the room.

"All of you are awful people. Let's go Herbert." Beatrice said.

She checked the hall then left. Herbert and Ernest allowed silence to fill the room. Amy sneezed.

"I'm sorry, Ernest. For Beatrice. She just wants to blame

everyone else for Linda's behavior so no one thinks she's a bad mother. But you're right. None of us should be around Amy. I'll do what I can to help you and Linda and Amy have a life together. I can't do much to stop Beatrice. You're a good father. And once all this blows over, I know you'll take care of Linda." Herbert said.

"Thank you, Herb."

"I'll see if I can calm down Beatrice. Assuming she'll let me talk. Sometimes it's best to let her talk until she tires herself. That's the only way I've found to get her to be quiet. Good luck with everything."

Herbert left with a calm resolve. Ernest set Amy on the bed, and she returned to her toys. He stared out the window. The sunlight beam was no longer harsh in the blinds. He stood there lost in thought. Amy starting moaning and wining. He picked her up and patted her back.

"Are you hungry?"

Amy nodded.

"How about some crackers and cheese?"

"Yeah." Amy said.

Forty
June 7, 1977

Jed, Samantha, and Ernest waited outside a detective's office for the Kennebec County Sherriff's Department Major Crimes Unit. The detective escorted someone from his office thanking him for his time.

"Hello, Miss Belcher. Mister Kemp. Good to see you again Deputy Wells. I'm Detective Vaughn. I'm following up on the incident from a couple weeks ago at the house out in the woods. It shouldn't take long. I need a few holes filled and you can all be on your way. Deputy, if you don't mind, I'd like to speak to you first."

Jed walked into the office and Detective Vaughn closed the door.

"I've had to speak to police more in the last six months than I have my entire life." Ernest said.

"At least this time you weren't arrested." Samantha said.

"Not yet anyway."

"How are things with Linda and Amy?"

"Linda is still in jail pending a psychiatric evaluation."

"I'm sorry. That can be difficult."

"Amy's handling everything pretty well as long as she has her toys."

"She's probably too young to understand what's happened."

"Yeah. My parents and my in-laws came for a visit."

"The family Linda was running from?"

"Yep. It was the worst family reunion I've ever seen."

"Did they at least explain some things?"

"Not really. They all want to make our decisions for us. I don't really want them around right now."

"You're going through a lot. That's hard without family to support you."

"You're more supportive than my family right now."

"Are you saying we're family?"

"Not really, but I'd rather be around you and Jed than my real family."

Samantha smiled and looked down at her purse.

"I know how draining being around family can be. But you can't change or control people. All you can do is hope they change on their own." She said.

"I wish they'd stop trying to change and control me. And Linda. I wish Linda would tell me whatever it is she hasn't told me." Ernest said.

"I'm sure she will when she's ready. Sometimes saying things out loud makes them more real and that means you'll have to face them. That's scarier than pretending it never happened."

"That sounds like experience talking. You want to talk about it?"

"Not today."

"They smiled at each other then looked away. Ernest looked at the bare yellow walls. Samantha got some lotion from her purse and rubbed it around her hands. Ernest looked at his watch.

"I'm gonna get some coffee. Do you want a cup?" He said.

"Sure. Thank you."

Sitting alone, Samantha searched through her purse. She got out a small paper and balanced her checkbook. Ernest returned with two small cups of coffee.

"They're still talking?" He said.

"Yeah. I hope we don't have to explain the whole thing all over again." She said.

"It feels more like a debriefing. They call us in to make sure the paperwork is squared away then they tell us to never talk about it again. Forget it ever happened."

"If only it was that easy."

"You never forget. No matter how much you pretend it

didn't happen."

"So, you know something about that too?"

"Yeah, and I wish I didn't."

"Me too."

They sat in silence for a moment. The office door opened. Jed stepped out.

"Miss Belcher?" Detective Vaughn said.

She walked into the office with the detective.

"How was it?" Ernest said.

"Not as bad as I thought." Jed said.

"Did you have to go over everything again?"

"No. He had a few questions, then asked for more details that weren't in the report. Routine stuff for follow up questioning."

"It didn't take you that long. I guess we won't be here for hours."

"Probably not."

"Did he tell you anything new?"

"No. He wants me to stay out of it."

"What do you mean?"

"He doesn't want me doing any off-duty investigations. He did encourage me to work on becoming a detective through the department though. I guess he thinks I have potential."

"You definitely helped us out. I'm not sure how things would have gone down if you hadn't been with Samantha."

"Mmhmm. Things can go to Hell when you least expect it. This job has taught me a lot."

"I'll bet. I learned more than I wanted to from the Navy."

"You didn't like all the training you got?"

"The training is all good knowledge to have. The experiences that come after are some of the things I wish I didn't have."

"I think I know what you mean."

They both stared at the floor, each lost in thought. Ernest looked at his empty paper cup.

"I'm gonna get more coffee. You want one?" Ernest said.

"No thanks. I've already had two cups today." Jed said.

"Only two? I have two every morning before getting

dressed. How do you get through the day without more?"

"I like to sleep at night and not vibrate through the walls."

"Ha! Yeah okay. Maybe I should cut back. But not today."

"Maybe tomorrow?"

"Probably not tomorrow either."

Jed sat with his hands on his knees. He patted them a couple times then crossed his arms and put his right leg on his left. He exhaled a long breath then pulled out a small notebook and pen from his breast pocket. Ernest returned as Jed reviewed his notes. Samantha walked out before Ernest sat down.

"Mister Kemp?" Detective Vaughn said.

"Um, can I bring my coffee?" Ernest said.

"Of course."

Detective Vaughn closed the door behind them. Without a word, Ernest sat in one of the two chairs in front of the desk. Everything in the room was a mix of different shades of brown and mustard yellow. Ernest looked for someplace to put his coffee, then resigned to continue holding it. He tapped his heels on the floor as Detective Vaughn sat down.

"Thank you for agreeing to meet with me today. I'm sure you're sick of law enforcement by now." The detective said.

"I don't mind that much. Everyone's just trying to do their job the best they can." Ernest said.

"Still, it's all a bit annoying, right? Always getting accused of something. That'd make me frustrated."

"It's definitely frustrating. But I also know it's frustrating for them when they think they have their guy, and they find out they're wrong. That'd piss me off more than being falsely accused."

"Well, I can't argue with that. I did look into why you were detained. Many people accused you of various things. Some of which happened before you ever came to town. You've managed to piss off a lot of people since you got here, but I haven't found evidence of you doing anything illegal."

"I'm glad someone finally believes me."

"You are, however, getting close to being called a vigilante."

"What are you talking about?"

"Miss Belcher is a reporter. I'm used to hearing about her putting her nose where is doesn't belong. Deputy Wells has helped people with matters in his spare time and had that right as a deputy. You are a stock boy at the general store who used to be in the Navy. You're a civilian now. Like it or not, you're not on the battlefield anymore. I suggest you either join the police force or mind your own business and settle down."

"You want me to give up? We've gotten closer to finding those responsible for killing children than you have. You want us to forget about everything?"

"I would appreciate you sharing any information you have to help my investigation. I will handle things from here. That's my job. If I require your help, I will reach out. But you need to stay out of this and let the police do their job."

Ernest swallowed the last of his coffee and looked down. His heels were still tapping the floor.

"I understand." He said.

"Did you have any intention of killing or harming anyone that night in the woods?" Detective Vaughn said.

"Of course not. Why would you ask?"

"You were carrying a revolver."

"For protection. I expected to run into a bear or wolf before some crazy ass women. I didn't plan to fire it, but things got a bit weird."

"Do you carry it often?"

"Honestly no. That's the first time I've taken it out in public."

"I recommend you keep it at home for now. The last thing the townsfolk need is more reason to distrust you. Everything will work out. You take care of your family and I'll take care of these murders. Sound good?"

"Yeah, sure."

"I'll walk you out."

Forty-One
May 1876 - Malla Skov's Journal

Tuesday, May 2, 1876

It was the first warm day of Spring. I don't think I've ever been happier to go outside. It was a dull Winter as it always is. So many nights spent trying to stay warm by the fire. It's nice to not need three blankets to sleep at night. So many days spent peeling potatoes or sewing new clothes. I went out one cold day, sometime after Yule had ended, just to be outside. Bella said I would catch a cold and I did. The fun was worth it.

I didn't spend too many days outside after that. At least not for too long. I met several ravens that foraged by our home. I've always enjoyed meeting different animals, but the ravens were the first to come back and visit. I never gave them food. Maybe they enjoy my company. I always enjoy there's. Carla stepped outside once when many of them were near our home.

"What are all these things doing here?" She said.

"They're just grazing. Food is scarce in the Winter." I said.

"Well, they should go somewhere else. Go on! Shoo! Bother someone else you filthy creatures!"

One of the birds croaked at her. It looked at the others and made some clicking noises. They all flew away, and Carla stomped the snow off here shoes going back inside. I listened to the ravens croaking in the trees.

I spent the whole day outside today but didn't see any of my little black friends. I hope I see them tomorrow.

***

Wednesday, May 3, 1876

It was warm again today. I decided to go to the river for some hornwort and stonewort. I expected it to be like any other day collecting plants. I had been by the river for a while. I spent so much time scrutinizing each plant that I never noticed a horse pulling a wagon along the river. I was admiring nature and daydreaming when I heard them calling.

"Is that Malla? Hello! So good to see you again."

It was Isabelle. Benjamin was with her. It was too late for me to leave without seeming rude. I had only seen my sisters and forest creatures for months. I craved conversation with others. Part of me felt uneasy about talking with them, but part of me was also excited. I needed something different and here it was like a present from a secret admirer.

"Hello. I'm surprised to see you so far from town." I said.

"After how warm it was yesterday, I convinced father to give Benjamin the day off and escort me on a little adventure traveling along the river. We've been at it since this morning." Isabelle said.

"What brings you out to the river?" Benjamin said.

"Oh, I'm just collecting some plants." I said.

"Do you study botany?"

"Something like that. I've never studied botany properly. I've only read a couple books on the subject."

"I haven't read any books on it, so you know more than me. Have you read any Benjamin?" Isabelle said.

"I have not."

"What's the book you're reading currently?"

"*The Law and the Lady* by Wilkie Collins. Have you read it?" Benjamin said.

He asked me. I don't know why he seemed so interested.

"I'm sorry, I haven't heard of that one." I said.

"I'm not surprised. It's still very new. It was only published last year. I've only just started, but I'll tell you how it is when I've finished."

"I hope you'll let me read it when you've finished." Isabelle said.

"Of course, you can. Don't be silly."

"Oh, but Malla, you can read it first if you want. I don't mean to sound so greedy."

"That's alright. Thank you. You seem more interested than I do." I said.

"I'm so sorry, I didn't tell you what it's about." Benjamin said.

"No need to apologize. I'm just feeling a bit warm." I said.

"It is warm today. And so beautiful. I'm so glad father allowed you to accompany me. I would have hated to be cooped up in the house on a day like today." Isabelle said.

"I wanted some time out of the house as well. I enjoy being around nature and animals." I said.

"You looked comfortable around all those ravens." Benjamin said.

"I'm sorry?"

"They're all around the trees behind you."

I turned to see many of them. I wonder if they were watching over me.

"So, they are. They've been so quiet I hardly noticed them." I said.

"I've never seen so many before." Isabelle said.

"Nor I." Benjamin said.

"They often avoid people, so many of them stay out here away from town. They won't bother you if you don't bother them." I said.

"I suppose it helps one from feeling lonely." Isabelle said.

"It was nice to see you both again, but it's a long walk back to my home. I want to get back before dark." I said.

"May we give you a ride home in our wagon?" Benjamin said.

"I'm afraid there are no paths or roads for a wagon through the trees to my home."

"But how do you travel into town?" He said.

"We walk. We don't make the trip often as you've no doubt noticed." I said.

"Be that as it may, I think I speak for both of us when I

say we would love to talk with you again. Preferably sooner than later." Isabelle said.

"I would enjoy that as well."

"Do stop by the butcher shop the next time you're in town. Even if you don't want to buy anything. Tell father you're a friend of Isabelle's and he won't hassle you too much." Benjamin said.

"Oh, look Benjamin! There are a couple of Bullfrogs by the river. They must like Malla as much as the ravens."

"They do appear to be looking at us, don't they?" He said.

"I'm sure they're being cautious and watching so they know when to hop away." I said.

"Yes, that must be it." Benjamin said.

"Well, I should be off. Until our next meeting."

"Goodbye, Malla. Have a safe journey home."

"You as well. Goodbye."

Once I was hidden behind trees, I looked back at the river. Benjamin and Isabelle were out of sight. The bullfrogs were still by the river hopping around as if nothing had happened. A raven croaked at me.

"Thank you for watching over me." I said.

I heard many ravens flying through the trees as I walked home. This made me think of them as guardian angels. It was a pleasant thought. The ravens were kinder to me than my own sisters. Is it wrong to think poorly of one's siblings and family? I wonder if the ravens have disagreements with their families.

There were many bullfrogs around the trees when I returned home. None of them looked like the ones I saw at the river, but they did stare at me like the ones at the river. Before walking inside, I could sense that my sisters were angry with me. But they always seemed angry with me.

"Bella saw you at the river." Carla said.

"Of course she did, because you always send her to spy on me." I said.

"I wouldn't have to if you would listen to me once in a while."

"I always listen to you. Every day of my unnaturally long life I listen to you and only you. I'd love to listen to anyone else for a change."

"Don't be so dramatic. You know we three can only count on each other. No one out there will ever help us unless they're getting something from us."

"You're no different from them. You only do anything because you gain something from it."

"Stop trying to turn this around on me. You're the one who's done something wrong. I told you not to speak to other people. What if they learn where we live?"

"They won't. I would have drawn more attention if I had ignored them. I spoke to them so they wouldn't try to follow me. There's no need for concern."

"Bella said you all seemed very friendly and close. Perhaps you've fallen for that young boy." She said.

"It's not like that. I suspect his sister doesn't have many friends and that's why they were so eager to talk with me. I doubt I'll see them again before we leave." I said.

"You had better not because if you do see them again, I will see to it that this friendship of yours ends abruptly. Do we understand each other?"

"You have no empathy, do you? You're only concerned about yourself."

"I'm concerned about keeping us alive. That includes you. You should be grateful. I don't want to have this conversation again."

Bella had been quietly knitting in one corner.

"I don't know why you two never get along."

"Shut up, Bella." I said.

"Well, that was rude."

I spent the rest of the day outside. I didn't speak to my sisters, and they didn't speak to me. We ate supper in silence. It wouldn't have mattered if I said anything. They wouldn't have listened. And they knew I wouldn't listen to them. I hated spending so many years trapped in that house with them. How could they love it so much? Didn't they crave something new and different? Didn't they crave something more than we'd been given? Maybe I'll never know what they want.

Forty-Two
July 9, 1977

"How are you holding up?" Ernest said.

He sat across from Linda. The room was small with a single brown table and two chairs. The tile floor was white. The walls were mustard yellow. Linda didn't speak. She looked down at the table like a child about to be punished.

"I imagine the food here is about as good as military food. Do they let you have coffee or is that contraband?"

Linda didn't speak.

"I almost died a few weeks ago running from these crazy women that live in the woods and might be killing children."

Linda didn't speak.

"Okay. You don't want to talk so I'll just leave."

Ernest stood up.

"What? No! Please don't leave."

"Have you heard anything I've said?"

"I…no. I'm sorry. I can't make sense of anything that's happened anymore. Please stay. How's Amy doing?"

Ernest was still for a moment. He sighed and sat down.

"She's good. She's still discovering the world. She never looks sad when I leave her with the sitter. It's like she doesn't notice I'm gone but she's always happy to see me when I pick her up. She can be a little chatterbox though. Lord knows what's she's saying half the time."

Linda stared at the table smiling.

"They say I'm ill. Crazy. They think I'm a nutcase." She

said.

"You're not a nutcase."

"Are you sure? I'm in prison for Christ's sake. They want to move me to a mental hospital."

"They told me."

Ernest handed her his handkerchief.

"Thank you. They're gonna fill me up with drugs until I don't know who I am anymore." She said.

"That's not what the doctor said."

"Like I'm gonna trust that jackass. You know he thinks I'm crazy because of childbirth? What did he call it? Atypical depression in the postpartum. I told him Amy was nearly a toddler and he dismissed it. He dismisses everything I say! He doesn't want me to see my child until I'm over my psychosis! His words! Oh God. I'm so sorry. I don't mean to scream at you. That man is so frustrating."

"It's okay. I'll listen if you want to vent." He said.

"Did the doctor tell you not to bring Amy to see me?"

"No. I wasn't sure how she'd feel in a prison. I didn't want you to get upset if she was acting crabby. I didn't know the doctor doesn't want you to see Amy."

"You're right. I don't want her to see me like this. I guess she wouldn't understand or remember anyway."

"I'll talk to the doctor and convince him to let you see Amy."

"Well, you don't have a vagina, so he'll probably listen to you."

"We'll get a second opinion once you're transferred. I'm sure they have better doctors at the hospital."

Linda didn't speak.

"Your parents paid me a visit, along with my parents." He said.

"What!? Did they take Amy?" She said.

"No. Amy is still with me. Remember I said I didn't want to bring her here."

"I…of course…why were they here?"

"After they heard you got arrested, they insisted on coming

out. I told them not to several times, but they came anyway."

"They all came together?"

"No. And that made things more awkward when they all showed up a few minutes apart from each other. They started fighting over Amy like you said."

"Did you not believe me?"

"That's not what I meant. I did believe, I do believe you."

They sat in silence. Ernest rubbed the bridge of his nose.

"With, uh, with all the arguing, I realized they didn't care what you or I wanted. I don't think they even care what Amy wants. I told them they were all acting like children." He said.

"Did you really?"

"Yeah. They didn't like that. I also said none of them should be around Amy and that really pissed them off."

Linda covered her mouth as she giggled.

"Actually, your dad agreed with me. He said he couldn't do much about your mom, but he would help us as best he could."

"Wow. I don't think I've ever heard him go against anything mom said."

"He looked pretty surprised when your mom demanded a paternity test."

"She wants…"

Linda covered her mouth. Her eyes were watery. She covered her face and looked down.

"Why would she say that?" She said.

Her voice was muffled by her hands.

"I don't think your mom believes you were unfaithful. She was trying to scare my parents. She was angry and probably regrets saying that." He said.

Linda's shoulders rose and fell. She still hid her face.

"Listen, Linda. With everything that happened, everyone believing I died, I won't be upset if you were with someone else."

"I WASN'T! I'm sorry. I never really believed you were gone. I didn't want to be with anyone else."

He took both her hands in his.

"It's okay. I told you I believe you. I don't want you to be afraid to talk to me. I trust you, but even if you had been with someone, I'd still love you."

She pulled away from him.

"Stop talking about it. Please." She said.

"Okay. I'm sorry."

They sat in silence. Linda sat with her arms crossed looking at the wall. Ernest sat back and stared. He tapped his fingers on the table before taking out a cigarette and lighting it.

"Can I have one of those?" She said.

"They're not filtered."

"I don't care."

He slid the pack and lighter to her. She pushed them back across the table after lighting one. He flicked ashes into the ashtray. It was the same color as the walls, a yellow blob in the middle of the brown table. Cigarette smoke sauntered up to the fluorescent lights. They barely heard the hum from the high ceiling.

"I don't think I've ever seen you smoke before." Ernest said.

"You didn't start until after you enlisted." She said.

"Yeah. They always came with the MREs and care packages. I started smoking more often after I got to Cambodia."

"You never mentioned much in your letters. We got most of them several months late. Your mother was really upset when we got an old letter shortly after they told us you died."

"The mail service isn't the best in wartime. I'm sure there are a few letters you never got."

"Maybe. Was it difficult? In Cambodia?"

"It wasn't my favorite time in the service. I saw a lot of good men die. Many of them died because I couldn't get to them in time. I don't feel like I made much of a difference."

"I'm sorry. I have no idea what that must be like."

"I hope you never find out."

The ashtray was sullied with white and gray lumps. They sat inhaling and exhaling smoke. They didn't look at each other, each lost in their own thoughts. Ernest started chewing the cuticles on his fingers staring at the table. Linda rested her chin in her hand staring at the wall.

"What do you want to do now?" He said.

"Does it matter what I want?" She said.

"It does to me."

"I want out of this place. I don't want to live in a hospital. I want to be left alone. Those are the only things I'm sure about."

"What about Amy? Do you still want to give her up?"

"That's what's best for her now. I can't take care of her if I'm locked up."

"I can take care of her."

"I can't ask you to do that. Not by yourself."

"I've been doing pretty well so far."

"It's a full-time job. You can't go to work and take care of her at the same time. No one can do that."

"That's why I get a babysitter."

"That's not the same as raising her."

"Why are you lecturing me when you don't even want her?"

"I never said I didn't want her."

"Then why do you insist on giving her up?"

"Because it's the only way I can keep her safe."

"Safe from what?"

"From your parents. From my parents. From me!"

"You don't think she's safe with you?"

"I screw everything up. Of course, she's not safe with me."

"You haven't hurt her, have you?"

"Oh God, no. I've never hurt her. Do you think I've hurt her?"

"No, I don't. And I know she's safe with you. Why would you think she wasn't?"

"I…"

Linda covered her face and took a deep breath.

"I don't know what to do anymore. If I was fit to be a mother, I wouldn't be in here. Maybe I don't know what's best for Amy. Maybe we should let our parents decide who she lives with." She said.

"We're not doing that. They controlled my life growing up. Then the Navy controlled my life for twelve years. I'm in control now and they have no say in what I do with my family. I'm not happy about it, but maybe a paternity test is the only way to get your parents to back off. I can handle my par…" He said

"Please don't do that! I don't want this to become an ugly legal battle."

"It won't come to that." He said.

"Why don't you and your parents go back to California with Amy?"

"I thought you wanted to give her up for adoption."

"That's not what you want."

"And you said you didn't want her around our parents. Hell, I don't want her around our parents."

"She'll be okay if you're there."

"You're not making any sense. You tried so hard to get away from them."

"I've changed my mind."

"But why?"

"Because I'm crazy and I'm going to the nut house."

"You're not crazy. Stop this."

"I want you to leave."

"So, that's it?"

"Please leave."

"No. Not until you tell me whatever it is you haven't been telling me."

"I don't know what you're talking about."

"Something scared you enough to run all the way out here and it wasn't just our annoying parents. What happened?"

"Will you please leave!? I don't want to talk to you anymore."

"Fine!"

Ernest grabbed his cigarettes and lighter. He pounded on the door and the guard outside opened it.

"We're not done talking about this?" Ernest said.

He walked down the hall placing another cigarette in his lips. He continued toward the bus stop. A raven croaked from a tree branch above him. He looked up and the raven stared back at him.

"Are you the same one that's been following me?" Ernest said.

The raven was silent.

"Maybe you can help me figure out all this shit that's been going on."

The raven flew off as the bus approached.

"Or don't help me. I guess I should've expected that."

Forty-Three
July 12, 1977

"That'll be $6.35." Ernest said.

"That seems expensive. Why does it cost so much?" The woman said.

"I don't make the prices ma'am. I just work here."

"I'll bet you're charging people extra and pocketing the change. Maybe I'll tell your boss about it."

"Go ahead. He's standing right there."

"Stop giving him a hard time Gladys." Joe said.

She took her bags and left with a huff.

"You have a way with the ladies, Ernie."

"I'm pretty sure they'd like me more if I did." Ernest said.

"Most of the folks in town still think you're some kind of troublemaker."

"Is that what you think?"

"If I did, you wouldn't be working for me."

"Thanks, I guess."

"Can you restock the soup cans?"

"Yes sir."

Ernest organized the shelves with care, making sure all the labels were facing outward. A woman turned towards the aisle he stocked. She cleared her throat. When Ernest looked at her, she looked away. He returned to stocking. She cleared her throat again.

"Ex-excuse me? Can you hand me that soup please?" She said.

"The tomato or the minestrone?"

"The tomato of course."

She snatched it from his hand and sped away.

"You're welcome." Ernest said.

He sighed and returned to his task. He spoke under his breath in a mocking tone.

"*Thank you so much, young man.* God, I hate people. Maybe I should apply for work at the hospital again. Retail isn't for me."

Ernest carried the empty boxes back to the stock room. He saw the woman who asked for the soup at the register. She glanced at him then looked away, disgust written on her face.

"I don't know how you tolerate that man, Joe." She said.

"Don't believe the rumors you hear, Susan. He's a good man." Joe said.

"Why doesn't he have a real job? You should hire one of those teenagers to help you. You can help keep our youth out of trouble."

"Don't take this the wrong way, Susan, but who I hire is none of your damn business. Have a nice day."

"Really, Joe!? My husband will hear about this."

"Tell him I said hello."

Susan stomped her feet as she left.

"Keep that up and they'll hate you as much as me." Ernest said.

"Most of 'em are only nice to me 'cause they get their groceries from here. And to be neighborly." Joe said.

"You mean to save face?"

"Tomato, Tomahto."

A scruffy older man entered the store and went to the back refrigerators. Ernest looked outside and saw three teen boys eagerly watching the older man. Ernest walked up to him before he opened the cooler.

"You buying beer for those kids?" Ernest said.

"Ah, Hell. You caught me. They was gonna' let me keep one and the change from the three bucks they gave me."

"I'll give you five bucks to give them their money back and scare them off."

"You bet mister. Thanks a bunch."

The scruffy man ran outside. Ernest heard shouting.

"Hey, take a chill pill old timer."

"Come on, let's book it. This dude's freaky deaky."

The scruffy man passed Ernest at the door with a grin stuck to his face.

"What the hell did those kids say?" Ernest said.

"I don't understand anything kids say these days. What'd you say to that guy?" Joe said.

"I paid him to scare the kids off. They wanted him to buy beer for them."

"The other day a kid came in with his dad's driver's license. The kid didn't know I knew his dad. Dad didn't know his license was missing."

"I'll bet the rest of his Summer vacation won't be fun."

"No, it won't. His dad's a hockey coach and teaches kids how to skate at the ice arena. He probably has the boy helping with all that."

"That'll be good for him. Hard work builds character."

"Strong words from a man everyone calls a troublemaker."

"Thanks for the reminder."

"I'm just teasin'. Never stop the old folks from havin' their fun."

"I don't think I could stop you if I wanted to."

"Damn right. You'd just get yourself hurt."

"Well, don't laugh too hard and break a hip."

"Damn you and your youth."

They both laughed and smiled as Samantha walked in.

"You two are having a good time." She said.

"We're just a couple of crabby old men insulting each other." Ernest said.

"You're the only crabby one around here. I'm a delight." Joe said.

"That's because you're so neighborly."

"Throwing my words back at me. You're a cruel man, Ernest."

"I'm not sure if you're arguing or not." Samantha said.

"Just a bit of teasin' is all." Joe said.

"How are things otherwise?"

"I've had better days. I've had worse ones too." Ernest said.

"Yeah. How's the kid?" Samantha said.

"She got comfortable walking. I'm struggling to keep up with her. I don't know how mom's do it."

"Does she get into lots of trouble?" Joe said.

"Actually no. She's curious about things but she doesn't run off and she listens. I wasn't like that so she must get that from Linda."

"How's Linda holding up?" Samantha said.

"She's getting moved to a hospital. I don't know when. The doctor's a quack. Amy's almost two years old but he thinks Linda's behavior is because of childbirth. I hope the hospital has a better doctor so we can get a second opinion."

"That's terrible. I'm sorry. The Augusta Mental Health Institute is a good place. That's probably where she's going. They have good people there who enjoy caring for others."

"That's comforting. I'm sure it'll be a better environment for Linda."

"Isn't that where you're momma's staying?" Joe said.

"Um, yeah. They care for her."

"I'm sorry. I didn't know. You don't want to hear about my issues when you've got your own." Ernest said.

"It's okay. It's no trouble. But now you believe me because I have first-hand experience with the hospital."

"Yes, thank you."

"Well, I'll let you two chat. Hold down the fort. I got some paperwork stacked to my eyeballs I need to go through." Joe said.

"No problem."

"We didn't get to talk much at the Detective's office." Samantha said.

"Yeah. I didn't tell you the whole story from when mine and Linda's parents showed up."

"What's the whole story?"

"Linda's mother wants a paternity test."

"I'm sorry. Does she have a reason to ask for one?"

"She's trying to spook my parents. I mentioned it to Linda. She didn't take the news well."

"I wouldn't take it well either."

"She was so upset she started contradicting herself. I get the feeling there's something she's still not telling me."

"You think she's lying?"

"No, more like she's not telling me the whole story."

"I know how that feels."

The store fell silent. Someone walked in browsing the automotive section.

"May I ask why your mother's in the hospital?" Ernest said.

"My dad was abusive. Always drunk. Their relationship was complicated. A few years ago, he, uh, he shot himself and, um, my mother saw it happen. She hasn't spoken a word since."

Ernest stared off. A memory crept in, foggy at first then cleared. Bullets whipped past his head striking trees and dirt. A plume of dust filled the corner of his eye. His ears ringing from the grenade. He saw a Marine squatting behind a tree, holding his knees and rocking back and forth. In front of him was another Marine on the ground. The back of his skull missing.

"Ernest?" Samantha said.

"Sorry."

"I lost you for a minute. Everything okay?"

"Yeah. I was just thinking, death isn't an easy thing to see. I'm sorry about your mom."

"Thank you. So, what are you going to do?"

"About what?"

"Your family? The test?"

"Oh! I don't know. I'm not sure what to do. What would you do?"

"Well…I guess I'd get the test. If I was a man, I'd want to know if I was or wasn't the father. Since I'm not, I think the true father deserves to know too."

"Yeah, I guess."

"Whatever the results, the love you feel for that little girl is real." She said.

"That is one thing I'm sure about." He said.

"And I know you'll take good care of her. And of Linda."

"I'll do my best at least."

"No one can ask for more than that."

She gave him a wink and they both smiled. A customer came up with some motor oil. Ernest continued the conversation as he rang up the transaction.

"How's the story going? That'll be a dollar 37." Ernest said.

"Well, the police don't want reporters snooping around." She said.

"Thanks. Have a good one. Did the detective tell you to stay out of things too?"

"Yeah. I have a little more freedom than you do, but not much. I did hear from Jed they have the house taped off and an officer standing guard."

"I'm sure those women have other places to stay. I don't think they'll go back now that we found their hideout."

"Probably not, but I've hit a wall on this story. All we can do is wait for something else to happen."

"What are you doing in the meantime?"

"My editor has plenty of stories for me. The paper's going to have lots of stuff for Old Hallowell Day coming up."

"What's that?"

"Everyone celebrates the town. They do it every year. I think it started eight or nine years ago."

"Sounds like a day for large crowds. That'll be a big nope for me."

"It's not all that bad. I'm sure you'll be fine."

"It's been a few years since I've celebrated anything. You know I'm not great with socializing."

"We'll just have to force you into it. I need to get back to the office. Say bye to Joe for me. See you later."

"Okay. Be safe out there."

Forty-Four
July 16, 1977, 10:00 am

Ernest fought against the crowds on their way to watch the Old Hallowell Day Parade. His gait was fast enough to pass someone jogging. He found a spot clear of people and stopped. He closed his eyes and took a deep breath. With shaking hands, he lit a cigarette while keeping an envelope wedged in his armpit. He savored the smoke burning down his throat closing his eyes again. He looked at the envelope addressed to him from a medical lab in Augusta. He stuck his finger in the flap to open it then stopped. He walked on with the envelope still sealed.

The traffic was less hectic as he moved away from downtown Hallowell. He stopped and waited a few minutes before catching the attention of a taxi. He dropped his cigarette and stepped on it.

"Hey friend. Haven't seen you in a while." Harold said.

"How you doin'?" Ernest said.

"Same old. Same old. Where to?"

"The institute in Augusta."

"The nut house? Why you goin' there?"

"My wife's there."

"Hey man, I'm sorry. I didn't know. Is she gettin' help or somethin'?"

"Well, it was either go there or stay in prison."

"That's rough man, I'm sorry. I guess you're not feeling up to the festivities today."

"Not really. I'm not too good with crowds."

"I know how that is. I got a cousin who'll park six blocks away just to avoid a crowded parking lot. He says he likes walkin' though. How you holdin' up with all these mosquitoes?"

"Okay, I guess. I don't go out much."

"That's the way to do it. I'm lucky I got the A/C in the cab. I just recharged the R-12 too. It's not too cold back there, is it?"

"It's fine by me."

Harold carried on with small talk the rest of the way. Ernest didn't say much.

"Keep the change."

"Man, you tip good. Good to see ya again. Good luck with everything."

"You too. Take it easy."

Ernest stared at the entrance. He pulled out his cigarettes and stared at them. With a sigh, he returned them to his pocket and walked in. The nurse at the front desk told him where to find Linda's room. He passed a couple orderlies going down the stairs and wondered if the hospital needed help. He hadn't used much of his training since his enlistment ended.

He liked Linda's room. White walls and a wood floor. White sheets on the bed. There was a small desk and chair. Linda sat in a rocking chair facing the window. The door was open, but he knocked as he went in.

"Hey."

"Hey."

She stood and hugged him. He dropped his envelope on the bed.

"This is definitely more comfortable than prison." Ernest said.

"Anywhere is more comfortable than prison. Sit down with me." She said.

Ernest sat on the bed to face Linda in the rocking chair.

"How's the view?" He said.

"It's nothing special, but it's nice. I never see the sunrise or sunset."

"Does that mean the room doesn't get too hot?"

"They always have the air on, but I don't need blinds to

block the sun. The moon gets too bright sometimes. The shadows from the blinds in the moonlight make the window look like it has bars. That's when I remember this is just a nicer looking prison."

"The doctor said over the phone they won't be giving you any medication."

"Yeah, but I'm sure they'll change their minds after a few days. I've only had one session with the doctor, but I bet he thinks the same thing the quack form the prison thinks."

"At least you have a nicer bed and better food for now."

"Don't forget the view. It's not overwhelming or underwhelming. I'm just whelmed. Is that a word?"

"I don't know."

They both chuckled without much sound.

"What's that?" Linda said.

Ernest picked up the envelope.

"It's a…paternity…test." He said.

"You haven't opened it."

"No. I just got it today."

"Don't look so anxious. Sometimes tests are wrong. You can't always trust those labs with however they do that stuff."

"You don't want me to open it. Why?"

"I never said that. I read once that someone got some bloodwork, or something, done and the test was inconclusive because the blood was contaminated or something. It wasn't the person's fault. The lab messed up everything."

"Will you stop me from opening it?"

"Open it, but it probably won't say anything because of an error or something." She said.

"Only one way to find out."

Ernest opened the envelope and unfolded the paper. He read for a minute, flipped the paper over to the blank back, and flipped it back to the front. Linda stared out the window without interest. He looked in the empty envelope then back at the paper in his hand. His jaw was slack, mouth hanging open.

"Wha…how? 47 percent? There's a 47 percent chance I'm the father. How the hell does that work? Am I the father or not?" He said.

"I told you. You can't trust those labs. It's an error or a mistake." She said.

"I saw plenty of these in the Navy. Sailors wanting to know if they got some Asian girl pregnant. I only saw 98 percent or zero. There was never room for doubt. If there was an error, the results would say inconclusive. We'd send another sample, and those results would be fine. What the hell does 47 percent mean? I've never seen that on one of these."

Linda continued looking out the window, cheeks wet.

"There's a chance it could still be wrong, right?" She said.

"Who's the father, Linda?"

"You could have the test done again."

"Look at me."

"They say get a second opinion with doctor's, right?"

"Answer the question."

"Getting another test…"

"Linda!"

She jumped in her seat and looked at him. She covered her face and started sobbing.

"I don't know. I don't know. I don't know." She said.

Ernest knelt in front of her looking up to see her face. He put a hand on her shoulder.

"Linda. Please talk to me. What aren't you telling me? Were you with someone else when you thought I was dead?"

She wiped her face. Ernest handed her his handkerchief.

"Thank you. After the last time you were home, before they said you were dead, I don't remember how long after you left that it happened." She said.

"What happened?" He said.

"If I tell you, you won't want to be with me anymore. You'll hate me."

"Nothing you've done or could do would make me hate you. If you were with another man, I need to know."

More tears welled in her eyes.

"I didn't want to, but I was scared." She said.

"Of whom? Who scared you?"

"I was staying with your parents. One night, your dad

woke me. I don't think he wanted me to wake up. He was…he… he was…touching me. I must have screamed or something because he put his hand over my mouth. He was shushing me. He told me everything would be okay if I stayed quiet. I tried to move his hands away, tried to fight him. He slapped me so hard. I asked him to stop, I was crying. He told me to be quiet or he'd hit me again. Then he lifted my nightgown and he…he…did everything he wanted. When he was done he said he'd kill my parents if I told anyone.

"When I found out I was pregnant, I didn't know if it was his or yours. I hid the pregnancy for as long as I could. When everyone found out, your dad became very concerned about me and the baby. We heard you were dead and that's when your dad started making demands for Amy. I could tell he thought it was his. That's why I ran. I thought he'd take Amy and kill me."

Ernest stared at her. His eyes watered. His knuckles were white as his hand held the arm of the rocking chair.

"Are you mad at me?" She said.

Ernest shook his head.

"You don't hate me?"

Ernest shook his head.

"I was so afraid to tell you. I'm so sorry."

He leaned up and held her as she sobbed and mumbled into his shoulder.

"I need to go. I'll come see you again later." Ernest said.

"Where are you going?"

Ernest didn't answer and left the room.

"Ernie wait. Ernest. Ernest!"

Forty-Five
1876-1877 - Malla Skov's Journal

Sunday, July 16, 1876

Despite their misgivings, I've ignored my sisters' warnings. It's been so long since I've had real friends. For many years I've only seen my sisters. I've always avoided other people out of fear. I feel no such fear around Isabelle and Benjamin. I was cautious at first, but soon all I thought of was them. Over the Summer I devised a plan to meet them. I sent a raven with a message. I asked them to meet me by the river to the South of town. There was one clearing in the forest I always liked and wanted to show them. I invited them to lunch.

On the day, I feared maybe they didn't get the message. Or maybe they didn't want to come. But they did. We shared food and talked of books. I was on edge the whole time. I feared my sisters might find us. I asked my raven friends to distract any bullfrogs before they came near us. I was surprised how well they kept up this task. Even when I was alone, they would snatch up any frog they saw. I've never felt such loyalty from another living creature before. I decided I would continue to meet them in secret. They are my friends.

***

Wednesday, August 9, 1876

I was nearly caught today. Isabelle and Benjamin had given me a book. I was happy to read something new. Bella saw me reading.

"That's a new book. Where did you get it? Who gave it to

you? If Carla finds out…"

"I…I stole it. I'm sorry. I know I shouldn't have because it could draw attention to us, but I desperately needed something new to read. You know how much I love books." I said.

"Where did you steal it from?" Bella said.

"A man stopped near the river to refasten his horse to his wagon. I saw he had some books and apples in the wagon. When he wasn't looking, I took as much as I could carry. I'm sorry. Please don't tell Carla."

"Share an apple and I won't say a word."

"Thank you."

In truth, I had gotten the apples from Isabelle. And I had in fact seen a man fastening a horse to a wagon by the river as I returned home. I like keeping this secret from my sisters. I feel like I finally have something that I can call mine. We share everything. I don't know what it's like to have my own things.

***

Thursday, September 7, 1876

I must be more careful when I meet Isabelle and Benjamin. I found one of my raven friends this morning dead near our home. I didn't think much about it at the time. I gave a burial to return my friend to the Earth. My sisters saw me.

"What are you doing?" Carla said.

"The creature died. I returned it to the Earth as we do when all creatures die." I said.

"The birds have attacked my sweet frogs." Bella said.

"You must be joking. The only birds that eat frogs are hawks or eagles." I said.

"I suspect one of the bullfrogs ate one of the smaller ravens, perhaps a baby, and the ravens retaliated. Bella believes something more sinister is happening." Carla said.

"But don't you think it's strange? The ravens have acted oddly all year." Bella said.

"Then keep an eye on them. Both of you. If anything seems out of place, tell me at once. Do you understand?"

"Yes, sister."

"Yes." I said.

I told the ravens to leave the bullfrogs alone for a while and I decided to limit how often I would meet Isabelle and Benjamin. I don't know what I'll do, but I fear the worst if my friendship with them is discovered.

***

Monday, October 9, 1876

We've begun preparing for the Winter. It grows colder and snow will begin to fall any day now. I've spent the last couple days tasked with collecting the remaining firewood we would need to last the Winter. My sisters watch me closely. More than usual. They would burn this journal if they knew I was writing. Of this I am certain.

I have not met with Isabelle or Benjamin in several weeks. I would not be bothered if we were not going to town soon. We must obtain flour and vegetables as our gardens did not grow enough this year. Carla blames me for this. She said I spent too much time reading instead of tending to the gardens. I fear my friends may try to speak with me while my sisters and I are in town. We need nothing from the Butcher's so perhaps we can avoid any awkwardness or arguments.

I've realized my friends the ravens will become easier to see in the snow. They do not migrate in the Winter, and while I enjoy their company, I fear my sisters will learn of their alliance with me. I was kind to them, and they repay that kindness with loyalty. I do not wish to lose that trust. I will have to think of something, but tonight my exhaustion overwhelms me, and I must sleep.

***

Friday, October 27, 1876

I suppose I should be grateful how things turned out. All anyone will think is my sisters are overprotective and rude. We went to town yesterday for everything we would need to survive the Winter. I was tasked with getting flour and more thread and new needles. I was surprised neither of my sisters accompanied me. I was almost on my way back when I saw Benjamin.

"Fancy seeing you in town, Miss Malla." He said.

"Benjamin, hello. Are you not working today?" I said.

"I'm getting more parchment for my father. He gave me a reprieve from the meat cutting."

"Lucky you."

"Indeed. Are you enjoying the book we gave you?"

"I finished it then read it twice more."

"Really? Three times?"

"I'm just happy to have something new to read."

"We are always happy to send more books your way."

"Thank you. I should be going."

"Will you be coming to town again before Winter forces us all indoors?"

"No, I'm sorry."

"Isabelle will be sad, but we look forward to seeing you in the Spring."

"Malla!"

Carla was calling me.

"I'm sorry, I must go." I said.

"Tell me you weren't fraternizing again." Carla said.

"He was being polite. That's all."

"Have you been sneaking around with this man?"

"Of course not."

"Do you wish to bed with him?"

"No. What's wrong with you?"

"If I learn of any secret rendezvous, I will put an end to him. You know how men can be. You know they only want one thing from girls like you."

"And what kind of girl am I?"

"I'm trying to protect you, little sister. From others and from yourself."

"Job well done, Carla. The world will never know I existed."

"Promise me you won't see that man again."

"He was only a polite man with whom I crossed paths."

"He seemed familiar with you."

"He mistook me for someone else. I promise I won't see him again.

"For his sake, I hope not."

I suspect Carla didn't believe me. And I know Bella will take her side because she always does. I have until the Spring to sort this out. I want to part ways with Isabelle and Benjamin properly. I don't want to cause them any pain.

***

Sunday, April 1, 1877

There is still a lot of snow on the ground though it's getting a bit warmer. We no longer fear the roof collapsing from the weight of the snow. Every day my thoughts drift towards Isabelle and Benjamin. The only thing I can think of to ensure their safety is to tell them to stay away from me. The roads and walking paths have cleared enough to be safe, and I dared to travel to town alone. I left early before sunrise and before my sisters woke. I do this often so they wouldn't find it peculiar, especially now that some of the snow has melted.

I've never traveled to town without my sisters. I can't recall the last time I went anywhere without them. I hadn't even the chance to write in this journal for months because of being cooped up with them in our home. Traveling to town alone was both terrifying and thrilling. When I wasn't worrying of my sisters catching me, the walk was peaceful. I had chosen to speak to Isabelle or Benjamin in person. I couldn't only send a note and expect them to stay away.

The town was lively when I arrived. And I was fortunate to find both of them at their father's butcher shop.

"Malla! It's so good to see you. I hope the Winter was kind to you." Isabelle said.

"I wonder if I might speak to you both." I said.

"Of course."

"I think it would be best if we didn't speak to each other anymore."

"That's ridiculous. For what reason?" Benjamin said.

"My sisters are overprotective, and they think there is some kind of secret romance between you and I."

"That's absurd." Isabelle said.

"I know. And I've spent all Winter trying to decide what to do. I think this is the best course of action."

"I understand if they feel you and I are too familiar, but Isabelle shouldn't have to suffer the loss of your friendship." Benjamin said.

"It's more complicated than that."

"I do enjoy your company. Perhaps if we speak to them, they will understand." Isabelle said.

"That won't work. They won't listen. They already believe I'm hiding things from them. I'm afraid they might do something. They might try to hurt you to keep you away from me."

"Well, let them come."

"Benjamin?" Isabelle said.

"I won't stand by and let someone tell my sister with whom she can or can't be acquainted. We will remain your friends. And if we see you in town with your sisters, we will say hello."

"Please. For your sake, let this be. Don't make this more painful than it needs to be."

I walked away before they could speak. I felt I was betraying them. They had been so kind. They didn't deserve this. But I had to protect them.

***

Thursday, May 24, 1877

Benjamin is dead. That's not even the worst news of the day. I wouldn't have known if Bella hadn't blurted it out.

"Reading the book you got from your little friends again?" Bella said.

"What do you want Bella?" I said.

"You shouldn't have gotten close to him."

"To whom?"

"Your secret love."

"I told you I'm not acquainted with anyone. Oh, it doesn't matter now. I told them to stay away from me. You should be happy."

"Them?"

"Yes. Isabelle and her brother Benjamin."

"I don't know about this Isabelle, but Benjamin, as you call him, was sneaking around the forest yesterday."

"What?"

"He was looking for you but found Carla instead. She sent him away and made sure he won't come back."

"What did she do? Where is she?"

"She's seeing to other matters. You know we're leaving in a few months. That's why you shouldn't have asked your suitor to meet you."

"I didn't. I told him to stay away from me. I told them both. I don't know why he was here. Please tell me Carla didn't hurt him."

"Why do you care about this stranger so much?"

"He was kind to me. He doesn't deserve to be punished for kindness."

"Kindness is a weakness."

"Then why are you kind to your frogs?"

She didn't answer.

"Where is our sister?" I said.

"At this moment, I don't know. She left for town this morning but should have been back by now." Bella said.

"I'm going to find her."

"You'll leave me here alone?"

"You have your frogs."

I ran off before she could argue more. It was a long walk, and I feared the worst. I kept imagining different possibilities. The Sun was setting when I finally got to town. There was commotion in one of the streets. A crowd of people all talking or shouting. A man stood over them.

"Everyone quiet down please. Quiet! The doctor's diagnosis says the young man died from Scarlet Fever. An affliction that usually affects young children. Those afflicted are usually ill for several days, however this young man was in good health yesterday."

"Witchcraft!" Another man said.

This made the crowd angry. There was more shouting. A raven appeared near me and croaked. There were many ravens on buildings and tree branches. Then I saw the bullfrogs filling the street. The raven croaked again. Other people noticed the animals and started screaming. More people were shouting witchcraft. I saw Carla shouting at me. I ran to her.

"What have you done?" I said.

"What I had to, to keep you safe. No one will take you from me." Carla said.

"This. This isn't safe."

"That's why we must go."

"Did you kill Benjamin?"

"We don't have time for this."

"Answer me!"

"The man in the crowd was talking about Benjamin. He died from Scarlet Fever. There's nothing unusual about people dying from illness."

"I hate you."

"We can talk about this on the way home."

Someone shouted over the crowd and noise.

"There are women who live outside of town. They have no husbands, brothers, or children. It must have been them. They seduced my poor boy." The man said.

"Run before they see us." Carla said.

We didn't speak the whole way home. I cried and am still crying. I barely knew him, but I never wanted him to die. He was kind. I've never known such kindness from another person.

Forty-Six
July 16, 1977, 12:00 pm

Ernest had walked for over an hour. His fists had stopped shaking. His breathing was normal. He approached the motel his parents had stayed for the past month. He saw their rental car, a brown Chevy Nova. Next to it was a yellow Plymouth Satellite. It looked like Linda's parents' rental car. He stared at the cars and lit a cigarette. He didn't move for several minutes lost in thought. He took one final long drag from the cigarette and flicked it on the ground.

"Fuck it."

He moved with purpose at a fast pace. He startled a cleaning woman as he swept past her. The door was open to his parents' room. Voices floated outside. Linda's parents were here. Ernest knocked on the door. Everyone turned to him as he entered.

"Ernest? Is something wrong?" Gail said.

He ignored the question, walked past her towards his father and punched him. His father staggered back catching himself on the wall by the window with wide eyes clamping his jaw.

"Ernest!"

"What the Hell are you doing!?" Robert said.

His mother stepped between them with arms out.

"What's gotten into you?" Gail said.

"You bastard! This whole damn time you've been the problem." Ernest said.

"You're not making sense, Ernie."

"Shut up! Everything that happened with Linda is because

of you! Do they know what you did? Are you gonna tell them, or should I?"

"Tell them what?"

"What you did to Linda."

"I don't know what you're talking about. Whatever she told you…"

"I got a paternity test. I'm not Amy's father. Linda said you are."

Gail covered her mouth with both hands. Fear shook in her eyes. She looked at her husband.

"Robert? Is it true? Tell me you didn't sleep with Linda."

"He raped her!" Ernest said.

"Are you actually listening to this? You're gonna believe some whore our son married."

Gail slapped him in the same place Ernest had punched him. He covered his face eyes wide again. Everyone was silent. Ernest's fists were shaking. Linda's parents stood pale, with blank expressions, like mannequins in a department store. Gail fought back tears pushing through the quiver in her voice.

"Is it - is it true, Robert? D-did you rape her?"

"I didn't rape anyone."

"Horseshit!" Ernest said.

"I didn't!"

"Then explain the paternity test."

"I…she…she didn't tell me to stop."

"Oh, God, Robert!" Gail said.

"It wasn't rape!"

"You still had sex with your son's wife you sick devil!" Beatrice said.

"We thought Ernie was dead."

"Linda said it happened right after I left for deployment three years ago. That's why the timing seemed right when she was pregnant. And maybe she didn't tell you to stop, but that doesn't mean she wanted it."

"She's obviously lying to you. You didn't see the way she looked at me after you left. She was lonely and she wanted me because you couldn't satisfy her. A son of mine should know how to keep a woman happy."

Gail slapped Robert repeatedly in the face, chest, and shoulder. The large man cowered away from his small wife.

"You don't know anything about keeping a woman happy, you bastard! I hate you! How could you do this to our family!?"

Ernest held a small smile while his mother hit and shouted at his father. Herbert pulled Gail away getting Ernest to hold her back.

"Thank you, Herb. We men have to stick together." Robert said.

Herbert spun around throwing all his strength and body weight into one punch. Robert fell back into the wall a second time.

"Beatrice. Gail is staying with us for a while. And I don't care if you're angry I didn't discuss it with you first. I'm putting my foot down. And that's how it is." Herbert said.

"Oh, you handsome idiot, I'm not angry at all."

She kissed him surprising him and almost knocking him over.

"I didn't think he had it in him." Ernest said.

"Neither did I." Gail said.

"What do we do about him?"

"Leave him here. I'll get my things. Herb and Beatrice's room is on the other side of the motel."

They all ignored Robert's protests. He shouted at them but never got up from the floor.

"I'll help carry your things over." Ernest said.

"Thank you, sweetie. We'll sort all this out." Gail said.

"I know momma."

Ernest carried Gail's two large suitcases across the motel. He set them on the floor in Herb and Beatrice's room before falling into the chair by the door.

"These things are heavier than my Navy duffel bag. How much did you bring?" Ernest said.

"Stop being dramatic. You're not even breathing hard." Gail said.

"There's not much for closet space, but you'll have the

second bed all to yourself." Herbert said.

"I can manage. Thank you again."

"I think you surprised everyone today, Herb." Ernest said.

"I surprised myself. I'm still a little wound up after all that."

"Well here, have a seat. I'm not that tired."

"Thank you, but I need to move around a bit. Um. So, now that we all know – what we know, what's to become of Amy?"

Ernest remained seated and stared at the floor. Gail absently played with her necklace with closed eyes. Water welled up under the lids. Beatrice whimpered in the bathroom with her face in her hands. Herb moved in silence picking up things around the room and moving them around.

"Amy should be with her mother. And since Linda is my wife, she'll stay with me until Linda is able to come home." Ernest said.

"What about your father?" Gail said.

"That son of bitch will never see her again. I like it in Maine. I think Linda, Amy, and I could make a life here."

"Are you sure that's what you want? I'll support any decision you make. I just want to know you're doing what's best for you."

"I spent months searching for my family. Now that I have them, I'm not giving them up. As far as I'm concerned, Amy is and always will be my daughter."

"You've made up your mind, then?" Herb said.

"I had a lot of time to think on my way over here. This is what I want."

"Well, let us know if you ever need anything. Bea and I will do whatever we can."

"Thanks, Herb. I need to get back and get Amy from the sitter. Hopefully the streets are clear now."

"I can drive you. Bea didn't you want to see what all the festivities were about?"

Beatrice wiped her face and cleared her throat before facing everyone.

"Sure. Let's go." She said.

They all filled the Plymouth and made their way downtown. They parked and walked to the front of Ernest's building. He stopped. His eyes fixed on something across the street.

"Ernest? Is something wrong?" Gail said.

A bus passed. The three sisters stood across the street staring back at Ernest. The brunette waved at him with a smile. The redhead held a grimace on her face leering at him. The blonde looked away, her hair hiding her face. Several cars passed and the three sisters disappeared. Several bullfrogs stood in their place watching flying bugs.

"Do you know those girls, Ernest?" Gail said.

"We need to get inside." He said.

Ernest ran to his room before anyone could ask anything. He found Amy and the babysitter playing. He walked through checking everything, the closet, the bathroom, and under the bed. Everyone had caught up by then.

"What's the matter, Ernest?" Gail said.

"Probably nothing."

He looked out the window and the three sisters stared back. Bullfrogs at their feet.

"Did anyone come by while I was gone?" Ernest said.

"No. It's just been me and Amy." The sitter said.

He looked out the window again. The sisters and bullfrogs were gone.

"Mom. Herb. Beatrice. I need a favor." Ernest said.

"What do you need?" Gail said.

"Take Amy back to California. Leave today if you can."

"What? Why? Are you sure?"

"It might be nothing. Maybe I'm being paranoid. Just keep her safe."

"Does this have to do with those girls outside?"

"Maybe. I'm not sure. But if I'm right, they might come after me. They might come after Amy."

"Why don't you come home with us?"

"I won't leave Linda behind. I know a detective in town. I'll go talk to him and figure out how to keep myself safe, but it's best for Amy not to be anywhere near here. Please."

"Of course. Young lady, would you mind helping us pack her things?"

"Yeah, sure." The sitter said.

"Call me when you all get home." Ernest said.

"Where are you going?" Gail said.

"To find the detective."

Forty-Seven
July 16, 1977, 1:00 pm

Ernest arrived at the sheriff's office. He reached for the door and noticed his hand shaking. He pulled his hand away and took out his cigarettes. The first drag was a long one. He took his time exhaling the smoke. He closed his eyes and kept taking long, slow breaths. A car backfiring startled him, and he dropped his cigarette.

"God dammit!"

He picked it up taking another long drag. He rubbed the bridge of his nose between his eyes. He took one more drag then dropped the cigarette twisting it with his shoe. He went inside to the reception desk.

"Can I speak with Detective Vaughn, please?" Ernest said.

"I believe he's out of the office. Let me double check." The deputy said.

He dialed a number and rested his elbow on the desk listening to the receiver. After about a minute he replaced the receiver in its cradle.

"Sorry. He's still out."

"Do you know when he'll be back?"

"What's this about, sir?"

"I have information that might pertain to an ongoing investigation."

"I can take a statement if you…"

"That's okay. Is Deputy Wells around? Jed Wells?"

"I'm afraid he's off for the week. He always goes camping

this time of year. If you'd like to leave your statement and…"

"No, thank you. I'll try calling Detective Vaughn a little later."

Ernest sped out of the building.

"Fuck. Fuck. Fuck."

Without thinking, he raced down the road on foot. He walked for about fifteen minutes before spotting a taxi. He waved them down. He'd never seen the driver before.

"Do you know where the Kennebec Journal office is?" Ernest said.

"The paper? Ayuh, hop in."

"Thanks."

The ride was quiet and uneventful. When the taxi stopped, Ernest gave the driver twenty dollars.

"Can you stick around for a bit? I'm not sure if my friend is there, I might have to go somewhere else." Ernest said.

"Ayuh! I'll wait all day if you need it."

"Thanks."

Ernest ran in then ran out within less than a minute. He jumped back in the cab and gave the driver Samantha's address. After another uneventful five minutes, Ernest was ringing the doorbell at Samantha's house. He waited. He didn't hear anything on the other side of the door. He tried the doorbell again then knocked. Nothing happened. He tried looking through the front windows, but the curtains were drawn. He walked back to the taxi.

"Wanna try another place?" The driver said.

"I think I'll just wait here until they get home. You can keep the change."

"Hey thanks. You take care now."

"You too."

Ernest paced on the porch and smoked several cigarettes for 20 minutes before Samantha's car pulled in the driveway.

"Finally!"

"Hey Ernie. Everything okay?" She said.

"No. I tried to talk to Detective Vaughn, but he wasn't in his office. I guess Jed's camping and you weren't at your office, so I waited till you got home."

"How long have you been here?"

"Maybe 20, 25 minutes.

"Sorry to make you wait. What's going on?"

She opened her trunk and picked up paper bags of groceries. Without being asked, Ernest picked up a couple bags and followed her inside as he spoke.

"I saw them again. Outside my place. They were grinning like some kids who got away with a prank. I don't know what they did."

"Whoa! Slow down. Who'd you see?"

"Those sisters. I thought they did something to Amy, but she was fine."

"Where's Amy now?"

"She's with my mother and Linda's parents. I told them to take her back to California."

"I thought you didn't want them around her." She said.

"It's a long story. My father's a bastard. I'll tell you about it later. I don't know what to do. How did they find me? How'd they know about Amy? Have you seen them anywhere?" He said.

"Okay, take a breath and sit down. I'll make some coffee. I haven't seen them, and we don't know if they're coming after Amy. She'll be safe if she's on the other side of the country, right?"

"Yeah, right, that's why I told my mother to take her."

"Okay. Let's think things through and we'll figure this all out."

"Oh God, why did I leave them? What if something happened while I've been gone?"

"I'm sure they're all fine."

"Those women could take Amy and there's nothing I can do. I won't be able to save her. I can't save anyone."

***

Ernest sees a dead Marine to his left. Samantha's kitchen is gone. He's back in the jungle. He's on the ground panting, eyes wide, looking everywhere and nowhere. In front of him is a screaming Marine, blood and dirt covers his face. The Marine's left leg is missing. Dozens of bodies lay around him. One body is trying to crawl away. The others lay motionless. Ernest's ears are

272

ringing. He rocks his upper body back and forth trying not to look at anything. He stares at his knees. Someone taps his cheek hard a couple times. Their voice is muffled.

"Hey? Hey!? Snap out of it! That Marine's gonna die if you don't stop his leg from bleeding out! Get over there and do your goddamn job! If he dies, that's on you!"

"I can't!" Ernest says.

"Bullshit! You're the only one here who can! Or are you some chickenshit hippie!?"

"I can't save everyone!"

"No shit! But you can save one! Just like one shot, one kill! One medic, one saved! Say it!"

"One medic…one saved!"

"Say it again! Louder!"

"One medic, one saved!"

"Again!"

"One medic, one saved!"

"Now get over there and save his ass!"

The jungle fades away. Ernest is back in Samantha's kitchen.

***

"Ernest? Ernest, are you here?" Samantha said.

She set a coffee mug in front of him.

"One medic, one saved." Ernest said.

"What?"

"Sorry. I was just thinking of something my old Gunnery Sergeant said. I can't save everyone, but I can save my daughter."

"Okay. We'll sort this out."

"Yeah. Can I use your phone to check on Amy?"

"Of course."

Samantha busied herself with putting groceries away. The call with his mother was short. He returned to the kitchen after.

"Everything okay?" She said.

"Yeah. She sent the babysitter home. They have Amy at Linda's parents' motel room." He said.

"What's the plan?"

"I'll head back. Make sure everything is safe until they

leave."

"Let me finish up here and I'll give you a ride."

"I'll help. Just tell me where things go."

"I don't know about you, but I keep my milk in the fridge."

"Okay, but what shelf do you want it on? Some people are picky about their kitchen."

"Are you saying that because I'm a woman?"

"No! I'm saying that because I'm picky about my kitchen."

"Okay. Milk goes on the top shelf."

"Okay."

They finished and left without saying much.

"Do you mind if I smoke?" Ernest said.

"You ask every time you're in my car. And every time I say yes, just crack a window." She said.

"Just because you were okay with it once doesn't mean you always will be."

"Fair point. But from this day forward, you never have to ask to smoke in my car. My house is another story."

"Yes, ma'am."

The remainder of the drive was uneventful. Samantha parked her car and Ernest opened the passenger side door. He paused before getting out.

"Thank you." He said.

"I don't mind giving you a ride." She said.

"No, I mean for bringing me back to reality when I was getting too…excited."

"That's what friends do. They sing you your song when you've forgotten the words."

"I like that. That's a good way to put it. I'll see you around."

"Give me a call when your family leaves. Let me know they made it out okay."

"Yeah. I will. Thanks again."

Forty-Eight
July 16, 1977, 2:30 pm - Samantha

I left for home after that. I drove a couple blocks and then I saw a flock of birds flying along the street. I had never seen so many birds together flying that close to the ground. They turned and disappeared between two buildings. I slowed to a stop to look down that alley. One of the Skov sisters, the blonde, stood there and stared at me. The birds stood all around the alley, perched on buildings and trash cans. I parked and walked over. The birds and the woman were still there. I approached her. As I got closer, I realized all the birds were ravens. They croaked at me as I passed.

"That's far enough." The woman said.

"Your name is Skov, isn't it?" I said.

"My name is not important. I bring you a warning. The man you were with at our home in the woods. My sisters want his child. He must take the child and leave."

"So, you are the ones killing children?"

"I take no pleasure in these acts. I wish to stop, but I can't stop my sisters. They are stronger."

"If you come with me, we can stop them."

"No! We are cursed. Stay far from me. If that man's child is gone, they will find another. There is still time before the next lunar eclipse. I can't save every child, but I can save his."

"If you tell me where to find your sisters, we can stop them before they harm anyone else."

"I've told you too much already. They're always watching."

"Don't leave. Your name is Malla Skov, isn't it? I've read

your journal."

The woman paused for a moment, half-turned away.

"Beware the bullfrogs." She said.

"Please wait." I said.

I tried to follow but the ravens took flight. A tornado of black birds surrounded me for a short time then they all scattered into the sky. There was no raven in sight. I ran to the end of the alley. I looked every direction but didn't see the Skov woman anywhere.

I returned to my car. I looked across the street and saw several bullfrogs watching me. They didn't move or break their gaze as people stepped around them. I drove away. In the side mirror, I saw the bullfrogs had turned to watch me leave.

Forty-Nine
August 1977

August 5

Ernest and Samantha walked down the hall in the Sheriff's station. When they got to Detective Vaughn's office, Jed was waiting inside. Detective Vaughn was on the phone. He waved them inside before Ernest could knock.

"Yes, sir. Thank you." Detective Vaughn said.

He returned the receiver to its cradle.

"Thank you all for coming. Before we begin, does anyone have any new information since we last met?"

No one spoke.

"Okay. Miss Belcher informed me that the next eclipse is about six weeks away, is that correct?"

"Yes. The night of September 26." Samantha said.

"That gives us some time to prepare. We are taking every precaution to keep the children safe, but we can't guarantee someone won't be abducted. If they follow the same pattern as the last two murders, they won't take anyone until a few days before the eclipse. It is possible they've already chosen a target.

"Mister Kemp, though we have not confirmed whether you or your daughter are targets, we are assuming you both are. The Hallowell and Augusta police are cooperating with us, and we will have an officer or deputy outside your place each night until this is all over. Just as a precaution we'll have someone watching Miss Belcher's place as well. You said you daughter is currently with your mother in California, is that correct?"

"Yes, sir." Ernest said.

"That's probably the safest place for her. I see no reason to worry for her safety if she's on the opposite coast. That should also satisfy the warning Miss Belcher received. Am I correct in assuming this woman has not made another attempt to contact you?"

"No attempts I'm aware of." Samantha said.

"Good. If she attempts to contact you, or if any of you see them somewhere, do not approach them or speak to them. Do not try to detain them or restrain them. Call the police and file a report. Deputy Wells, you're to call for backup. Do not attempt to arrest them alone. If any of you fails to follow my instructions, I'll have you arrested for obstructing a police investigation. Does everyone understand?"

"Yes, sir."

"Yes."

"Yes."

"Okay. That's all I have for now. I'll be in touch. Thank you all for your time."

***

Ernest held the phone receiver between his ear and shoulder while folding clothes.

"No mom. Linda is fine with you watching Amy." He said.

"You're sure?" Gail said.

"Yes. I explained everything. Herb and Beatrice visited her before you all left. Linda's been doing a lot better. They don't even give her medication."

"Does that mean she'll be getting out soon?"

"I haven't heard anything yet. She has a review or evaluation or something next month. They might decide what to do at that time."

"Well, I'm glad she's doing better. I'll bet she misses her baby girl."

"Yeah, we both do. Amy probably doesn't really understand what's happening, but I wish Linda and I could be with her on her birthday."

"You just be sure to call us on the 28th, okay? And see if

Linda is allowed to make a call."

"Yes ma'am."

"So, Ernest have you heard anything new about those occultists?"

"What? What occultists?"

"You know. The ones who make the sacrifices. The ones you think are after Amy."

"Mom, you don't have to whisper. Amy doesn't know what you're saying."

"Children are like sponges at this age. She can't hear about these inappropriate things. Now what's going on? Are you safe?"

"Yes, mom, I'm safe. The police are taking every precaution and handling everything. They even have a patrol car watching my place around the clock."

"That makes me feel better. It's about time those police did something useful for a change. How many times were you wrongfully arrested?"

"I wasn't arrested, mom. They took me in for questioning. I was never charged with anything."

"It was still a poor job on their part. I mean, you were a medic, you saved lives."

Ernest glanced at the drawer that hid his revolver.

"Not always." Ernest said.

"I'm sorry, honey, can you say that again? Amy's crying. I think she needs a diaper change."

"Um, it's nothing, never mind. I'll let you go so you can change her. I'll call you in a couple days."

"Okay, sweetie. You be safe. I love you."

"You too."

Ernest dropped the receiver on the cradle with a loud ring. He rubbed his face and took a couple deep breaths. He reached for his cigarettes on the nightstand and found the pack empty.

"Dammit."

***

August 17

"None of you have seen them anywhere? Or heard other people talk about them?"

279

Detective Vaughn surveyed everyone in his office. Everyone shook their heads.

"They must have realized we're looking for them. They're probably laying low, or they left town." Jed said.

"I don't think they left town. We may have located where they murder the children for their rituals. We found samples of blood that match both victims where the second victim was found. I suspect they'll use this same clearing in the woods for the next eclipse. I'm hoping to find them before that happens."

"What do we do in the meantime?" Samantha said.

"Stay quiet and keep searching. And don't report anything! I don't want these occultists getting wise to our plans. You can publish after their caught. Something wrong Mister Kemp?"

"Hmm? No. I've just been hearing that word a lot lately." Ernest said.

"What word?"

"Occultists."

"Something about it bother you?"

"No."

"Well, it should. Satan worshiping nut jobs should bother any normal person." Detective Vaughn said.

"What do we do if a child is reported missing?" Samantha said.

"We know where they'll be going. We'll set up a stake out and wait for them. We'll stop them before they have any time to harm the child."

"And what if they realize you're there and do it somewhere else?" Ernest said.

"It's a possibility but we'll cross that bridge when we get to it. If you don't like that plan, you better hope we find them before the eclipse."

Ernest and the Detective stared at each other for a moment.

"I hope you do." Ernest said.

"That's all I have for now. Let's meet this same time next week. Thank you for your time." Detective Vaughn said.

***

August 28

"Hey, mom. Is this a good time?" Ernest said.

"Well, hello! Your daughter is covered in pink and yellow frosting. It looks like a wild animal attacked the cake."

"Does that mean it's a bad time?"

"Oh, no, I'm sorry. Beatrice is going to get Amy cleaned up. What's that? It's Ernest. Okay. Herb says hello."

"Hi Herb."

"He says hi Herb."

"Everything going well?" Ernest said.

"Yeah, everything's okay. Nothing too eventful. How are things on your end?"

"The same, I guess. Nothing new. I'm working and get followed around by police. I'm living the dream."

"They haven't found those psychos yet?"

"Not yet. They're probably hiding somewhere with so many police around."

"Maybe, but you'd think they'd have found something by now with all those officers running around. I'll bet half of them just sit on their tail all day. You know, I was talking with Susan from down the street the other day…"

"Here we go."

Ernest rested the receiver on his shoulder. His mother's voice was clear despite covering the earpiece.

"…and her sister is married to a cop, and she says he's the laziest man she's ever seen. He has a big belly and eats too many sweets. Don't the police have standards for physical fitness like the military? I think it's more about character though because you still look fit but you're not in the military anymore."

"Okay, mom. Is Beatrice still cleaning up Amy?"

"Oh, hold on I'll go check."

There was a clatter on the other end of the line then silence. Ernest rubbed the bridge of his nose before getting some aspirin and swallowing the pills dry. He closed his eyes and took a deep breath. There was another clatter over the phone.

"Okay, here she is. The birthday girl. Say hi to da da. Can

you say da da?"

"Hi Amy. How's my girl doing?"

"Hi."

Ernest smiled to himself.

"You wanna talk to daddy? Oh, she pushed the phone away. She's staring at the cake on the counter." Gail said.

"Well, I didn't expect her to have much to say."

Wines and screeches pierced through the phone receiver.

"She's being fussy again. Bea, can you take her?" Gail said.

"Has Linda called yet? They said they'd let her use one of the payphones at the hospital."

"She did. We, uh, we got to talk for a while. I owed her a big apology for everything. She was excited to listen to Amy's gibberish."

"I'm glad she got to talk with everyone. I think that'll help."

"She definitely sounded like she was doing better. Hopefully we can get our little family reunited soon."

"Yeah, hopefully. Well, I'll let you go. I got some stuff to take care of. I'll talk to you later. Say bye to everyone for me."

"Okay, dear. Well Herb got one of those new polaroid cameras, so we'll have lots of pictures to show you from today, okay?"

"Thanks mom, bye."

"Goodbye, Ernie. Take care of yourself."

Ernest put the phone down. He laid down on his bed and took a deep breath dropping an arm over his eyes.

Fifty
1877 - Malla Skov's Journal

Wednesday, May 30, 1877

Everything has fallen apart. We've had to travel to different towns where no one knows who we are. We make longer trips to other towns only when needed. We never go to the same town twice. Word is spreading of Benjamin's death. Carla said other townsfolk are looking for us. No one knows what we look like, but our names are in the papers. Living deep in the forest has kept us safe thus far. I expect they'll find us soon. I barely speak to my sisters now.

Shortly after Benjamin's death, all I did was scream at them.

"Why would you do this!? He wasn't a threat." I said.

"He was manipulating you. If he had not become ill, he would have forced you into marriage and forced you to carry his child." Carla said.

"He never made advances towards me! He thought his sister was lonely! He wanted me to be her friend!"

"More manipulation. How can you still be so naïve after everything we've been through?"

"How can you still be so angry after all these years!? Just because you were fooled by some man doesn't mean I will be! You're the one who brought this curse on us, not me!"

Carla slapped me for that. Tears grew in her eyes.

"How dare you? You do not get to blame me for putting our lives in danger this time. We cannot return to that town because of you. Never speak to me of this again." She said.

She stomped out of the room. Bella stood still in shock. All I could do was sob on the floor. Was wanting companionship such a sin? Why wouldn't Carla admit to harming Benjamin? All she said was he became ill. She was far too pleased with herself for it to be just an illness. Bella tried to comfort me, but I pushed her away. I know she helped Carla without question like she always had.

I didn't speak but I did as I was told. I did my chores and read to pass the time. For the first time that I can remember they didn't scold me as long as my chores were finished. It felt like they were nicer to me than ever before. The last few weeks they haven't allowed me to leave our home. For my safety they say. The townsfolk are screaming witchcraft and many of them would recognize me from talking with Benjamin and Isabelle. I think my sisters just lack trust in me. I don't have the energy to argue anymore.

***

Friday, June 8, 1877

My sisters are always around. Since they won't allow me to leave the house, it's been difficult to write in my journal unnoticed. I used to go out by the river on warm days and write. I'd see my raven friends and sometimes read. Now I'm a prisoner. I was only able to write today because Carla and Bella went to another town. I'm not sure which one, but they said they'd be gone most of the day. Perhaps we all needed some time away from each other.

I've continued my silence. I never realized how much they both talk. I wonder if they dislike the silence. Bella has scolded me several times for not speaking. To my surprise and Bella's, Carla always defends me.

"Leave her be. She'll speak when she's ready."

I must be a fool for thinking this, but she appears nicer. She no longer demands things from me, but simply asks me to do things. I would do them either way to avoid conflict, but it's nice to be asked as opposed to ordered. At first, I thought they were giving me space because I was grieving the loss of my friends, but Carla continues to be polite. If memory serves, something like this happened once before. I don't recall the details, but the politeness of Carla's was short lived. I expect she'll be back to her old cruel self in a month's time.

***

Monday, June 18, 1877

Carla and Bella have gone to another town. They never tell me where they're going. For all I know, they could have continued going to Hallowell all this time. Although, once Bella did tell me they went to Manchester, but I don't recall when.

Since his death, I have found it difficult to read, or even look at, the book Benjamin gave to me. I should return it to Isabelle but I'm not sure how or when. They were both so kind and all these terrible things happened because of me. I expect she'll never forgive me. I should try to return the book to her. It's the proper thing to do.

I find myself taking on the chores that are more consuming, so I have little time to read anymore. I have found solace in sewing and knitting. Most of the time I'm mending clothes, but now and then I'll build a new dress or knit a blanket. I'm part way through with making a quilt for myself. Bella isn't happy about it because she has to pick up my work in the garden. She thinks I should focus on all my chores before anything else. Carla is still playing nice and tells Bella to leave me be.

That is how it's been for several weeks. I stay quiet, Bella complains about something, and Carla tells her to stop. Our time away from each other is more pleasant than I expected. I'm sitting outside near the garden and all I hear are the birds and the wind. It's so peaceful. I wish this would never end. Without days like this, I would never be able to manage being trapped in my home. I'm almost afraid to ask my sisters how things are in town. Are people still looking for us?

***

Wednesday, June 27, 1877

Carla was acting very strange this morning. It was still early when she came and woke me.

"Wake up Malla. Malla?" She said.

"What? It's barely twilight. Why are you waking me? And

285

why are you already dressed?" I said.

"I have some matters to attend to. Before I go, I need you to answer something?"

"What? What's the matter?"

"You've been home more than Bella and I."

"You told me not to leave."

"Yes, I know. In all that time, has anyone come around? Have you seen anyone in the forest?"

"No. Of course not. No one knows where we are."

"You're certain? You're not keeping anything from me?"

"Why don't you just tell me you don't trust me?"

"I'm not trying to argue with you Malla, please answer."

There was something urgent and fearful in her eyes. I'd never seen her like that.

"No. I swear I haven't seen anyone. What's this about?"

"It could be nothing. I'll be away most of the day. Bella will go into town today to gather some supplies. If you see anyone in the forest, do not speak to them and hide. Do you understand?"

"Yes, but why?"

"So, you are safe. I need to know you'll be safe. Please?"

"I will."

"That's a good girl. I'm off. Oh, and…I told Bella not to pick any fights with you while I'm gone. Please do the same with her."

I nodded and she left. It was such a strange exchange. Bella left for town sometime later. There is something strange in the air, but I cannot place it. The birds are quiet today. I don't think I've ever noticed the forest this quiet. I never thought I'd feel this way, but I hope my sisters return soon.

***

Thursday, July 12, 1877

So much has happened. I'm not sure where to begin. Over the last couple weeks, Carla grew more paranoid. She would run outside and search around the house. Once she claimed she heard a noise, but Bella and I never heard anything. It seemed her fears were unwarranted.

After a few days of her strange behavior, we confronted

286

Carla. We wanted her to tell us what was going on.

"I've seen men in the woods. I believe they're looking for us." She said.

"Why would they still be searching for us after all this time?" Bella said.

"I've only been back to town a few times. Mostly to get the newspaper. There have been several infant deaths from fever and a two men went missing a couple weeks ago. The townsfolk are blaming witchcraft and they're looking for us."

"I wonder why they'd accuse us of giving children fevers." I said.

Carla noticed my tone but ignored me. She's been very good about avoiding arguments lately.

"We might need to leave sooner than planned." Carla said.

"How soon?" I said.

"By the end of the month, I suspect."

"We don't have enough supplies to make a trip like that." Bella said.

"And we'll have plenty of time before Winter to get them once we make our way North. This is no different than what we did for the last cycle. We're just doing it sooner. I don't trust these men so be ready to leave at a moment's notice. Each of you have a bag ready in case we must leave in a hurry. Do you understand?"

We nodded and that was the end of the conversation. Carla would never tell us more. I supposed she could have told Bella more in private, but I don't think she did. That was a few days ago. We were preparing for bed tonight when we heard gunfire. We all heard the single shot.

"Ready your things. Malla put out the candles. Wait for me." Carla said.

She ran into the forest and disappeared into the night. Bella and I sat waiting in silence. The cicadas starting buzzing again not long after the shot. Fireflies floated in the darkness. Far from us, flames from torches danced between the trees. There were too many for it to be a lost hunter. Bella and I looked at one another but didn't speak. Something was running towards us. Leaves were rustling and twigs were breaking. Carla burst from the darkness.

"We have to go. They're here. We have to go now." Carla said.

We scrambled for our remaining things and trotted North away from the torch flames to the West. I don't know how long we had been walking when my foot caught on a tree root, and I fell forward. My bag flying at Bella. She came to help me up and Carla gathered my things.

"Perhaps this isn't the best time to be clumsy." Bella said.

If it hadn't been so dark, she would have seen the scowl on my face. Carla held my things and was looking at this journal.

"I thought you got rid of this." She said.

"I never said I did."

"Your clumsiness proves that anyone can get their hands on this."

"I've told you none of our secrets are in there. It's mostly trivial things like what I did each day. It was something to talk to that wasn't one of you." I said.

"Is that how you feel about us? Get rid of it. We can't have anything linking us back to this town. Do you understand?"

"But why –"

"Malla, please! Listen to me this once."

We stared at each other for a moment. Bella looked prepared for an argument. Carla spoke before I could.

"There's a clearing up ahead. We'll rest there and you can take care of this journal. We should be far enough away from the townsfolk, so take as much time as you need. I don't care what you do with it, but don't keep it and don't write where we're going in it. Can you do that please?"

"Yes."

"Thank you. We'll see you there."

She handed me my things and they walked on ahead. And that's where things are now. I decided to have one of my ravens deliver this and the book I borrowed to my friend Isabelle.

***

Dear Isabelle,

I'm so sorry for everything that's happened. I don't know if you have any interest in hearing from me or would want to read my journal. I believe you probably hate me. I never wanted any harm to come to you or Benjamin.

I leave this journal with you so that you might understand me a little better. It's your choice if you wish to read it or not. I want to thank you and Benjamin for being kind to me. I care for both of you and wish things had been different. You were the first friends I've had in many years. I can't even tell you how many years.

I'm going away and you may hear terrible things about my sisters and I. It's your choice if you wish to believe them. I hope you'll read my journal before making any final judgements. You'll never see me again, though I fear you have no desire to.

I'm so tired of running. I wish I could have stayed with you and Benjamin. Choices I made too many lifetimes ago prevent me from having a normal, happy life. My sisters and I are bound for an eternity and another cycle is about to begin. I don't want anyone else to be affected by our curse. I wish you a long and happy life. I'll never forget you.

Malla

Fifty-One
September 23-25, 1977

September 23

Detective Vaughn's office was stuffy with hot air and cigarette smoke. Ernest pulled out a cigarette as Detective Vaughn was putting one out. Samantha glanced at the closed windows. Jed reviewed his notebook as Detective Vaughn spoke.

"There's nothing. Not a single trace of these sisters for six weeks. And no children have been reported missing in all that time. All the other victims were abducted about a week before the eclipse and the next one is in a few days."

"They broke their pattern because we started looking for them. Maybe they went somewhere else for their rituals." Jed said.

"Or they abducted a child from another town or county." Ernest said.

"You may be right about that. I'll put in a call to find out if any surrounding areas have reported missing children. I have a hunch they'll come back here for their ritual. I don't have proof, but I suspect this area is sacred to them." Detective Vaughn said.

"I don't know about sacred, but I think they do consider this their home. I also think they don't want to be caught." Samantha said.

"Is this intuition coming from the one-hundred-year-old journal you discovered?"

"I'm not suggesting they're over a hundred, but the one who gave me the warning did react when I mentioned the name of the journal's owner. Perhaps it's one of their ancestors. I think that journal has some clues to what's happening now."

"What happened to the woman from the journal?" Ernest said.

"The three sisters were accused of witchcraft, but they were never found. According to the journal, they fled to the North, but it never mentioned where. The writer was told by her sisters not to write the location and to get rid of the journal."

"Well, that's not helpful."

"Is there anything about rituals or sacrifices in that book?" Detective Vaughn said.

"No, but there are a few mentions of curses and cycles. Some things were intentionally left vague and that's what I've been trying to interpret."

"I don't think it will provide any insight but let me know if you find anything. Let's meet again tomorrow if you're all available."

Detective Vaughn walked over and opened a window.

"I wish you had done that earlier." Samantha said.

"You can always ask. I sometimes don't notice all the smoke in the air."

"I'll remember that."

***

September 24

The next day in Detective Vaughn's office, the air was clearer. Samantha noticed a window was open when she arrived. The detective had a haze around him as he lit a cigarette right after putting one out. His eyes were dark with bags under them. The small trashcan by his desk was filled with empty paper cups. Steam rose from another paper cup sitting on his desk.

"There are no reports of any children currently missing in the tri-state area. The search of the house you all found turned up nothing of value. The place was run down with a century's worth of dust. Their ritual site didn't offer much, and we can't dig up anything just in case they return. Everything's a dead end. All we can do now is stay vigilant and wait." Detective Vaughn said.

"Is it too much to hope they just gave up and left?" Ernest said.

"We won't know for sure until after the eclipse."

"What do we do now?" Samantha said.

"Let's plan to meet again on Monday. I'll be in and out of the office all weekend. If you see these occultists or learn anything new, call first. If I'm not in, leave a message with the officer at the main desk, then come to my office. And like I always say, do not approach those women."

***

The rest of the afternoon dragged. Ernest was in his room pacing and smoking one cigarette after another. He would clean something and finish it too fast. He cleaned his whole room in thirty minutes. The phone rang and he answered before the first ring finished.

"Hello?"

"Hey Ernie."

"Hey Lindy."

"You haven't called me that since we were kids. Is this a good time?" Linda said.

"Yeah, it's fine." Ernest said.

"You don't have to work?"

"No. I took a few days off, but now I wish I had more stuff to do."

"You never were good at sitting still. How's Amy doing out in California?"

"I talked to her last week. I never know what the hell she's saying but she's happy that someone's listening."

"I feel like I missed so much."

"So do I. But we won't have to worry about that soon."

"What do you mean?"

"I'm thinking of staying in Maine. I've made friends here. And once this is all over, the three of us can be a family."

"You still want to be with me?"

"Yes. I never stopped loving you. I understand you a little better, so maybe I can be a better husband."

"You've always been great. I'm the one who's a mess."

"I'm a mess too. There's stuff I'm not ready to talk about. I understand why you didn't want to talk about your stuff. I shouldn't have pushed you so hard to tell me. I'm sorry for that."

"I'm sorry too."

No one spoke for a moment. Static hung in the phone receiver.

"What about Robert, your dad?" Linda said.

"I'm trying really hard not to kill him. Mom kicked him out. I don't want to know more than that. If he tries to contact us or come near us, I'll get a restraining order against him. I want nothing to do with him." He said.

"What if – what if he tries to claim some right to Amy as the father?"

"I won't let him hurt Amy the way her hurt you. I'm Amy's father and that's all she ever needs to know."

Ernest heard muffled sounds from Linda's end of the phone line. She cried.

"I l-love you so much." She said.

"I love you too."

She snorted and there were soft thumps through the receiver.

"I'm sorry, my time is almost up. Other patients need to use the phone. Will you come visit next week?"

"Of course. Talk to you then."

"Okay, bye."

"Bye."

Ernest replaced the phone on its cradle. He took a deep breath and rubbed his face. He lit another cigarette and stared out the window.

***

September 25

The next day was uneventful. Ernest went to a diner for breakfast. He looked through the wanted ads in the Sunday newspaper. He circled some and crossed out others. He glanced over some places for rent listed in the paper but didn't spend too much time on that page. He never noticed the server refill his coffee but wasn't surprised when he lifted a full cup. He stacked his dirty dishes and refolded the newspaper sticking it under his arm. He gulped down the last of his coffee, paid for his meal and went back to his room.

The phone rang as he entered. When he picked it up there was only a dial tone. He hung up and went to open the carton of cigarettes he bought the day before. He was about to open a new pack when the phone rang again. He answered after the second ring.

"Hello?"

"Oh, thank God you're there! I've been calling all morning! I don't know what to do! The police haven't been any help! This is all so awful!"

"Woah, mom, slow down. What's going on?" Ernest said.

"It's Amy, she's gone! I've told five different police officers the same story and it's like they don't talk to each other! It feels like no one's even looking for her…" Gail said.

"Mom? Mom! What do you mean Amy's gone? Did she wander off?"

"No! Someone took her! She was playing in the living room! I went to get her some juice and she started screaming! When I got back into the room someone was running out the front door and Amy was gone! I ran outside and there was a car that took off! The police keep asking me what kind of car and all I know is it was blue!"

"Okay calm down. Let the police look for Amy. I'll call the detective here and see if he can get the police out there to move things along. I'll call you when I know something."

"Okay. I'm so sorry."

"Everything will be okay. I'll call you in a little while."

Ernest hung up then searched through the nightstand drawer. He found Detective Vaughn's business card. He dialed the number. After ten rings he slammed the phone down.

"Fuck!"

He grabbed his cigarettes and jacket and ran to the door, catching his jacket on the door handle. He fought with it for a second then ran down the hallway once he was free.

Fifty-Two
September 25-27, 1977

September 27, 4:05 am

Ernest ran through the forest clutching Amy, protecting her with his arms from the twigs and branches bombarding his body. The moon hung in the sky casting a red glow over the forest. The shadows looked darker in the red light. Amy cried.

"Daddy!"

"I've got you baby. You're safe now."

Gunfire echoed behind them followed by screams. Some of the screams came from men. The others sounded unnatural, like battle cries from wild beasts. Ernest stopped a moment to catch his breath. He looked around unsure where to run next. The forest was quiet. Tears ran down Amy's face, but she was quiet.

"Sweetie, are you okay? Are you hurt? Did they do anything to you?"

"No. I sleept."

There was another unnatural scream. Ernest ran. He ran away from the scream but otherwise had no idea where he was going.

"Find them!"

The deep voice was far off but behind them. Ernest didn't want to know who the speaker was. He jumped behind a large fallen tree and crouched down. He set Amy down.

"Shh. Stay quiet, okay?"

Amy nodded and covered her mouth. Ernest tried to slow his breathing. The situation reminded him of a night in Cambodia.

He and a few Marines hid behind trees and bushes waiting for the enemy to pass. The wait felt like an hour. Every noise had been magnified in the moment. Two Marines communicated with hand signals, but Ernest didn't know what any of it meant.

A twig broke bringing Ernest back to the present. He heard someone breathing heavy. He heard every step they took. They were close. Something fell and slid on the other side of the fallen tree. Ernest looked towards the sky but only saw leaves. He slowly lifted his head to look over the fallen tree. He didn't see anyone. He never heard them leave. He looked over the fallen tree. The blank stare of a dead fox looked at him. He heard steps and ducked down.

"They came this way. I can smell them." One voice said.

"Which way?" Another said.

"I don't know. The scent is gone. Overpowered by other smells."

Ernest didn't know who was talking. The voices were too deep to belong to any woman. Amy stared at him still covering her mouth. He put one finger over his lips. She nodded.

***

September 25

Ernest ran into the Sherriff's office.

"Is Detective Vaughn here?"

"He just walked in. What's this –"

"Thank you."

Ernest ran down the hall. Detective Vaughn was talking with another deputy, coffee in both their hands.

"Detective!"

"Mister Kemp. Is something wrong?"

"Out in California. My daughter. Kidnapped."

"Do the Cali police know anything?

"I don't know. If they do, they haven't told my mother."

"I'll give the San Bernardino Sherriff a call."

Detective Vaughn unlocked the door to his office.

"Have a seat. I'll make the call right now."

The San Bernardino Sherriff's department didn't have much information. They were assisting the San Bernardino city police, but there was no new information. Detectives were showing pictures of types of cars to Mrs. Kemp, but the process was moving slowly. As an extra precaution, Detective Vaughn contacted the surrounding counties in California and made sure they had a description of the three women they suspected had abducted Ernest's daughter.

"How do we know they haven't already left the state?" Ernest said.

"That would take a few hours by car. The State was made aware of the kidnapping too soon after. They're watching the highways and interstates. I'd guess they're laying low somewhere planning their next move. I doubt they plan to leave California." Detective Vaughn said.

"Weren't you the one who said they'd come back to the forest outside of town?"

"I didn't think they would go across the country because of a grudge."

"I think they'll come back here."

"If they manage to get out of California, I suppose if they drove nonstop, they could still get here before the eclipse. I'll check in with California every hour and let you know if anything changes. Stay by your phone. I won't tell you not to worry. I'm a father too and I'd worry no matter what anyone said."

"Yeah. I'll do my best."

"You're friends with Miss Belcher, aren't you? If she's free, maybe she can keep you company. It'll help pass the time at least."

"Sure. I'll give her a call."

***

September 27, 4:10 am

"I see something there." One voice said.

"I can't get a scent." Another said.

Ernest and Amy held their breath waiting for the voices to leave.

"I hear something nearby. Go." A third voice said.

The footsteps trailed off. Ernest peaked over the fallen tree. He got a whiff of the dead animal in front of him. He covered his mouth and nose. Amy still had hers covered. He took her hand, and they moved back the way they came when they were chased. The wind blew and tree branches rustled. The forest was still covered in the red glow from the abnormal moon. They stepped with caution avoiding fallen branches and leaves. The three women fell from the trees in front of them.

"Found you." One said.

They looked to have aged hundreds of years. Two of them didn't have any eyes. Ernest saw them properly now. He saw them as they truly were.

"You thought you could hide behind the scent of a dead fox, but I heard you breathing."

"Stay behind me." Ernest said.

He pushed Amy behind his legs. She wrapped her arms around one of them.

"Give us the child and we'll kill you quickly."

The old hag in the middle was the only one who spoke. The one who still had eyes was to her right. She looked from Ernest to the hag in the middle and back again.

"I'll kill you before you touch her again!" Ernest said.

"We can't die, you idiot. See how we look? We need that child to look young again and renew the cycle. It was the burden we were given. The price for immortality. Give us the child so we may finish the ritual. Then we will leave this place. No one else will die. Except you, of course."

"Why us? Why go so far just to kidnap my daughter? Was no other child good enough?"

"You found us and tried to stop us. This is the price for interfering. No one can stop us. No one can control us."

"You'll never get my daughter!"

"Look sisters. Another man thinks he can tell us what to do. They're all the same. Show him what we do to all men."

The woman with eyes turned around. She ran and tackled the woman in the middle. There was gunfire and a scream.

***

September 26, 11:00 pm

Twenty-four hours went by before any news came. Women were spotted matching the sisters descriptions at the state border between New Hampshire and Maine. Detective Vaughn had deputies watching the forest while the rest of the State searched every roadway. By nightfall everyone decided to wait in the forest. Ernest and Detective Vaughn made piles of cigarette butts, both unaware of the bags under their eyes. Ernest had to walk away several times so his pacing wouldn't make too much noise near the clearing.

"Kemp?" Detective Vaughn said.

Ernest walked over after lighting another cigarette. Samantha sat in a patrol car writing in her notebook. Jed stood out in the trees with other deputies sipping coffee.

"You know how to clean a rifle?" Detective Vaughn said.

"Yes." Ernest said.

"Good. Put your nervous energy to use and clean this one. There's a cleaning kit in the trunk of my car."

"Yes, sir."

Detective Vaughn leaned on the car smoking while Ernest rummaged through the trunk and took apart the rifle. He laid each of the pieces on a towel inside the trunk.

"You know more than the average Navy medic." Detective Vaughn said.

"Not by choice." Ernest said.

"What does that mean?"

"I saw some awful stuff during Vietnam. But the real horror started after the war was over. I ended up with a Marine unit in Cambodia. I had never been trained to be a combat medic, so I had to learn on the job. I can't count how many times I almost died. I never had to use a rifle before that. The Marines showed me how to use them and clean them. They said the enemy would come after me first before I could save anyone, so the enemy could kill everyone faster. They told me to learn to fight just in case. I never wanted to fight. That's why I became a Hospital Corpsman. And now that my daughter's in danger, all I want to do is fight and I can't. Thanks for the busy work."

"My pleasure."

"Did you serve?"

"Yeah. Korea. Army finance corps. I didn't see any action.

Not like you."

Detective Vaughn pulled out a flask, took a drink, and handed it to Ernest. Ernest took a drink and returned the flask.

"This whole thing has me messed up too. We'll get your daughter back."

"Damn right we will."

They stood in silence. Detective Vaughn smoked. Ernest cleaned the small rifle pieces with care and detail. He didn't light another cigarette while his last one burned unnoticed on the car bumper. The moon made the forest as bright and white as day with long shadows from the trees.

***

September 27, 4:12 am

Ernest stared at the three hags on the ground. Detective Vaughn and two deputies Ernest didn't know ran towards them from behind. Two of the women stood.

"Get off me!" One said.

The third laid motionless. Something black pooled under her. The red light from the moon faded. The black pool turned red as the moonlight turned white. The Earth's shadow covered half the moon again.

"No! Bella! Get up! I said get up!"

Another shot hit the woman's side while she kneeled down next to the dead woman. She didn't flinch or notice. Tears welled in her eyeless sockets.

"I can't hear her heartbeat anymore."

The woman who had eyes covered her mouth. The one without eyes tilted her head so one ear faced the sky.

"But I can hear yours."

She rose into the trees and disappeared. The woman with eyes blinked and looked around, eyes wide. She followed the other woman into the trees. The only sounds were leaves rustling. The forest was darker during the eclipse without the red light. No one could see anything in the trees. There was a peaceful quiet for a moment. Cackling laughter broke the silence echoing through the trees.

"I can hear all your hearts beating faster."

The laughter filled the forest coming from every direction. Ernest looked toward Detective Vaughn and saw a deputy behind him get pulled into the trees. His yell stopped as quickly as it started.

"Smith! Where'd he go!?" Detective Vaughn said.

He and the other deputy looked every which way except up.

"In the trees! They pulled him up!" Ernest said.

"What!? How!?"

A body fell from the trees landing with a thump on some bushes. The head was missing and there were four long lacerations down the entire torso. Ernest covered Amy's eyes.

"Jesus Christ!"

From behind Detective Vaughn, something bounced along the ground stopping a few feet in front of the detective. The blank stare on the dead deputy's severed head looked at Ernest. He looked down to make sure Amy's eyes were still covered. Her face was buried into Ernest's hand and pants. More laughter echoed through the trees.

"Close it in! Back-to-back!" Detective Vaughn said.

The detective and Ernest put Amy between them. They looked up into the trees. Detective Vaughn handed Ernest a revolver. The other deputy was still running towards them. One of the women dropped on top of the deputy and lifted him without touching the ground. Despite her speed, both Detective Vaughn and Ernest fired several shots before she and the deputy disappeared into the darkness. Amy crouched on the ground covering her ears, eyes shut tight. The deputy's screams stopped. Everything fell quiet. The wind and leaves weren't moving. They heard footsteps and grunting. Jed was limping towards them with Samantha supporting him.

"Stop! They're in the trees!" Detective Vaughn said.

Jed looked up with his revolver at the ready. Samantha stared at the deputy's body and severed head on the ground.

"Where's Currier!?" Jed said.

"They grabbed him and took him up!"

"How!?"

"Don't know, but that's what happened to Smith too!"

"What do we do!?" Samantha said.

"Try to get the Hell out of here! We'll come to you! Watch your rear!"

Ernest picked up Amy looking at the trees and moving slowly. Detective Vaughn followed walking backwards and watched behind them.

"STOP!" Jed said.

Currier's body hit the ground in front of Ernest. His head still attached, but bloodier than Smith's body.

"Keep your eyes closed, Amy." Ernest said.

***

September 27, 4:00 am

The eclipse made the forest darker. Several deputies were watching the sky. No one noticed anything in the darkness. It was faint at first, almost unnoticeable. The moon turned red. There was no longer a shadow from the Earth. The red light brightened the clearing in the forest. The women had already begun the ritual with Amy between the three of them. She laid still. Flames burst from candles spread in a circle around the women. They were no longer young women. They looked like shriveled corpses standing upright and moving. One of them held a knife walking towards Amy. They chanted but their words were faint.

"NOW!" Detective Vaughn said.

All the deputies ran into the clearing with revolvers and rifles pointed at the women.

"Kennebec County Sherriff! Drop the weapon!" Jed said.

The woman with the knife had no eyes, but the anger on her face was clear. She screamed causing everyone to cover their ears. Some dropped to their knees. Others feel over with blood dripping from their ears and eyes. The woman stopped screaming and walked towards Amy. A shot kicked the knife from her hand. Detective Vaughn, breathing heavy, was the only person standing.

"Step away from the child!"

The woman growled and leapt into the air falling towards the detective. He jumped out of the way falling backwards. Jed charged after the woman ready to tackle her. She swiped one arm at him sending him flying. He hit the ground hard and rolled several feet. Several deputies were trying to fight the other women and Ernest took advantage of the confusion running to Amy. He put his ear to her chest looking at her face. She was breathing. He glanced over her and didn't see any marks or signs of trauma. He picked her up and ran. He didn't know where he was running, but he ran. He heard shouts behind him.

"They've taken the child! Go!"

Fifty-Three
September 27, 1977

4:15 am

Ernest stopped moving briefly after the body landed in front of him. He stepped around it, looking to the trees. He heard Detective Vaughn's footsteps behind him. Straight ahead, Jed and Samantha kept their heads moving never looking the same direction as the other. The forest was still and quiet. Ernest felt the blood pumping in his ears, his arms, legs, and chest. He heard the leaves rustle, the crunch of dead leaves under his feet, and Amy breathing heavy. They passed the body of the dead woman and Detective Vaughn flipped the body over with his foot.

"This one is definitely dead. Let's hurry back to the cars. We all move at Deputy Wells' pace. No one left behind." Detective Vaughn said.

"What about those two?" Ernest said.

"We'll come back at daybreak. How are the other deputies back at the clearing?"

"Some are unconscious, but no visible injuries. Four didn't make it. Six if you include Currier and Smith." Jed said.

"Shit. Alright, Wells take point. I'll watch the rear."

Jed hopped while Samantha supported him, followed by Ernest and Amy. Detective Vaughn stepped backwards looking left and right as he went. The rhythm of crunching leaves surrounded them. They marched in darkness as the eclipse hit its peak. More than half the moon was covered in shadow. A scream broke the silence. They all froze. The scream came from behind far away.

"Do you think that was one of them?" Samantha said.

"One of them was shot several times. That didn't stop her from killing two deputies." Ernest said.

"Keep moving. We can talk in the car." Detective Vaughn said.

Jed hopped a little faster. Everyone else matched his pace. Another scream echoed longer than the first. No one stopped. Detective Vaughn turned forward staying behind everyone. They returned to the clearing. Several deputies were still on the ground. A few sat up holding their heads. They made it to the cars.

"Take my keys and my car. I'll stay here. Get on my radio and call for paramedics. You four get back to town." Detective Vaughn said.

Another scream interrupted him.

"No arguments. Go Now!"

Samantha helped Jed into the front passenger's seat. She opened the back door for Ernest and Amy.

"I'll drive. Don't let go of her." She said.

Samantha put the car in gear and sped off leaving a cloud of dust behind them.

***

12:00 pm

Ernest hadn't slept all morning. He made the effort but could only lay in the bed staring at the ceiling. Amy had fallen asleep a second time and had the entire blanket wrapped around her. Detective Vaughn had called earlier and said they recovered the fallen deputies, but all the women were gone, even the one they killed. Ernest was on his second pack of cigarettes for the day. Discarded cigarette butts formed a mountain in his ashtray. He checked his watch.

"Shit. I should call mom and let her know we're okay."

He sat on the bed holding the base of the phone in one hand and the receiver in the other. He used the receiver hand to dial then placed the phone to his ear.

"Hello? Ernest, is that you?" Gail said.

"Yeah, mom. Just letting you know Amy and I are okay."

"Oh, thank God! Is Amy hurt? Are you hurt? Did they catch

305

those terrible women?"

"Amy is fine. She's sleeping right now. I checked her out and she looks okay physically. I'm taking her to a doctor first thing tomorrow just in case."

"Okay. I'm happy she's okay. What about her kidnappers?"

"The Sherriff's department got one of them, but the other two got away.

"What will they do now?"

"I'm sure they'll keep looking for them for a while. I don't think they'll try anything anytime soon."

"What about you? What will you do now?"

"I think I'll stay here in Maine. I have to wait for Linda to be discharged anyway. The Detective out here suggested I apply to be a paramedic. I forgot how much I like helping people."

"If you're sure that's what you want then you have my support."

"Thanks. I have to try to get some sleep. I've been anxious all morning. It feels like the other shoe is about to drop."

"Oh, I understand. Well, you should sleep honey. Thank you for calling. I'm glad you're both safe."

"Okay, mom. I'll give you a call this weekend."

"Okay sweetheart. I love you. Bye now."

"Love you, too. Bye mom."

There was a knock at the door as Ernest returned the phone to the nightstand.

"Ernie? You in there? It's Sam."

Ernest opened the door and Samantha walked in without an invitation. She saw Amy sleeping on the bed.

"Sorry. I didn't mean to be so loud." She said.

"It's okay. A freight train wouldn't wake her up. How are you?" Ernest said.

"Pretty good compared to you and everyone else. Luckily Jed only sprained his ankle. It could have been a lot worse. For everyone. I'm really glad my cousin Francis had to work the front desk last night."

"I need some coffee. You want some?"

"Sure. I could use an extra boost. My editor wants a recap

of last night written up by this evening. I don't think I can write what I actually saw. Everyone else saw the same thing, but I can't explain half of it."

"I can't explain any of it."

"You think maybe we were drugged? Like it was some mass hallucination."

"I don't know. Let the detectives figure that out."

"Have you heard from Vaughn?"

"Yeah. He called me after dawn. He said the body of the woman that was killed is missing. They never found the other two."

"Should we be worried?"

"Not today. I think we'll have some breathing room before we see them again."

Ernest poured the coffee and there was another knock on the door.

"I'll get it. Are you expecting someone?" Samantha said.

"No, but I wasn't expecting you either."

Samantha stood at the doorway with her eyes wide and mouth open.

"I'm not here to hurt anyone. Please don't get upset. I just want to talk."

Ernest didn't recognize the voice. He approached the door and saw one of the sisters; the blonde. She held her hands out with palms facing them with fear flashing in her eyes as she looked back and forth between Ernest and Samantha.

"You're Malla?" Samantha said.

"Yes. My sisters are dead. Please. I swear I mean you no harm."

"Were you the one who threw the dead fox at us to hide our scent?" Ernest said.

"What?" Samantha said.

"Yes. I tried to help. I'm sorry I couldn't do more."

They stood in silence a moment.

"I'm willing to hear her out." Ernest said.

"Yeah, okay." Samantha said.

"May I come in?" Malla said.

Ernest nodded. He gave Samantha her coffee then sat on the bed in front of Amy. Malla sat at the table and Samantha sat in the chair between the bed and table.

"There's coffee if you want any." Ernest said.

"Thank you."

Malla looked at the coffee on the table but made not effort to pour any. She sat with her legs together and hands in her lap. She stared at the floor and didn't move.

"You said your sisters were dead. Were their names Carla and Arabella?" Samantha said.

"What!? Oh! I'm sorry. I forgot you said you read my journal. Yes. They – they both died last night. I gave them a proper burial." Malla said.

"You don't look very upset about it." Ernest said.

"Our relationship was, um, complicated. I hope they've found peace in death. I wanted to let you know before the ritual, I made sure your daughter wasn't harmed. I gave her something to drink that made her sleep so she wouldn't see or hear anything."

"Why'd you take her? Why not some other child?" Ernest said.

"That was Carla's choice. She felt some energy from you and saw you as a threat. She wanted to break you. She thought it might somehow break our curse because of a dream she had. I guess her dream was right because the curse broke last night when my sisters died."

"How do you know the curse broke?" Samantha said.

"You saw how we looked last night. The ritual helped us maintain a young appearance. I would still be cursed and look like an old woman since we didn't finish the ritual. I don't know how I look like this now or what broke the curse. Carla was obsessed with being young and beautiful. Someone hurt her long ago. 900 years ago actually."

"Nine hundred..." Ernest said.

Samantha shushed him.

"She wanted power to get her revenge, but the power came with a price. To keep that power and our youth, we had to take the lives of children. Carla didn't mind paying that price. But I couldn't keep doing it. And I did nothing to stop her. I have to live the rest of my life knowing that. I have nine centuries of atrocities for which to atone. I wanted to start by offering a gift to your daughter. Only if you agree. Give it to her when she comes of age, or you can throw it away. I understand if you don't trust me. It won't cause her any harm."

She put a small box on the table.

"What is it?" Ernest said.

"A protection charm. It will keep her safe. Consider it my way of thanking you for breaking the curse that held my sisters and I for so long. I don't know how the curse was broken, or if it just changed somehow, but I'm grateful. My sisters suffered enough and can find peace."

She stood and walked to the door. Ernest stood but didn't move.

"You won't see me again. I wish long and happy lives to you both."

She left. Samantha and Ernest looked at each other. He picked up the box Malla left on the table. Inside was a necklace. The charm on the necklace was a coin with a raven stamped on it. Ernest saw a raven perched outside his window watching them.

"There's a lot of this the journal won't print. But I feel like people should know this story." Samantha said.

"Maybe write a book."

"But it's not my story. Not really. You should write it."

"That's not my cup of tea. Can I pay you to write it for me?"

"Sure."

They both laughed. Amy's breathing was slow and heavy. She had blankets and pillows surrounding her. A little drool hung from her mouth.

The End.

Letter from the Author

This is the first story I've written at this length. Before this, the longest story I had written was about half as long. I learned a lot on this project. Since I was born in '86, and have never been to Maine, I had to do a lot of research to make things in this novel as accurate as possible.

Some things may not be accurate to the exact time period. For example, the alpha-numeric phone number system was still in place in some areas in the U.S. in the late 1970s, but not in others. I don't know which areas still used the old system at the time, but I took some creative license and assumed Ernest might be someone who didn't like All-Number Calling.

Another inaccuracy is the paternity test. Everything I researched said if a father and son might both be the father of a child, the test results for both men would be closer to 98%. I took some creative license again for this scene as a way to get Linda to reveal what had happened to her without her feeling threatened or interrogated. Hopefully any lab techs who read this won't be too upset.

I hope you enjoyed this little world I created. I have not decided if I want any of these characters to appear in future works. I may consider something that takes place in modern times, but we shall see. Thank you for reading and I hope you'll write an honest review. I hope this book gets you excited about my future works.

James

About the Author

James Pack is a member of the Horror Writers Association and has published several collections of poetry and short fiction. Learn more about James and his collected works on his personal blog thejamespack.com. He lives in Tucson, AZ.

9 798985 934243